ALEX TOXIC

KILL OR DIE

Have a nice game!
Alex Toxic

BOOK ONE

MAGIC DOME BOOKS

THIS BOOK IS ENTIRELY A WORK OF
FICTION.
ANY CORRELATION WITH REAL PEOPLE OR
EVENTS IS COINCIDENTAL.

TABLE OF CONTENTS:

CHAPTER 01

WOODS ALL AROUND. Birds singing, sunlight filtering through the leaves. Unfamiliar woods. Neither spruce, nor birch — some other type of trees. *"Well... I'm no botany expert,"* he thought. But if he wasn't a botany expert, then who was he?

He blinked. Spots swam in his vision. Gradually they grew clearer until they crystallized into a UI. This had a calming effect on him for some reason. As if walking around the woods with a user interface was habitual for him.

HP, MP, XP... the standard trifecta. So he was in a game. What remained unclear was what game it was and how he ended up in it. It wouldn't hurt to find out how to get out of it as well.

The inventory was empty. On the map, his green dot floated alone amid the unexplored darkness. All stats at level one. A newbie. A noob. The name "TargetAi" glowed above the dot. An unfamiliar handle, yet his it seemed.

He opened the quest log last. To his surprise, there was already an active quest in it. The first and only objective read: "KILL ANNA."

*   *   *

Walked right into it. Deliberately skirted around the courtyard from the other side and still walked right into it. Even through my headphones, I could hear their whistles.

"Yo, Drone! Hold up!"

There they were in full force: Sullen and his bros. Five street punks slouching on two benches they had dragged over from the building entrance and arranged facing each other. Sitting on the bench-backs, feet on the seats, taking turns swigging beer from a plastic bottle, almost empty. Ugh, how trashy.

Running is dumb, although seeing as it's 5 v 1, it's the smart thing to do. But I'm not used to running. Besides, where would I go? I live here. If we don't run into each other tomorrow, we'll run into each other the day after. So I just stop and wait for them to approach.

The punks come swiftly off the benches and gather around me from all sides.

"What's up, Drone?" Sullen tries to give me a hug, wrapping his arm around my neck, but I already know this move and just step back out of range.

I hate my name. I hate that it can be turned

into Andy, Drew or Drone. And I hate Sullen, even though we were classmates once. I went on to high school, and he dropped out, rallying all the local numskulls around himself. Even adults were afraid of them, while the local drunks were downright deferential, addressing Sullen respectfully by his patronymic "Victor Sergeich" and bowing when they encountered him.

"Hey, Vic," I address him directly to the delight of his gang.

"You got some loot for me?"

"Are you sure you're not mixing something up?" I'm flabbergasted. I knew the conversation was going to be about money, but Sullen got to the point too quickly even for himself.

My fist clenches on its own. I could belt this cheeky bastard a couple of times in the face and give it a little color. Then I wouldn't care about my broken ribs so much. It's broad daylight after all — maybe they won't stomp me for too long.

"Don't get worked up, your dad owes me!" Sullen declares triumphantly. "A week ago, he borrowed money 'till tomorrow.' Ain't that so, boys?"

The punks grunt approvingly and nod their heads.

The worst part is that this could very well be the truth. When he's drunk, my father will borrow money from just about anyone. Even the neighbors harass my mother over my father's debts. So Sullen is within his rights here.

How I want to wipe that disgusting smirk off

his face. All I gotta do at the moment is lean in and throw down. I could KO this scumbag with a single hook. I know how to hit someone so they won't get up. My dad taught me.

I've been beating Sullen since elementary school. He was a jackass even back then, picking on everyone, looking for weaknesses. Why the hell am I hesitating now?

My father's face appears before my eyes, strong and invincible, carrying me on his shoulders in childhood, smashing bricks with a punch. Then I see my father sitting as a defendant in the courtroom. Just like that, with a single punch, he shattered his own life and ours — his family's.

I loosen my fist.

"How much does he owe?" I force myself to ask.

"Five hundred," Sullen grins. "Come on, hand it over!"

In my pocket, blindly with my fingers, I count out five hundred rubles. No need to show the rest or they might start insisting on interest and processing fees. I couldn't care less about Victor's "reputation." I just don't want this scumbag mocking my father. It's disgusting to imagine my dad standing there, enduring their insults, kicks and slaps. It's even scarier to think that he might fight back.

Four years ago, my father — an engineer, top of his class, a former marine — stood up for a girl at a banquet in his honor. He beat up three assholes who were trying to drag her right from the dinner table to their car. Later one of the assholes turned out to be the son of a local politician. The girl withdrew her statement to the police and a few weeks later bought herself a new car. My father got five years. In court, it turned out that he was the only guilty party — a drunk and a brawler.

He came out of prison two years later, but he was different. Broken. He lost his job at the factory. Every day he hung around with other alcoholics, looking for money for booze. He came home covered in dirt and scabs. My mother screamed and cried and threatened divorce. She stayed with him out of pity. I guess both she and I could still see a shadow of the former strong and kind father figure in the stooped sickly shadow he'd become.

"There, take it," I hand him the crumpled bills.

"I thank you humbly from my heart, my soul and my spirit!" Sullen says with a chuckle.

He tries to give me a friendly slap on the back, but I slip past him and quickly walk home.

A Land Cruiser stands parked near the entrance, a big black SUV with tinted windows. I wonder who it belongs to. None of our neighbors could afford a car like this. As I climb the stairs to my apartment, I realized who it is. Olga, the girl from the apartment across from ours, passes me on her way down for her date. In high school, she used to follow me around like a little puppy. Back then, I seemed grownup and cool to her. But back then, I ignored her advances. How could I not? She was a year younger. She doesn't even say hello now. Pretends not to recognize me.

She looks provocative. "Damn fine," Simba would say. A short jacket that barely covers her stomach. A pierced belly button. No danger of her freezing outside — she'll jump straight into that Land Cruiser. Her skirt looks more like a wide belt. Standing a flight below, I notice that she is wearing stockings instead of tights. *"Easier to have sex in them,"* a quiet voice whispers in my head. *"No need to take off the panties — just push them aside, and you're good to go."* I shake my head to dispel it, but the voice goes on, *"And what kind of panties could she be wearing? Probably just a thong. Or sheer lace. Not much space in a car so you gotta dress for the occasion."*

Obscene images keep popping into my head, making me grit my teeth. Olga and I only kissed once, in tenth grade after a dance party — but now I feel ashamed of my untucked jacket and old battered sneakers. She walks past me, engrossed in her cellphone and envelopes me in a pungent scent of sickly sweet perfume. My day is definitely not going well.

* * *

"Are you going to have lunch?" asks my mom.

"Yeah," I reply, tossing my backpack in the hallway. I wash my hands and take a seat in the kitchen.

Some spaghetti, two hot dogs, firm and crumbling in the mouth like meat jelly, and sauerkraut — that's my whole lunch. My mom sits across from me, a look of anxiety on her face. It's clear that she is wrestling with whether to ask me something or not. Finally she can't hold back any longer.

"Have you seen your father?"

"Nope," I shake my head, "what's the matter?"

"I can't find my payroll card," she says and adds hopefully, "Maybe I left it at work."

"Block it," I suggest. "You can do it over the phone."

"And how are we going to buy groceries?!" she exclaims. "What are we going to eat until they send me the new one? Tell me!"

I don't respond, stuffing the last bits of spaghetti into my mouth. Mom's been getting upset for no reason as of late. My feelings aren't hurt. I feel sorry for her.

"Thanks for lunch, Mom," I stand up and to my own surprise, kiss her on the head. She flinches slightly from surprise and suddenly starts weeping, quietly, a small tremor in her shoulders.

Unable to think of anything else to say, I head to my room, collapse onto the worn-out couch and put on some music.

My mom's anxiety infects me. After lying down for half an hour, I put on some rough camouflage pants, a simple gray t-shirt with a university logo, and an old jacket of faux leather that's cracked in cobwebs on the shoulders.

I plod through the residential courtyards heading for the city's industrial zone. I'm always welcome here, among the warehouses.

"Andrew's here!" Stepanych waves at me. He always calls me just "Andrew." He knows that I like it. "Come on and join us! The truck just arrived."

I greet everyone except Petrovich. The scruffy-looking guy my age is Dimaga. There are two more unfamiliar guys who don't introduce themselves, but who cares about them. I grab a clinking crate of vodka. I take ten steps. I pass it to Dimaga. A few minutes later, my mind shuts off, leaving only the clinking of bottles and the growing soreness in my muscles.

"That's a wrap, boys!" Stepanych counts out the bills. He hands me four hundred rubles — less than the others. "Sorry, Andrew," he shrugs. "You came late. We already unloaded a whole truck before you showed up. Want me to sweeten the deal with a share of the breakage?"

The breakage is the loaders' legitimate loot. A set percentage of bottles for every truckload is automatically written off as broken by the accounting department. Yet we warehouse workers carry vodka as carefully as a baby, so nothing actually gets broken during the unloading.

"Is there any canned meat among the loot?" I ask, recalling today's plastic sausages.

"No, it's canned for a reason," Stepanych laughs. "The cans don't break."

I agree to take some vodka and stash two

bottles in my pockets. It's vital I hide them at home so dad doesn't find them. I can give some to Simba. He can turn anything into cash, especially booze. I'm feeling a lot better as I head homeward.

"You bastard... you monster... you piece of... shit... You're not a human, you're shit!" I hear from the kitchen. Mom is yelling at dad. He just grunts in response, drunk to the point of incoherence. I hear her slapping him across the face. Dad tumbles as sloppily as a sack of potatos. The stool creaks as he falls back on it.

I can't listen to this. Quietly, so as not to slam the door, I step into the hallway and climb the stairs to the top floor. Through the hatch, I make my way onto the roof. Tucking my legs, I sit on the very edge. The city roars below, and I listen to its breathing. Somewhere out there, people are driving expensive cars. They are taking beautiful girls to fancy restaurants. They bang them on luxurious beds or in saunas or just bent over the hood. They tip the waiters the equivalent of my monthly paycheck. They go to the beach for a weekend getaway to soak up the sun. Meanwhile, the peace I sought by coming here is nowhere in sight. Instead, rage and sorrow grow like a fire in my chest.

"Hey, got a smoke?"

I flinched. Simba moved as silently as a lion. Quite impressive for his build.

"Don't trip," I replied. "You know I don't smoke."

"Figured I might get lucky," Simba, whose

real name was Simon Baranov, shrugged wistfully. "Doesn't hurt to ask. What if you took it up since last we met?"

"You mooch."

"Slander!" Simba objected. "Vile calumny. I'm no mooch, I'm just thrifty. Money burns a hole in others' pockets, whereas in mine it thrives and multiplies."

Simba was one of those people who could sell snow to an Eskimo. He pushed Korean facial creams and Turkish thongs to the girls in our group — and stolen Nikes and refurbished gadgets to the dudes.

He tapped a cigarette out from his soft pack, lit it, and squatted down beside me.

"What's going on with you?" I asked him.

"My ma's got a new flame," Simba smirked. "He decided to teach me a life lesson. I was on the verge of fucking him up. So I got out of there."

Simba was desperately saving up for a place of his own. A studio apartment, a rented room, even a shack, as long as it was his own. However, the banks wouldn't give a punk like him a loan at any interest rate. His mother, whom he always ironically called "ma," desperately refused to grow up. She dressed like our friends, hung out in bars and clubs, and hooked up with guys half her age. Having an adult son didn't fit into her lifestyle and Simba's mere presence caused her confusion and resentment.

My friend finished his cigarette and flicked it over the side. The bright red star tumbled into the darkness. Make a wish if you like.

"What if it lands on someone's head?" I asked.

"Who gives a shit?" Simba hocked a loogie after the butt. "I'll piss on their heads too!" He jumped up, yanking at his belt, "Hey! I'm up here, pissing on your heads, you idiots!"

"Settle down," I chuckled.

"Sure," he agreed easily. "Listen, someone offered me a side gig. Easy money. Seriously, money for nothing."

"Where?" I perked up.

"As a beta tester for an online game. They actually want to pay me to play!"

"Sounds like a scam," I lost interest.

"Why?" Simba persisted. "You used to play. It'd be cakewalk for you."

"I used to play," I agreed, "but that's in the past."

Esports had grown into a massive entertainment industry in recent years. Ever since the military began granting access to their VR server farms, all traditional sports had taken a backseat. A person's body, placed inside a gaming pod, transmitted all the necessary sensory data into a simulated environment. You could taste, smell, touch — feel heat or cold and even pain. People weren't just playing games in virtual reality now, they were living in it.

Racing, flight, combat — insane stunts on the edge of life and death — suddenly became accessible to everyone. Even if your car's burning on the side of the road, or your plane's crashed into the ground, you're alive, healthy, and ready to keep fighting.

But the Gladiator Games were the most intense. One-on-one duels, team deathmatch, free for all. Any map, any weapon, even barehanded. When it came to popularity, they surpassed boxing, mixed martial arts, and all forms of combat sports. Speed and knowledge of virtual combat mechanics were the deciding factors. Paradoxically, not a single real-life mma fighter achieved even average results in esports.

Four years ago, I joined the regional junior esports team. We crushed everyone in the league. But before the semifinals, my dad was sent to prison. My family was hard on cash and renting a VR pod isn't cheap. "Any sport is an investment," my coach told me. "Parents are the first to invest in their child. They spend money on training time, equipment, gear, and proper nutrition. Then, if the bet pays off and the kid makes it to the big leagues, they'll get everything back a hundredfold."

I got out too early. In the junior league, recruiters are just beginning to eye promising gladiators. I fell short by just a hair. And then I simply walked away, never to return, trying my damnedest not to dwell on my shattered career. I immersed myself in ordinary online RPGs, roaming as an archer in one or as a druid in another. Strangely enough, to the disappointment of millions, there never was a VR RPG. New projects would flare up from time to time — and inevitably turn to vaporware while still in alpha.

Something didn't gel, but the developers never talked about what exactly. Could this be another one of those projects? But whatever, to hell with it…

"I've gotta go," said Simba, unoffended. "I'll tell you about it later, maybe you'll change your mind."

I went back home after midnight, but the light in the kitchen was still on. Mom wasn't asleep. Her face haggard, she sat silently at the table, her eyes fixed on a point on the wall as if someone had died.

"Would you like some tea?" I asked.

She nodded with a waxen expression. I flipped the switch on the electric kettle, waited for it to boil, and poured the hot water over two tea bags. The extent of my tea ceremony. My mom didn't move once.

"What's happened? What's wrong?" I sat down across from her.

The mugs steamed between us, too hot to touch. Waiting is a part of the tea ceremony too. It allows for time to have a conversation. And that was when my mom replied.

"Everything happened, everything's wrong," she squeezed her face between her hands, unable to look at me. "He blew it all: the utilities, the emergency fund, your university tuition… We have nothing. We're destitute, Andryusha."

INSTEAD OF GOING to the university in the morning, I crossed the road, hopped on electric bus number seven and headed to the other side of the city. Nine stops. It was a good thing that there were no transfers. Here, towering above the rows of ramshackle apartment blocks, loomed a massive office complex. I had no idea what was here before, but I had no reason to know. Now that I did, however, it wasn't any clearer because there weren't any signs on any of the office towers. You'd expect some signage at an office complex. Nothing of the kind here though.

On the other hand, a crowd had already gathered at the entrance to the main tower. A long line snaked down the stairs, almost to the very bus stop where I got off. The fans' discipline was a marvel to behold, since they looked like complete slobs by and large. But I quickly realized what was going on. Security personnel in identical black jackets and sunglasses patrolled the line with an air of importance. Damn Agents Smith. Like sheepdogs, they were funneling the flocks of job applicants into the building.

The sight of the crowd alone was enough to spoil my mood. I didn't really want to go through with this. It was all nonsense. A con for fools. They'd show us a fantastic new world for half an hour, and then start trying to sell us VR pods and modules on credit that would end up costing more than a two bedroom apartment. And there were always fools who'd sign up. And that was the best-case scenario. There's no such thing as a free lunch.

"Andryusha!" I heard Simba's voice. "Over here!"

I looked around and saw him waving from the head of the line. He was already mere steps from the entrance. Simba sure was a gem.

"Changed your mind?" Simba stepped back a bit, making room for me. "What are you waffling for? Get over here! I saved a spot for my buddy," he added, turning to the people around him. They grumbled but didn't dare argue. The weight categories were too different.

"You thought I'd ditch you? And who's going to get you out of trouble?" I grinned. "How's the wait been?"

"Almost an hour. They're letting people in slowly."

"What about over there?" I nodded to the left.

"Any faster?"

An identical but empty entrance was framed by two guards and an office chick dressed in a short, trendy fur coat. She kept shifting from one foot to the other. Every once in a while, someone would approach her, show her something and then head inside. The chick would nod and make a note of it on her tablet. I didn't have anything to show, although I really wanted to. She was one of those types that executives like to keep around for looks and prestige. From the slightly upturned tip of her nose and stylish glasses, to her pointed boots, she exuded efficiency and professional ambition.

"That's the VIP entrance," Simba grimaced. "Special invitation only."

Just then a bright yellow sports car rolled into the parking lot. I couldn't make out the model. Some kind of Tesla. Electric cars had seriously encroached on combustion vehicles as of late. Four individuals climbed out of the roadster and hurried towards the VIP entrance. Colorful jackets, wide-legged trousers, bangs almost down to their noses. One had a pink hairdo, another had a blue one. The entire crew looked like it'd just come from a street race on the outskirts of Yokohama. The chick with the tablet nearly jumped out of her fur coat from excitement. The tallest of the crew, the one wearing a flashy black jacket with white sleeves, leaned in and whispered something in her ear. She smiled and blushed.

"What the..? That's not Lance, is it?" I

couldn't believe my eyes. Just a few years ago, when I was deeply immersed in the world of online gaming, that face would pop up on every other website dedicated to esports.

"Yeah, it's Lance," Simba spat on the ground. "The champion of the capital city and the surrounding region."

"And you think we stand a chance?"

"Well, the game's brand new," my friend grumbled. "Everyone starts out on a level footing."

We weren't the only ones who recognized Lance. A lot of the crowd yelled his name, waving their arms and squealing with excitement.

"Lance... Come over here!"

"Lance... Lance... We love you!"

"Lance, can I get your autograph?" cried an adorable girl next to us.

Lance finally deigned to notice his fans' excitement. He came closer, flashing a wide, toothy smile, shining with perfect teeth, and waved as if he were a politician or a movie star. A chiseled profile, the look of a champion, a meticulously styled fringe that appeared artificially gray. The girl next to us broke out from the line, ran up to him, handed him a marker and hiked her cropped jacket, revealing her belly. The champion smoothly signed his autograph across it. With a squeal of happiness, the fan dashed back, eager to show it off to her friends.

"Hey, what's taking so long?" losing my patience, I hollered into the buildings' depths.

As if in hearing my plea, the line jumped

forward by several people at once. We were already inside when suddenly the crowd behind us began squealing again: "Anna... Anna!"

From inside the lobby I saw a black sport bike roll into the parking lot. A figure clad in tight leather raced up the steps, removing her helmet on the go. I managed to catch a glimpse of long black hair cascading in a wave down her shoulders before the sliding doors closed.

Simba and I made our way along the lobby's marble tiles, peering around. We signed some contract without reading it and followed the arrows. Smiling girls at every turn pointed us in the right direction, while stern-faced guards peered through their glasses in silence. At some point Simba and I got separated, and like tadpoles in a stream, we moved along with the flow.

"You play sports?" the nurse asked me.

"Sometimes," I grunted.

No point in telling them about the warehouse or the trucks of vodka. Daily physical labor didn't make me a muscle-bound hunk. I couldn't boast about my abs or biceps. But I was sturdy and resilient. At least she noticed that much.

"How old are you?"

"What?"

I shifted my gaze to the nurse, then quickly looked away, staring at the floor: A waterfall... I'm thinking about a waterfall... I hear the sound of water...

I was undergoing a medical examination, stripped down to my underwear, and all I could think about was not getting an erection. There wasn't anything about her clothes. She didn't look like a porn actress. It's just that her nurse's coat hugged her figure as if it had been tailored specifically for her, and she herself looked as if she had auditioned for television. The two nurses looked alike, like twins. Or maybe I just didn't notice anything else besides their white coats and slender legs.

One of them sat at a desk, recording the results. The other was conducting the exam, touching me occasionally. The touches sent shivers down my spine. Waterfall... I see a waterfall...

"What's your age?" she asked patiently with a faint sparkle buried deep in her eyes. Surely she was aware of the impression she was making on me.

"Nineteen," I replied.

"Lie down on the couch. We have to do an EKG on you," she said, running her fingers across my chest.

Oh Lord, give me strength!

* * *

"I almost came," Simba told me. "Where did they find so many cuties? Were yours like that too?"

"Uh-huh," I nodded.

As always in an unfamiliar environment, a feeling of tension had come over me. It happened before every test, competition, or stage performance. It wasn't fear, no. Just focus. I didn't feel like talking. Luckily, Simba's eloquence sufficed for the two of us.

"So I ask her, 'Are you on IG?' and she just laughs…" my friend kept going, "She said if I didn't calm down, she'd be forced to give me an enema!"

TESTERS 175 TO 195, PLEASE PROCEED TO THE IMMERSION HALL…

It looked like we passed the medical exam. We were each given a card with a number and directed to a huge waiting lobby. The place felt like a train station or an airport. Rows of metal, albeit comfortable, chairs and a large screen displaying a list of numbers adorned one of the walls. I got 212, while Simba got 224. Almost together.

"Hey, yo! Did you pass too? Come join us!" Simba waved at someone.

I spotted the girl who had gotten Lance's autograph.

"Do you know her?" I asked in surprise.

"I'm about to find out," Simba nudged me with his elbow.

The girl seemed puzzled as well and I got a better look at her. She was of average height, with dark hair and an unusual haircut. Her hair was intricately braided and arranged snuggly along her head. With her round, mischievous face, she resembled a sly kitten. Her lips were plump, and at first, I even thought they were artificially enhanced, though perhaps it was just her genetics being kind to her. The puffy jacket didn't allow a glimpse of her chest, but everything below seemed just fine. Her short pleated skirt reminded me of the Japanese schoolgirls from the anime that Simba and I used to watch in our senior years. Slim legs, a juicy booty... Simba didn't miss out on a good catch.

The girl was looking us over as well. Her gaze brushed over me, but it seemed like she approved of my friend. Simba always made sure to dress stylishly and impressively. "Appearance is a salesman's main showcase," he'd say.

"Have a seat," he said now to the girl, removing his bag from the neighboring chair to make room.

"Do you like esports?"

"Ab-so-lutely!" the girl laughed, and I couldn't take my eyes off her lips. They couldn't possibly be real.

"Andrew here is also a pro," Simba lied desperately, nudging me with his elbow so I wouldn't slip up.

"Oh yeah," I nodded.

The girl fixed her eyes on me. I was no longer some gloomy guy in an outdated jacket. On the contrary, I had become cool and mysterious. The kitten even licked her lips out of curiosity.

"I'm Simba," my friend continued his successful introduction. "And what's your name?"

"Zoia," she blushed slightly. It seemed like she didn't particularly like her own name. "But everyone calls me Yumi. That's my handle. I'm also a pro... Well, sort of."

"I'm Andrew," I said, and she blushed so

cutely that I couldn't look away. Simba noticed this and began to tease us.

"Andrew is cool and all, but Lance is the coolest!" he declared, as if he hadn't spat at the mere mention of the champion's name half an hour ago.

"Ohhh, yes!" Yumi agreed.

I didn't like to rile my esports memories, treating them like an old wound. It felt like picking at a scab that could start bleeding. But suddenly, I felt something else, something I'd completely forgotten. Excitement. Just like in the old days when we sat in the locker rooms before the gladiator duels, joking, encouraging each other, making plans.

"Show me that autograph!" I asked Yumi.

"Right here?" she hesitated to my surprise.

"Just come closer, no one will see," Simba backed me up.

Yumi stood up and, feigning reluctance, lifted her jacket. Lance had boldly written his name in English and drawn a heart at the end.

Unexpectedly, even to myself, I raised my hand and touched the inscription, tracing its lines with my finger.

"Oh!" she exclaimed softly. "That tickles."

I could feel the delicate girl's abdomen trembling under my finger. I outlined the heart and paused at its lowest point.

"When I win, I'll give you my autograph too, deal?"

Yumi blushed again and squinted her eyes,

just like a girl in an anime.

"Okayyyy... *If* you win," she giggled.

The pause lingered, but Yumi didn't hurry to pull down her jacket, and I didn't hurry to remove my hand.

TESTERS 195 TO 215, PLEASE PROCEED TO THE FULL IMMERSION HALL. I REPEAT, TESTERS...

Damn it! What a disappointment! Simba even burst out laughing with delight. No wonder — I had to go and these two would remain together. My friend would get another fifteen minutes to flirt with those delicate ears.

"Good luck, Yumi!" I smiled generously.

"Good luck to you too... Andrew?" she pronounced my name with a questioning tone. "What's your handle?"

"You'll hear it eventually," I answered enigmatically.

What was my handle? I definitely didn't want to recycle the old one. I'd buried Ratmir four years ago. Then again, it sure would be funny if Lance ran into the same person who beat him once at the Moscow Cup. Yet he'd been getting better all these years, while I... I'd been unloading trucks full of vodka. So I had better stick to the shadows and not stand out for now. In which case, what should my handle be?

I followed the arrows down the stairs to the basement floor. The path led to a changing room, much like in a gym. VR tech required that I lie down completely naked in the pod: A metal capsule with a coded lock. And why not, where would I store a key in my pod? I changed into a fluffy white robe and surprisingly comfortable slippers. Then I went plodding to my next destination as if I were at home and not in some corporate facility.

There was soft music playing. Some kind of lounge or ambient, though I don't know much about electronica. But it was very pleasant and soothing. The light fixtures bathed the sterile white tiles in warm and cozy light. It felt like I was about to enter a sauna, not a VR pod. I even wished I had a nice cold beer with me.

The door from the changing rooms led to another hall. I entered and froze. Nothing had prepared me for this.

"Come in and give me your card." A cheerful guy in a gray coveralls standing right at the entrance extended his hand. "Everyone reacts like that. It's impressive, right?"

His badge read: "Sergio Ivanov. MosTech Corporation."

"No kidding!" I shook my head, trying to take in the enormity of the space. Whereas ordinary office buildings have underground parking decks, this subfloor contained a brightly lit hall outfitted with long, neat rows of VR pods. Everything was white: the floor, the ceiling, the walls... The place resembled a deck on a star cruiser. In sci-fi movies, this is where the crew would linger in cryosleep while their ship travelled to a distant star.

Sergio waved my card over a scanner. There was a beep and the scanner lit up with a green light.

"All parameters nominal, Tester 212. Follow me to your pod. Do you have any experience?"

"Two years as a gladiator," I nodded.

"Excellent," Sergio exclaimed, "then you won't have any problems."

"Problems like what?" Never pass on a chance to chat up the staff. Where I was going, every bit of info could come in useful.

"Many people are afraid of the pods," the technician didn't disappoint. "They say it's like being in a coffin. Gives 'em claustrophobia."

So there are many newbies was what I gleaned from that. My experience, although outdated, would give me an edge. "*Easy frags, fresh meat,*" whispered an inner voice. I ignored the nudge. After all, the point here was beta testing, not winning — right?

"Get undressed. If you're shy, I'll turn away. Oh, by the way, in case you're squeamish, the pods are disinfected after each immersion."

"I know how it works," I nodded.

We approached the pod. A coat hanger had been provided to hang my robe. I looked around: All around the giant hall, technicians were helping players settle into their VR pods. There were only men here, however. The girls' pods were somewhere else, in another hall.

"Have a good trip," Sergio said and shut the pod's lid.

DEEP IMMERSION SESSION INITIALIZED. PLEASE ENTER YOUR NAME…

I still hadn't decided what handle to choose. "*As you name thy ship, so shall she sail,*" I recalled a bit of nautical wisdom. My old nick, Ratmir, is out for obvious reasons. So, what then?

"Tar-get-Ai!" I dictated loudly, syllable by syllable, so that the dumb system wouldn't make any typos.

HAVE A NICE GAME, TargetAi!

A black-and-white spiral whirled before my eyes. It drew me in, immersing my consciousness and sucking it in as into a bottomless well. We used to call this the Hypnotoad screen back in the day, reminiscing about an old cartoon.

The spiral adjusted the brain to control the new virtual body. That's how the engineers explained it. The real body, in the meantime, was submerged in a dense saline solution, becoming weightless and imperceptible. In that moment — while your consciousness hurled through a spinning two-tone corridor — the body had neither arms, nor legs, nor anything else.

EARN EXPERIENCE AND IMPROVE STATS.

A voice spoke from somewhere inside my head. Pleasant, uncanny, oddly androgynous. No doubt women perceived it as masculine and men as feminine.

PRACTICE AND ACQUIRE UNIQUE SKILLS.

The phrases imprinted themselves into my brain. The flickering bands of black and white plunged me into a trance. My consciousness drifted.

BUILD REPUTATION AND COMPLETE MISSIONS.

The spiral spun faster. For a moment, I felt weightlessness, like when you swing on a swing and freeze at the highest point. And then... WHOOOOOOSH!

CHAPTER 03

AND HERE I AM, kneeling like a runner at the starting line or a killer robot from the future in an ancient movie. The second thought makes me chuckle and look down at my body.

No, I'm not naked. I'm wearing a rough shirt without buttons, like a sweatshirt, or whatever you call such clothing. Below the waist, there are pants that could be better described as "trousers." My feet are bare. They didn't even give me some worn-out sandals.

The sun is scorching down mercilessly. Initially, the most shocking thing is the transition from winter to summer heat. Summer smells like dust and wildflowers. I lean down to pluck a blade of grass, rub it between my fingers, and inhale the fresh, spicy scent. There was nothing like this in esports. There, the arena always had a perfect plastic surface, streamlined and pared with nothing superfluous. But here it's just like reality, but on maximum settings.

My body behaves strangely. At first, it feels like the settings got messed up during loading. My arms and legs are weak, as if I'm sick. Every movement is difficult. I try to touch a finger to my nose. It takes me three attempts to succeed.

Moving my eyes wakes the UI. It's unfamiliar, not like the one in Gladiators. In addition to the life bar, there's mana and experience. And Stamina, of course. There's no list of special moves or combos. Apparently, I'll still have to earn those, but I am certain now that this is an RPG.

I explore the other buttons. In the profile section, I admire myself in 3D. In these starting rags, I look like a runaway peasant who decided to become either a soldier or a bandit. That said, the system simply copied my real appearance without allowing me to make any changes. Well, the girls will be disappointed. No dolls to play with for them! I wonder if they start in the same rags too.

I find the stats panel. Every stat is at one. That's why I'm so weak! Stats aren't just numbers here. They impair my physical condition. It feels pretty lousy, honestly. Just a little more, and my legs will give out.

I've spawned in some secluded alley. Tall wooden fences stretch along either side. I don't see any other players nearby. I spot a small boulder near the fence. I try to lift it and discover that I'm *really* weak — I have to strain really hard to even budge the boulder. My only consolation is that the others should be the same.

My prior experience as an esports player was supposed to help, but it's only confusing me now. We used to do warm-ups before every match: to get the brain to adapt to the virtual body, to see how quickly it reacted and how powerful its response was. I started doing the same thing now, muttering to myself from time to time. This is like switching from a sports car to a beater.

And I still don't know what to do! How do I get quests in this place anyway? After waving my arms and stomping my feet enough, I noticed a flashing envelope in the left corner of my peripheral vision: That's the the quest log.

GET A QUEST FROM THE MAYOR

BUY A WEAPON AT THE STORE

KILL ONE MOB

You have 30 minutes to complete all the quests!

A timer was counting down below. It was no longer at 30, but at 27 and falling. Time to get moving.

Well they sure don't bother with lore here! No intros or cutscenes. It's understandable — we're beta testers, not players. Our job is to test the game mechanics and then write a report. The "nice features" will be added by the screenwriters for the big spenders who'll splurge on the finished product.

The quest log used the word "mayor," so the setting is definitely European. Otherwise, it would be "shichō" or some other term. So, let's go find the mayor then.

The quest giver was waiting for me just around the corner. The alley led to a wide street, and that street, like a river, brought me to a large square. There were other players already converging on it, just like me, popping out from different alleyways and passageways.

Already, a mob of us had formed around the mayor. The only thing indicating his importance was an exclamation mark hanging over his head. There it was, a bright orange icon sticking out in the air. Are you serious?! This is what they call full immersion? This feels more like a tutorial for dummies.

Pushing through to the mayor turned out to be its own challenge. The beta testers didn't bother to form an orderly line here. To the contrary, they jostled with their elbows and shoulders, wrangling among themselves. I tried to squeeze my way in from the side into the crowd. Useless. Our low stats made us as helpless as newborn kittens. The testers shoved each other with their weak little arms and slapped each other's backs with their feeble fists, creating an impassable mass. The rare lucky ones who reached the NPC were desperately shouting and couldn't find their way back out. The crowd rarely let anyone out.

I decided to follow the lucky few who did escape.

Like ants, a thin stream of them trickled to a neighboring street and into a building with a prominent sign: a sword and an ax crossed. There were various ways to interpret this. It could be a guard barracks, a mercenaries' guild, or some kind of martial arts school. But judging by the fact that the testers were darting into it, it was sure to be an weapons store.

Scoffing at the morons stuck in the square and exulting in my own resourcefulness, I too stepped inside.

"Excuse me! Hey, sir!" I tapped on the counter, trying to get the attention of a hulking lad in a worn leather vest. Judging by his biceps, he not only traded weapons but also forged them.

"Hey!" I waved my hand in front of his face. No response.

The feeble stream of players kept coming. They entered the store, made their purchases, glanced over at me, and went on their way without saying anything.

"A sword."

"I want a sword."

"Sword, please."

"Give me a bow."

"Oh, honorable merchant, would you..."

"Hey, buddy!"

"What you're doing — it won't work," one tester finally grumbled. "He won't see you if you haven't started the quest. You think you're the only wise guy around here?"

What a bunch of tosh! Even browser games have more flexible plots these days. I had to go back to the square. Not only had the crowd not thinned out, but it had become denser, more tightly-packed, and more impenetrable. New beta testers were pouring into it by the minute. One guy even gave up entirely and dropping to all fours, began crawling among the crowd's legs. I was about to follow his example when suddenly I heard a shout from behind.

"Hey, Andryusha!" Simba waved his hand. He looked exactly the same as in reality: big and loud, like a friendly teddy bear. "Why are you still here? Were you waiting for me?"

Crapola! This meant that at least fifteen minutes had passed already! Simba had been among the next wave to be let in. I looked at the timer:

14:52... 14:51... 14:50...

Half of my time was already gone and I hadn't made any progress at all!

"Of course, I'm waiting for you!" I didn't feel like telling my friend that I had wasted all that time idly. "What if you got lost?"

"Tar-get-ay," Simba read aloud the handle hanging over my head. "Did you make a new nick or what?"

"Forget it, I'll tell you later," I hurried him. "Let's get a move on."

"Wait, have you seen Yumi around here somewhere?" Simba looked around.

"Simba, check the quest log. This one's got a timer."

Simba's eyes clouded over for a moment. Then he abruptly took off running, slammed straight into the crowd in the center of the square

— and bounced off like a rubber ball. What I like about him is that he acts first and thinks later. Strategy is not his strong suit. But in view of his explosive nature and significant body mass, tactics are usually enough. It's just a shame it didn't work in this case.

The timer is ticking and failing such a stupid tutorial would really be embarrassing. Even though I don't really care about this beta testing gig, I still need the money. Those who can't finish the quest won't get a single penny. It's a way to weed out the useless.

I try to prod my brain into action. The problem is not that we're too weak. It's just that everyone has equal strength. If I push the guy next to me with my mass of one, he pushes back at me with his own mass. Our forces are equal and no one makes any progress.

Now, how can I increase my strength? Leveling up is one way, but I can't possibly do that in 15 minutes without any weapons or knowledge of the map. Of course, stats could be increased without leveling — as in Legendary Moonlight Sculptor, for instance. But there's no time for hardcore grinding either. Then what if we simply… combine our strengths?

"Over here Simba!" I yell, running towards the crowd. "See that guy? Grab his left arm. I'll grab his right and then — on the count of three?"

Simba joins me without any further questions, positioning himself beside me. We grab a feisty old man with a bald patch. He's a bit too old to be a beta tester, but to each his own.

"One... two... heave!" We pluck him out of the crowd like a carrot. He flies aside, lands on his rear and erupts in expletives. We've forgotten all about him however: "One... two! One... two!!!"

Girls and boys, irrespective of their age or appearance, begin flying out of our way, clearing a path before us. After a dozen such tosses we find ourselves face to face with the mayor without even having broken a sweat.

"Are you ready to fulfill your duty, hero?" the haughty NPC scans me disdainfully from head to toe. I admit, my appearance is far from presentable. But there aren't many options here. Everyone is dressed the same way.

"I am humbly prepared to serve your will, Your Highness!" I crow energetically and incoherently, standing at attention. Simba chortles beside me.

The mayor's sour expression softens into a paternal smile.

"Serve with honor, young one!" He hands me a scroll and nods. Quest received.

+1 REPUTATION WITH THE MAYOR.

CURRENT STATUS: 1/10 (PASSING INTEREST).

Blessing Received: The Mayor's Encouragement (+20% to all stats)

"Do as I do," I whisper to Simba. He flaps his eyes in surprise but then obediently blurts out some "heroic" platitude as I had.

"Wow, we hit the jackpot!" he says, rejoicing

at the blessing notification.

Working our shoulders and elbows, we make our way out of the crowd. Getting out is easier now because we understand how and because we have the mayor's buff. The quest scroll dissolves in my hands, and immediately the inventory icon begins to blink in my interface. The scroll appears in one of the slots, along with five coins next to it. I guess that's the money for the sword I'm about to buy.

We sprint as fast as we can to the store. Thankfully I already know the way, and Simba follows me without wasting time on questions.

7:45... 7:44...

"A sword... a sword!" we exclaim almost at the same time.

Mentally commanding my interface, I grab the coins in my inventory and toss them onto the counter. This time, the merchant responds as he should. Two identical swords appear before us. Simba immediately stashes his in his inventory, but I can't resist. It's been so long since I held anything like this. Then again, I used to have a deep fondness for Eastern blades — whereas this one is short and straight, like a Roman gladius. It's as heavy as a railway rail and so poorly balanced that it threatens to slip out of my hands at any moment. I flick my wrist to twirl it and test the balance...and drop the hunk of iron to the floor with a clang. Simba laughs again.

"Fek! How are we supposed to fight with this thing?"

"Let's go," my buddy urges me on. "We can

figure that out in the heat of battle!"

But where do we go? After a second's thought, I think to unfurl the scroll.

"Venomous spiders have infested some houses on the edge of town. Slay at least one of the creatures. Show your willingness to serve the town."

The quest list changes again, leaving only the last item. Immediately, a map icon lights up. I open it, and a new marker appears. It's the same yellow color as the highlighted task — so that even an idiot can understand what's expected of him.

We set off running again, almost depleting our Stamina. We scour the streets, panting heavily as if we just finished a PE exam, until finally we stumble upon the spiders' lair.

Once upon a time, a house like any other stood here. Now, however, only its foundation and the ruins of the first floor remain. If there was once a fence here, it's long gone. The desiccated trees before the ruins gesticulate with ugly branches, and a thick layer of cobwebs entangles the ruins and remains of a garden. Beneath this layer, something is constantly moving and shifting, as if the entire cover is alive somehow.

"Ugh..." Simba turns to look at me, speaking for both of us with a single grunt. Disgusting.

Thank goodness we don't have to go inside. There are enough spiders about. Large, hairy creatures the size of small dogs scurry along the path leading to the house, over the lawn sprinkled with cobwebs, and even out to the pavement. They are as industrious as ants, constantly weaving, moving, and dragging... something.

I feel even more uneasy when I realize what that something is. The spiders are wrapping human bodies — fallen beta testers — in cocoons. It looks like, there'll be a feast in the spiders' lair tonight.

"I'm not going in there... No way... Nope... Anything but that!"

A cute girl is standing next to us, horror-stricken as she gazes at the ruins. She tugs nervously at the hem of her gaming t-shirt, revealing a cute belly. Tears well up in her bright eyes, as blue as fields of cornflowers. I don't even know how such a beautiful image could occur to my cynical brain. I have only seen fields of cornflowers on TV. Perhaps there's something about the girl that suggests that she comes from the country. She's thick, as they say, corn-fed yet not overweight by a country mile. At the same time, her breasts and ass are remarkably generous in size. I would even have suspected that this sweetheart had tampered with the character editor, but the system didn't give us that option earlier — so, I have to assume she's all natural.

"AngelCake" — I automatically commit her handle to memory. Although, if she's this afraid of spiders, I don't think I'll ever run into her again. I doubt the admins will hang onto anyone who can't complete the first quest.

5:28... 5:27...

"Aaaaaah!" With a gurgled cry and without

waiting for me, Simba rushes into battle.

I eject the busty girl from my mind and grip the sword more comfortably in my hand. How can anyone hold this contraption comfortably? And what is it with this thing anyway? It looks perfectly fine, but...

Then it hits me — it's the stats! The weapon isn't the problem — I am. With my abysmal skills, it's pure torture to wield any weapon at all.

The spiders meanwhile stay calm, ignoring us, and that works to our advantage. I choose a lone spider who has crawled out further into the cobbled road. It taps the cobblestones with its spindly legs as if searching for something. In fact its behavior is more reminiscent of ants than spiders, but let's leave that inconsistency to the developers. I grab my unwieldy sword with both hands and bring it down onto the spider's convex abdomen, which is covered in fine red hairs. At the last instant, the spider jumps aside. My sword's inertia tugs me past my target. Son of a...!

The next instant, the spider's sharp, needle-like jaws sink into my leg below the knee. A burning pain ignites within my leg. Venom. This mob is venomous!

YOU HAVE BEEN POISONED (-1 HP/S).

My life bar turns a sickly green. It starts shrinking in jerks, though thankfully very slowly. I jump back and raise the sword again for an attack. This is like trying to kill a mosquito with an iron crowbar. I hear Simba bellowing nearby. It sounds like things aren't going well for him either.

3:33... 3:32...

Well this isn't much like esports at all. In the Gladiator Games I had all my skills at my disposal right out the gate, but in here we're like helpless cripples. We need to increase our Strength and Dexterity. To have any effect in this place, we'll need to grind and level up. It's the first time hardcore mode seems tempting to me. Poor noobs — they'll be eaten alive!

I back up and — now having some space to work with — dash sideways. As I suspected the spider refuses to stray too far from its nest. Seeing that I've moved far enough away, it raises its front legs menacingly, then turns around and skitters back.

I watch a beta tester rush into the thicket of spiders, crying in a frenzy and swinging his sword like a scythe. The spiders clamber all over him, covering him from all sides, knocking him off his feet. The wriggling mass of them completely engulfs the player's body. He's still twitching as they wrap him in their silk.

"Someone save him!" the blue-eyed beauty screams at the top of her lungs, pointing at the writhing cocoon.

This is why it's customary to shoot panicking soldiers in war. Fear is too contagious.

And why the hell am I trembling?! Wasn't I a champion esports player once? I take two deep breaths and calm myself down. Every opponent has strengths and weaknesses. If you can't find the weaknesses, you have to neutralize the strengths. The spiders are too nimble for us to hit them directly, so we need another approach.

Simba is stalwartly on the defensive, holding his sword before him. He struggles to fend off his opponent. Meanwhile, the spider eagerly scurries around him, trying to bite his legs like an enraged Scotch terrier.

I run over and dive onto the spider's reddish back like a soccer goalie.

"What are you doing?!"

"Strike now!" I shout.

I roll onto my back, unexpectedly exposing the spider's pallid belly to Simba. Even to the naked eye, the armor is softer there. The spider struggles desperately. It snaps at my arm with its crooked pincers. My wrist goes numb, and the pain shoots up towards my elbow. I won't be able to hold on for much longer.

"Aaaah!" Simba swings at me with everything he's got. My life bar immediately drops by half.

"Damn it, be careful, you dolt!"

"Son of a...! I'll stick that sword where the sun don't shine and twist it!" he curses, and I'm not entirely sure who my buddy is threatening, the spider or me.

He tosses the weapon aside and starts punching the spider with his bare hands.

"Die! Die! Die, you bastard... Die!"

The spider wriggles weaker and weaker in my hands, suggesting that the blows are doing their job.

"There!" Simba finally shouts. "I did it!"

I don't see much difference between the living spider and the dead one. But I guess Simba's gotten a system message prompting his celebration. I get up to my feet.

"The timer, Simba! I have two minutes left!"

Without a further word, he repeats my trick — with the grace of a falling hippopotamus. Our next victim manages to escape from under him, but Simba jumps and grabs its hind leg. The spider screeches desperately.

"Come here, you bitch... Stop struggling... We're going to dance now..." Simba says, pulling the spider towards himself. Now it's me who chuckles. I feel like tossing away the disobedient sword and just throttling the damn creature.

As strange as it sounds, I feel a little inadequate with this weapon. It's not the sword's fault that I'm such a noob and clumsy. It's an honest sword. To save face, I must now drench it in blood, even if it's the green goop of a spider.

Pressing the point into a gap in the spider's chitinous armor, I push hard with both hands. The sword cracks through the creature's armor. I throw my whole body into it, splitting it open like a butcher. The spider's acrid blood splashes on my face.

You have slain a venomous spider. The tutorial quest is complete.

1:35... 1:34...

There's still time.

"Hey, you! What's your name...AngelCake! Come over here!"

Simba turns around in surprise and locks eyes with AngelCake, then gives me a knowing wink.

"I can't... I'm afraid of spiders." The cutie wrinkles her nose. Then, after a fierce internal struggle, she takes a few steps forward. Oh what the hell! She's even holding her sword like a pitchfork, as if she's about to chase a scary turkey out of her garden.

A debonair smile appears on Simba's face. He's already arranged this simple girl in every possible position — in his imagination.

"What are you standing there for? Help us!"

My friend hesitates for a moment and then lunges at the nearest spider.

"Grab it... Grab it... I'm chasing it your way!"

What was terrifying suspense just a couple of moments ago now turns into a circus. Using the tested method, I tackle the spider on its back. Simba rushes in, grabbing its twitching legs. Using our four hands, we splay the creature out on the cobblestones. This time, we manage to do it without taking any bites.

"Take that! And that!" AngelCake peppers the spider with a hail of strikes.

"Damn it, be more careful!" bellows Simba like a wounded bear. "You hit my arm!"

"Oh, sorry!" the blue-eyed girl panics, lowering her sword and freezing in place.

0:27... 0:26...

"Stop waffling and start attacking, you dummy! I'm running out of time!" I explode.

The cutie lifts her nose again and approaches the spider, trying her best not to look in my direction. Oh, heavens, she's offended!

"Aim for the head, aim for the head," Simba advises.

The blue-eyed girl positions herself, apparently aiming to knock the enemy's head off with a heroic strike.

Whack! I feel a sharp pain in my shoulder, followed immediately by a system message:

YOU HAVE DIED.

PLEASE CONTACT THE SYSTEM ADMINISTRATOR TO REINSTATE YOUR ACCOUNT.

Pshhh... The VR pod's lid rises on a pneumatic actuator. Saline solution drains away from me with a slurping sound, leaving an unpleasant dry crust on my skin. Around me, other players are emerging from their pods. Their laughter and chatter reverberates under the arches of the vast hall.

They sound happy, so they passed the test. And here I am without a clue. On the one hand, I finished the quest. On the other hand, I died. What does this mean? Some penalty or straight elimination?

The conditions were never explained to us. How can you play without knowing the rules? Irritation slowly turn to anger inside me. I try to control it with my willpower.

Wrapped in a robe and lazily shuffling in my soft slippers, I head to the shower. A slight apathy sets in, as always after a battle. All my emotions have remained back there in virtual reality. Now, for a while at least, my life here will seem particularly dull and bland.

I wash away the remnants of adrenaline along with the saline solution under a current of scalding water. My body returns to life in meatspace. I'm craving food wildly, and pardon the details, something quite opposite too. I recall seeing a door with the coveted letters somewhere along the way. I quickly get dressed and set off in search of it.

The restroom, like everything here, is designed on a grand scale. There's no one inside. Each step echoes off the tiled walls. I barely have time to do my business when I realize I'm no longer alone.

It's clear that the people who've just entered are trying not to make noise. I hear quiet whispers. Stifled laughter and the rustling of clothing. The sounds pass by my stall. The door of the adjacent stall slams shut.

"Oh, stop... you can't do that here..."

"I can do anything..."

And almost immediately after that, I hear a soft gasp or moan. I wish I could leave discreetly, but the voices sound familiar to me. Berating myself for my curiosity, I very quietly lift the seat, stand up on the edge of my toilet and peek over the partition.

CHAPTER 04

I DIDN'T SEE ANYTHING unexpected. The couple in the stall next to me was banging. The girl was standing in a position commonly referred to as "doggy style." One hand rested on the toilet tank, while the other passionately pressed against the wall. Hasty sex doesn't look very erotic, especially in tight spaces. But the girl was putting in a lot of effort. She dropped her jacket to the floor and lifted her shirt, revealing a cute and firm breast for all to see. I could barely see it myself, but her partner not only watched but also enjoyed groping her. She bent one leg at the knee and placed it on the closed toilet lid, making serious efforts not to slip. Even in this position, she looked very seductive.

She hiked her skirt almost to her waist, exposing her defenseless white rear. The girl moaned softly, encouraging her partner. With each thrust, her pigtails bounced on her shoulders in a playful manner. The most interesting part was hidden from me, as the guy's back was covered in a leather jacket. He didn't bother undressing. I immediately recognized both the pigtails and the jacket. Lance was banging Yumi. Taking his time, enjoying it, he was relieving stress with a fan after the first battle. And Yumi diligently moved her buttocks, accommodating him. She probably felt pretty special at that moment.

Without making a sound, I climbed down and left the restroom.

"Did we give them a hard time or what, eh Andryusha?" Simba caught up with me in the corridor. "Why are you looking so down?"

"I'm not sure who gave who a hard time," I replied. "I actually got killed there at the end."

"Yeah, I know." I didn't hear any sympathy in Simba's voice. "But I didn't let the spiders have you! Anastasia and I moved your body aside."

"You and who now?"

"Well, the busty one, AngelCake. Her name is Anastasia." Simba had managed to cement the random encounter. "She was really upset that she accidentally hit you with her sword. Almost chopped off your hand. So, be prepared, she might come to apologize."

The thought of the curvy blue-eyed girl lifted my spirits a little. Why am I getting so worked up about Yumi? We hardly even know each other. The fact that Lance is having his way with her right now instead of me? Well, that's the law of nature. The alpha male takes the females he wants, and the rest pick from among the leftovers.

"Never cross those who are stronger than you," my father used to say in moments of hungover clairvoyance. "They'll trample you, crush you, break you, and throw you away. Live, work, save your pennies. Know your place and be happy that no one bothers you."

I listened to him, seeing his trembling hands, hearing his shaky voice. I listened and nodded. But now, a long-forgotten anger flared to life inside of me. And for the first time in a long time, I didn't feel like smothering it. I enjoyed feeling that cold, fiery rage burning inside of me.

*   *   *

"Don't just walk away!" a smiling girl in an office suit waves at us. "Come in and submit your results. Type up your test reports!"

Heeding her command, we enter a large room that resembles an internet cafe or a computer class.

"Your ranking depends on the quality of your reports," she says in a seductive tone.

We find some free seats. Beta testers around us are typing up their reports, coming up with something, furrowing their brows. It's strange, it feels like some kind of exam. I still can't figure out if we're the ones being tested or the ones doing the testing.

I entered my personal info, got some questions in response, and started to think. There are two types of tests. In the first one, it's recommended to answer the questions honestly, or else you risk getting some kind of unpleasant surprise. For example, they might enroll you in a book lovers' club, a crochet circle, or the university volleyball team without your consent.

In the second type, on the contrary, it's better to guess what they expect from you. Otherwise, at best, they might get offended, and at worst, they'll send you to a psychiatric facility. I wonder which type of test this is?

There weren't any specific questions. I was asked to evaluate the game based on several categories and leave my comments for each one.

REALISM.

At first, I wanted to give it a 5 out of 5. I remembered how the sun burned, how the fresh grass smelled, how desperately the spider escaped from my hands, and how its stiff red hairs pricked my palms.

But then I recalled the orange exclamation mark glowing in the air above the mayor. A ridiculous and stupid symbol straight out of ancient multiplayer games, completely shattering the illusion of immersion. It was like they were deliberately hinting: don't take what's happening seriously — you're in a game. Realism? Really? I ended up scoring it a 3 out of 5 and explained my reason.

PLOT.

Was there even a plot? Can you call a mindless dash through a gauntlet without any choices or options a plot? It was too primitive even for a tutorial. A starting location should not only teach the player basic skills but also set up a scenario. It should allow the player to immerse themselves in the events of a new world and become a part of it. There was nothing of the kind here. When it came to plot, this game hardly deserved a 1 out of 5.

COMBAT SYSTEM.

Not bad, considering we didn't even see the extent of it. Maybe I'm a bit of a masochist, but I enjoyed how the lack of stats affected my physical condition. It really made me want to level up and get stronger. I can only imagine how much of a difference reaching Level 2 would make. And the further you go, the more substantial your advantage will be. That's the kind of hook that makes you grind for days, collect legendary sets and seek out unique skills.

It's one thing when competition is expressed in stat numbers or rankings, and a completely different thing when it genuinely makes you feel omnipotent. When you're striving for dominance not in a world of 3D dolls that you see from the outside, but among humans who feel completely real, you get that much more into it.

On the other hand, it's unclear how real-life fighting skills would translate into the game's combat mechanics. If I know how to fight or wield a sword in the real world, wouldn't it help me in the game? Playing it safe, I scored it a 4 out of 5. More intuition than anything else. I liked it —

that's all. Maybe I just missed gaming.

NPC BEHAVIOR.

1 out 5. They're as dumb as bricks. They fall for rank flattery and don't interact at all unless it's a quest event. They look human and all but their behavior gives them away completely. In this day and age, when there's an AI running my vacuum cleaner, these NPCs are painfully scripted. Heck, a car nav has more personality than that mayor.

INTERFACE.

Yes, it's ordinary. Maybe a bit intrusive, but it doesn't bother me much overall. The prompts are clear enough. I only used it for a half hour, but it quickly became intuitive. Still, some stubborn part of me prevents me from giving it the highest score. You never know what kind of glitches might come up later. After all, this isn't the final stage of beta testing, right?

I gave it a 4 out of 5 and the average score popped up on my screen: 2.6. For some reason the numbers glow red and are accompanied by an unpleasant sound.

The office girl glanced at me disapprovingly. Was I borking her numbers or something?

"How now," Simba exclaimed, surprised. "Don't you think you've overthought it? I just gave it straight 5s down the line."

"Crap. Really?" I said. "You could do that?"

"Yeah, you bet," Simba chuckled. "Anyway, forget it. Let's go find the cafeteria."

"Let's eat," I agreed, following him. He seemed to have some mysterious internal navigation system that effortlessly led him to various cafes, cafeterias and fast food stands. Perhaps it was nature's way of ensuring this huge organism stayed well-fed, endowing him with a gift for finding grub wherever he was.

We found the cafeteria on the first floor, not far from the front lobby. Despite the long line, Simba and I wound our way through quite easily, thanks to our student habits. The prices were affordable, so we grabbed some budget-friendly sausage rolls and a glass of some pale beverage, neither fruit punch nor apple juice.

People around us were gathering in groups, sharing their impressions. I caught snippets of other people's conversations. Many had fallen into the spider's nest, figuratively speaking. And some hadn't even managed to get the first quest. I felt a bit better hearing this. Maybe I wasn't doomed after all.

"Hey, Yumi, we're over here!" Simba yelled suddenly. He rushed after the girl, who didn't bother to turn around.

Damn it! I couldn't stop my friend in time and hurried after him.

"Yumi," Simba reached out to touch the girl's shoulder — and encountered Lance's steely gaze.

"Who are you?" Lance asked, surprised.

He seemed calm at that moment, holding a tray neatly heaped with plates of cutlets, salads, buns and a bottle of some carbonated drink.

"Oh, he's just confused," Yumi mewed. "I don't know him."

As Simba stared dumbfounded, one of Lance's friends jolted his elbow, knocking the glass of pale liquid onto Simba's trendy yellow jacket.

"You got a spot there, deadbeat. You should really clean that," sneered the imbecile with the fashionable pink bangs. The whole clique burst into raucous laughter. Even Yumi chuckled. Lance was the last to laugh, politely and regally, as if acknowledging a fine jest.

A red warning light flashed in my brain. *"He's baiting him,"* occurred to me. *"Don't feed the troll!"* But it was too late.

Simba bellowed like a wounded bear and slammed his hand directly into Lance's tray. Like a slow-motion fireworks display, bowls, plates, and their contents flew in all directions. The coleslaw spattered the imbecile with the pink bangs. The soda pop erupted in a gush of foam that whipped right at Yumi. And a bowl of some thick soup, maybe gumbo, maybe minestrone, tipped over onto Lance.

"I'll tear you apart, you bastard!" Lance's friend tried to shove Simba, but it would have been easier to move a boulder from its place. Yumi let out a piercing shriek.

"Guards, guards!" the townsfolk cried all around us.

The security guards arrived quickly and positioned themselves between us, ready to intervene if any punches were thrown. The chief security officer appeared almost immediately. I recognized him by his prominent belly and insolent gaze. He didn't waste time with explanations.

"Both of you, out!"

"Everything's fine, we've quashed it," I raised my hands, demonstrating friendliness. "We're just waiting for the results."

"You're the lippy one, eh?" The tubby guard squinted at me. "I've got your result right here: Both of you are kicked out!"

"But we were told the results would only be available in thirty minutes!"

"Lippy and a smart aleck!" seethed the chief. "Boys, get this dreck out of here!"

He turned and headed for the exit. Two guards approached Simba. He tried to fight them off, but they twisted him into a painful hold and walked him away. I didn't try to be the hero. This fight was not only meaningless but also futile. However, I didn't make it easy for them either. When the security guards took hold of me, I went completely limp, becoming dead weight.

Anyone who's ever carried a drunk friend on their back, knows how difficult and uncomfortable it is. Muttering under their breaths, the meatheads began dragging me out while I snagged every piece of cafeteria furniture along the way. I don't know what I was counting on: a miracle or just my innate stubbornness.

People were staring at us, whispering and filming with their phones. I'd be shocked not to see myself on YouTube later today. The office girls gasped, covering their mouths with their hands. Apparently, they had never witnessed such a spectacle in their lives.

The meatheads dragged us into the lobby and then on to the front entrance. Simba was still trying argue his case, while I had the clear realization that in just another minute, my VR adventure would come to an end.

"Where are you taking them?"

The question was posed with such incongruously cheerful curiosity that even the security guards paused.

A short man in perfectly polished shoes, pressed trousers, and a polo shirt was observing the scene with interest. A tiny Lacoste crocodile was the only spot of color on his otherwise completely black outfit.

At first glance I took him for old. His hair was completely gray and cut in a short military buzz, and deep wrinkles covered his face like a baked apple. But there was some mischievous restlessness in his posture and sly blue eyes that dissuaded me from reaching this conclusion. He rocked back and forth on his heels, comically puffing up his cheeks and generally behaving completely unseriously.

"I asked you, where are you taking them?" The grizzled man raised his eyebrows in a simple, rustic manner, expressing his surprise. I locked eyes with him, and suddenly, unexpectedly, he winked at me, as if all of this was somehow amusing.

"None of your business." The tubby security guard stepped forward.

The grizzled man puffed out his cheeks in deep thought, and squinted as if he was trying to see the tip of his own nose.

"But the results haven't been announced yet, right?" he finally asked.

"I've announced the results for these two personally," replied tubby.

"Really?" the grizzled man insisted. "How come?"

"Because I can," the tubby guard yelled angrily, spraying saliva.

Then everything happened very quickly. The grizzled man nodded, as if he had expected exactly that answer, and with a swift movement, he stepped right up to the main security guard. He raised his hand, joined his index and middle fingers together, and lightly poked the chubby guard on the forehead.

Some kind of deep sense of unreality engulfed me. It was as if the grizzled man had just shattered the pattern of everyday life for everyone present.

"What are you doing?!" the tubby guard exclaimed in shock.

He wasn't the only one — everyone around us was gaping, stunned.

"What I want to," the grizzled man chuckled. "How come? Because I can, right? And I can do this too!"

He flicked the tip of the guard's nose.

"Ow!" the guard's squeal sounded like a

piglet's. "Why, I'll...!"

"Why you'll what?" the grizzled man asked softly and swiftly and sharply punched the tubby guard in the nose. Then he immediately jumped to the side, out of the way of the squirting blood.

Amid the stunned lobby, the quiet smack sounded like a bomb exploding. The security guards suddenly lost all interest in us. They relaxed their grips, dropping Simba and me to the floor like two lifeless sacks. Yet even then, they seemed completely bewildered as to what to do. Only one of them lunged at the grizzled man without thinking. The grizzled man crouched, letting the assailant's fist pass over him, then deftly twisted, tossing the heavy guy over his back, and slammed him to the floor. A second later, he stood there again, rocking on his heels and toes — though now his posture did not seem silly at all.

"Get him!" the tubby chief bellowed.

His entire shirt was soaked in blood. But his minions hesitated. This was a bit tougher than sparring with Simba, I thought spitefully.

"Could you show us your ID please?!" one of the guards finally managed.

"Well, finally!" the grizzled man sighed with relief. "A thinking person among this sophomoric gang."

He took out a tiny card from his pocket, the size of a credit card or an electronic pass, and handed it to the guard. At the mere sight of it, the guard suddenly drew up straight and bowed ceremoniously. I had only seen something like it in movies about yakuza or in manga.

"It is an honor to serve you, Master," he said, pronouncing the word "Master" in a way that made it clear that it was not just a polite address, but rather a name or even a title.

"I'm not your master and you're not my student," the grizzled man replied sharply. "But you're definitely the smartest one in this flock, so you have a chance. In the meantime, take over his duties." The grizzled man pointed his finger at the tubby ex-chief. "In case you dim lot don't get it, the rest of you are fired. For cowardice and stupidity. Actually, this one can stay too." He pointed his finger at the bull lying at his feet. "At least he's brave."

"ALL BETA TESTERS, PLEASE PROCEED TO THE WAITING AREA FOR THE ANNOUNCEMENT OF RESULTS..." a loud neutral voice suddenly said over the speakers.

"What are you sitting around for?" The grizzled man looked directly at me and winked. "That applies to you too."

The atmosphere in the large lobby where we had recently waited to enter the game had changed dramatically. The seats had been pushed out of the way and a large information board had been hung on one of the walls. Through some strange irony, I encountered Lance's name on it before anyone else's.

128 points. Holy crap! Someone explain to me how anyone could rack up 128 points in that stupid quest. Did he fuck the spider queen? Or did

he marry her and adopt her whole brood?

And yet Lance's score wasn't the most interesting part because Lance was only in second place. The first place read: "Anna – 200 points." As for myself, I couldn't find my name anywhere at all and was starting to get nervous when Simba beat me to it. He put his hand on my shoulder and said:

"Well, this is bullshit, isn't it?"

Chapter 05

MEANWHILE, NINE FLOORS overhead, a meeting was under way in the office tower's executive suite. The long wooden table in the middle of the spacious and opulent space was only a quarter full. This was the finest suite in the entire office complex and it was no wonder therefore that it belonged to the VP of MosTech, or that it emphasized its occupant's status in every way: The suite was furnished with plush leather sofas and boasted abstract paintings on its walls, all kinds of high-tech devices, a thick rug on the floor, and a luxurious bar, offering the finest selection of liquors and spirits. The occupant of the office loved to surround himself with quality, and most importantly, expensive things. At the moment, however, he was sitting on the sidelines, sweating profusely and secretly rejoicing that he hadn't already been canned.

One of his playthings, by contrast, was currently very much center stage — under the withering scrutiny of several pairs of predatory eyes. The VP's plaything had a name, and her name was Marina. She was the head of PR at MosTech. She looked very good on screens large and small, in the back seats of company limousines, as well as in sundry saunas and country clubs that the VP patronized. Short, curvy and pert, the blonde with a trendy short bob smoothly complemented any number of interiors.

Those waiting in line at the office tower's entrance that morning would have recognized the office chick in the short, trendy fur coat, standing watch at the VIP entrance. By now, however, Marina had changed into a white blouse and a prim pencil skirt that accentuated her excellent behind. She now nervously unbuttoned an extra button on her blouse just in case, revealing a glimpse of designer lingerie. This trick had served her many times with the VP and she figured it might work on the ones currently watching her too.

Marina's anxiety was not unfounded. The company board members sitting at the table exuded an aura of power and wealth. Sensing it, the young girl felt both fear and excitement. Only the lone woman sitting among the men at the table terrified her to her core.

Besides the VP (whom no one cared about anyway) there were three men at the table. The one sitting at the head of the table was called Doc by the rest, although he didn't look like a scientist or a doctor at all. Rather, he resembled a successful entrepreneur or a business coach. Even now, despite his evident displeasure, his charisma was overpowering. With her keen eye, the aspiring PR maven noticed more and more signs of wealth and status about him: a tan in the middle of Russian winter (and clearly not from a tanning bed), perfect white teeth, an expensive brand-name suit, a pristine white silk shirt with the collar casually unbuttoned and a watch of a brand that was unfamiliar to her, yet clearly very expensive. Gray hairs salted Doc's thick black hair, yet the PR girl couldn't tell his age. He could've been as easily 35 as 50.

The second man was called the Master. The oldest among the group, he was also the most restless. As he listened to her presentation, the Master constantly fidgeted in his seat, furrowing his brow at his own thoughts or raising his eyebrows in surprise at what the others said. Marina felt that he was the most out of place among those present, but the others treated the Master with marked deference. Dressed entirely in black, he made the girl feel especially timid. Anytime his gaze paused on Marina, he looked at her as at a small, tame animal that he could either pet or strangle, without being able to decide which.

The third person at the table belonged to a category men that Marina knew quite well and did not consider to be men at all. He was an IT guy and to be fair to him, he did stand out from among the other members of his dull profession, as far as she was familiar with them. He had a beard and glasses and generally dressed as if he had found his clothes at a garage sale. Nonetheless, his beard was neatly trimmed, his glasses boasted a fancy frame, and among his accessories, Marina spied individual items that she herself could only afford during special sales.

He was constantly torn between his laptop, his tablet, and two smartphones, and he maintained a very stern demeanor the entire time. Perhaps due to his youth he was called variously Benjamin, Ben, and even Benny by the others. As for Marina, she didn't dare address him by anything other than his last name. Mr. Benjamin Zvyagin was in charge of all technical matters in the beta test and was the only one present who had already crossed paths with Marina. And crossed paths in this case meant that he had yelled at her twice over the phone and once personally called her a "headless chicken."

The only woman among these guests — all of whom behaved like they were at home — had still to utter a single word. Instead, she curled her plump lips in dissatisfaction and made notes in an old-fashioned paper notepad. The others treated her as if she were the Queen of England, addressing her only respectfully as Dr. Skuratova. As they took their seats at the table, Doc had pulled out the chair for her, while the Master busied himself with the electric kettle, brewing some special tea, which he then served to her with a slight bow. Marina noted with glee that the woman was no longer young — and then observed with chagrin that she was still very beautiful. Dr. Irina Vladimirovna Skuratova's well-groomed, aristocratic features showed no signs of plastic surgery, but the PR maven knew very well that looking like she did required either lots of money or outright sorcery. Dr. Skuratova's dark hair was styled in an elaborate updo, and her lilac pantsuit would have served its wearer equally in a boardroom or on the red carpet at a film festival.

"In total, we had 824 beta testers take part in this initial round of the beta," chirped Marina, "of whom 112 were disqualified due to health reasons and 18 were disqualified during the test..."

"Disqualified due to what?" Doc immediately asked. He seemed like a very punctilious person.

"Personal violations," Marina explained with a blush.

"They tried to fuck the girls," observed the Master.

Dr. Skuratova made an exasperated "pffff" sound with her lips...

"Did they succeed?" Benjamin asked with interest.

"Nah," the Master shrugged. "They got them naked all right, but their pods didn't have mature content modules installed."

"Why were they disqualified, though?" Doc wondered.

"For what reason?" Marina didn't understand.

"Did the rules state that they couldn't undress other players?" Doc clarified.

"No, but…" Marina grew completely confused.

"A woman in the Middle Ages was an extremely vulnerable object," declared Dr. Skuratova unexpectedly, looking at Marina attentively and making her uneasy.

"Benny?!" Doc redirected the question to the IT guy.

"Why ask me?" Benjamin backpedaled. "My guys only handle the technical matters. The one in charge of the beta's personnel is this headless chicken here."

The head of PR blushed deeply. There was a pause. Desperate to put the moment behind her, Marina hurried on with her presentation.

"All told 276 players passed the test with positive results, with scores ranging from one to two hundred points," she chattered. "Points were awarded for completing game tasks as well as for the comprehensiveness and loyalty demonstrated in their responses to the evaluation questions. We had advertised the beta test on social media two weeks prior so that our beta partners could receive personal invitations."

"Our who?" Doc interrupted again, displeased.

"Our preferred partners in the beta testing program," explained Marina with a sweet smile. "Gaming influencers and esports champions."

She considered the beta partner program her signature achievement. Even now she could not fathom why her idea to invite TV crews along with the most popular media influencers to the beta test launch had been rejected. She wanted to redeem herself and was ready to fight for her opinions tooth and nail.

Doc frowned in displeasure.

"And how did your esports champions perform?" he continued to probe.

"Superbly!" Marina exclaimed happily. "Every one is at the very top of the rankings. The champions I invited all had the best results."

The interactive display on the wall blinked twice and displayed Lance and his buddies in futuristic Kevlar armor joyfully dismantling unfortunate spiderlings. The panicked arachnids fled in every direction trying to hide amid the ruins and among the trees. The braver among them managed to regroup and even attempted desperate counterattacks — only to perish hopelessly under the champions' blades.

"What is this?!" Doc exclaimed, staring at the screen.

At that moment, the camera caught Lance from a particularly favorable angle. From the broad back-plate of his blackened-steel armor, his glyph — a snarling white lynx — winked at the viewers.

"A champion passes the test," the Master quipped with a smirk.

The PR girl spied a tiny remote control in his hands. With its help, the man casually fast-forwarded the image.

"That's not vanilla," said Benjamin, looking up from his laptop. "The starting loadout for the beta test doesn't look like that."

"Well, that's what you gave them, Benny," the Master continued to his own amusement.

"Where did they get that gear from?!" Doc finally got to the point.

"That's their personal gear, which we remodeled for them," Marina began to explain, not realizing that this was precisely the moment she should keep quiet. "They refused to take part in the beta test without it! Oh how come you won't understand! We need their feedback and we need it to be positive! We need captivating screenshots for blogs and gaming portals! How would we get that with those... those... those peasants?!" She shot Benjamin a triumphant look, certain that the others would now see her wisdom and insight.

She remembered how Lance had handed her the drive with the loadouts and how he had discreetly caressed her firm buttocks as the data was loading into the system. A pleasant warmth spread through her body once again. How could anyone say no to that guy? And anyway it was all for the greater good of the end product!

"So where are all the other beta testers?" asked Doc. "Why are your champions the only ones on screen?"

"We sent the riffraff in later so they wouldn't ruin this topnotch footage!" Marina replied, still oblivious to the peril she was in.

"Fuck me," summarized Doc.

While Marina blinked in confusion, the Master fast-forwarded the video. Having played their allotted half hour, the esports pros vanished and the square where they had been began filling up with ordinary beta testers in their standard issue gray shirts and pants. The girls looked more appealing. They wore short skirts like tennis players and cropped tops barely covering their navels. No wonder some of the guys forgot the task at hand and aggroed the half-naked girls.

The video paused. The screen now showed a clutter of players jamming the square from every direction.

"I warned you," Benjamin shrugged before anyone could ask. "Given the limitations of the sandbox we're using, the plan was to stagger the beta test across four hours. total The local brainiacs finished it in two."

The Master zoomed in on the footage — two players were plowing through the crowd.

"Hey, look there…" Doc sat up, interested. "How did those two manage to do that?"

"They combined forces," explained Benjamin. "Each of them has a strength of one, but together they add up to two. So together they are twice as strong as every other single player."

"The incidents of attempted rape were also undertaken by groups," the Master added somewhat irrelevantly. "Another example of humans pooling strength cooperatively."

He winked playfully at Dr. Skuratova, who wagged a finger at him in reply.

"Self-organization is always focused on primitive instincts," said the Queen of England with a smile. "Security, hunger, sex. It was a mistake to disqualify those testers. Those individuals adapt and survive better than the others."

"We'll send in our head of PR for the next test personally," the Master proposed suggestively. "So that she can study the process, so to speak, from the inside."

"And we'll activate some mature content modules too," added Benjamin vindictively. "Since Lady Psychologist sees such utility in it."

Dr. Skuratova nodded regally, approving his jest.

Onscreen, the gridlock around the mayor began to dissipate. Following the others' example, the players found friends, formed groups, and began forcing their way through. The remaining stragglers pushed for a while, then gave up and formed into the semblance of a line.

The camera swooped over towards the edge of town. The spiders had a clear advantage now. Having been soundly routed by the esports pros earlier, they now took revenge. One by one, the beta testers disappeared into the depths of their lair.

"What a nasty business," Dr. Skuratova pursed her lips, revolted. "Why spiders, of all things? Couldn't you have chosen something more pleasant?"

"It was the psychologists' advice," Benjamin

chuckled. "They explained that arachnophobia is one of the most common fears among people. It is believed that every tenth man and every second woman is afraid of spiders. We *are* looking for a psychologically resilient candidate, after all."

The screen was just showing a cute busty girl freaking out and screaming. Another player threw away his sword and fled in a panic, while a third pressed the blade against his own stomach, trying to commit harakiri out of foolishness or despair.

"Who the hell knows who we're looking for!" Doc exploded again. "This is like working in a daycare! Champions... perverts... nutcases... We should send a SWAT team in there and be done with the whole lot of them."

"We already did send a SWAT team in," the Master replied with a frown. "We sent the very best — personally selected by me — and not one of them returned! You know that as well as I do. We have no idea what lies in wait in there! Spiders... monsters... ghosts... horned demons... It's all UN-KNOWN! All we know is that you-know-who shows no mercy. Dr. Skuratova, remind me please of our ideal candidate. Who are we looking for?" he addressed the woman.

"Adaptive... proactive... cool-headed... resilient... Someone who will survive in any conditions and not lose their sanity," said Dr. Skuratova, sounding like the Queen of England more than ever. "If such an individual even exists of course."

"If we can't find them, then we'll make them,"

the Master pressed his palm against the table. "We can't wait any longer. In six months, either the press or the lawyers will roll over us and crush us like a pancake. We're left grabbing at straws because that's all we've got."

"Look at those two," Benjamin pointed at the screen. "That guy is holding the spider with both hands, and the other one is pounding it with fists. Look, Master — it's your Moses again!"

"Now tell us, darling," the Master said to Marina, "how many points did that player score?"

"One moment..." the girl rummaged through her tablet. "One. He didn't pass."

"What?!" Doc couldn't hold himself back and jumped up from his seat. "ONE?! Based on what?"

"He demonstrated poor loyalty..." babbled the PR maven. "He gave the game low ratings and was critical in his feedback... And besides... He died. So, he didn't pass... In fact, he scored in the negatives, but the scores default to a minimum value of one."

"Have you ever played computer games at all, you idiot?" Benjamin asked playfully.

The only thing Marina played was Dates and Kisses on her mobile phone. But she thought it was an inappropriate moment to mention this, so she shook her head.

"N-n-no..."

"Dying doesn't mean anything," explained Benjamin syllable by syllable, as if he were suffering from mental exhaustion. "You could lose items or experience points for dying, but it's not critical otherwise. If he completed the quest, dying doesn't negate that achievement. This is why experienced players are not afraid of dying. Who on earth assigned this idiot to design the test evaluation anyway?" he asked, almost rhetorically.

The sidelined VP, whom Marina had spent a week persuading by all decent and indecent means to give her this project, lowered his head even lower. The crafty PR maven had calculated that she could advance her career by taking on this project. Besides, one of her girlfriends was crazy about Lance, and a selfie with the cyber celebrity was supposed to put an end to their long-standing rivalry.

"It's high time some personnel decisions are made around here," the Master grinned predatorily.

"Go for it," said Doc with a sigh. "You already got your start today."

When all was said and done, Doc was a kind person who hated having to fire people. The Master, however, took pleasure in it with unconcealed glee. "It's only the street, after all, not the cemetery," he liked to say, clearing a knot of toads from a bogged down office.

"I'll deal with this wimp later," he pointed his finger at the VP, "but you, darling," the Master shifted his eyes to Marina, "I would gladly transfer you to a brothel for junior executives — to broaden your horizons," he stood up from the table and approached the girl. "But since we don't have such a vacancy, I'll give you another assignment."

He whispered something into the PR girl's ear, causing her to blush profusely. A second later she snatched her tablet from the table and rushed out of the office.

Chapter 06

"FORGET ABOUT IT," Simba said to cheer me up. "This place is full of jerks anyway."

"Yeah," I nodded. "Jerks is right."

Various thoughts were running through my mind. I had hoped for a high score, allowing me to see my handle at the top of the rankings. But I also reckoned it was possible I'd score low, which would be okay for a first try. One trait I have about my character is that I don't like to rush into things. I prefer to wait on the sidelines first, observe how others fare, and then make a strong move. It's like the tactics that marathon runners employ — stick to the pack leader, push them hard and exhaust them, only to crush and leave them behind in the final stretch.

Simba scored eight points, which put him somewhere in the middle of the rankings. AngelCake managed to score five and even Yumi made the cut, remaining among the beta testers. As for me, I got eliminated. And there was no one to blame but myself. I acted like a fool, falling for the allure of pretty faces, and messed it all up. Stepanych at the warehouse was right: women were trouble. I'd met two of them today and both had spoiled my chances as a result.

The tables had been set up in the lobby once again. Instead of registration, however, the girls staffing them were now distributing money. They checked names on the list and handed out envelopes prepared ahead of time. There were many tables and the line moved quickly. Those who got eliminated didn't get a dime.

Simba went over for a few minutes and came back awkwardly tucking the envelope in the inner pocket of his jacket. He didn't even bother counting it in front of me. What a tactful guy.

We stepped outside to the front stairs. Simba pulled out a cigarette but toyed with it in his fingers without lighting it.

"What are you sulking for?" I asked. "Let's go. We can still make it to the last class at the university."

"Maybe we should wait for Anastasia?" Simba asked.

"So wait," I replied curtly and took off down the stairs.

I wasn't about to hold grudges against anyone. But the thought of running into the girl who had caused my elimination made me realize that I might lose my temper, yell at her, and then regret it. Let Simba seize his chance instead. For his part, knowing the way I was, he didn't try to rush after me. I took the electric bus alone.

* * *

Only now did I realize how much I had enjoyed that game. My hand still remembered the way the sword's hilt had felt — unwieldy, heavy and all too real. In stark contrast to the Gladiator Games designed for spectator esports, this world felt incredibly authentic. Aside from the two dumb NPCs, who had been deliberately designed to be unlike humans, all the other details had completely beguiled my senses. It felt less like a virtual world crafted by designers and more like a portal to another reality. And I wanted to be there. Craved it like an addict who'd been in rehab for four years and relapsed. Yearned for it to the point of withdrawal: adrenaline, battles, triumph... It was everything my current life couldn't give me.

I also wanted to stuff Lance's arrogant grin down his throat. Back in the cafeteria, I thought he recognized me. It had been a long time. He had over a thousand battles under his belt, but you could count those who'd beaten that bastard on one hand. Even if he was a snotty newbie back then; defeats always make a stronger impression than victories.

The university welcomed me with empty hallways. Classes had ended and the only sound was lively voices and cheerful laughter from where the faculty offices were. The graduate students were hitting on the freshmen. Both groups lingered after classes, some to do work, others out of curiosity and to make new friends.

I headed to the dean's office. My tuition payment for the second semester had been due two weeks ago. My mom kept procrastinating, hoping that "interest rates would come to the rescue." She used to tell me that "the rich make a living off this," going on about how they delay paying us our wages while using the banks to play around with the money they owe us. I doubted that any substantial interest could accumulate on a credit card, but arguing with my mom wasn't worth even that.

Our school was pretty poor. The linoleum was swollen with blisters where the floorboards underneath had rotted. Every other ceiling light was out. The doors were worn out, the desks were scribbled over with the wisdom of previous generations of students, and the lecture halls had such a draft that the students all had to wear their jackets to class in the winter.

The average GPA to get into sociology was low and there were only a few funded spots. As for the stipend, that was the lowest in the whole university. Who needed sociology in the age of triumphant bureaucracy? It was already impossible to find a job as a sociologist, but at least they hadn't started shooting us on sight.

I ended up in this dreadful major by accident. I was originally going for foreign languages, and my entrance exam results had been excellent. However, the sly bureaucracy running the university introduced an additional requirement — essay writing.

The applicants were divided into two groups right away. Those whose parents bribed the university president's office got into the state-funded program. The ones who hesitated and tried to be honest went into the paid group.

I realized my mistake only when my essay grade turned out to be lower than those who could barely speak Russian.

The choice was between studying sociology and spending my youth begging for a job. The older guys made an effort, took out a loan, and barely managed to get me into the paid group.

I made my way down the hallway with my carefully handwritten schedule, listening to the voices drifting from the offices. Not recognizing a single one, I resolutely entered the dean's office.

Ella, the secretary — a plump and kind graduate student with thick glasses — pointed to a chair and silently pushed a plate of cookies over to me. Someone was already in the dean's office — someone very loud.

"I'm asking you nicely, Dr. Ivantsov..." came from the door, "...you can't go on like this... We can't be welcoming beggars... Higher education is an attribute of the privileged class after all."

Ella glanced at my jacket and lowered her eyes. I didn't fit the look of someone from the privileged class. I felt uncomfortable myself. I wanted to sink into the chair and pretend to be a stack of documents or a pile of junk.

The door of the dean's office swung open and the university president emerged. I had seen him only twice during my studies — at the first student assembly and once randomly from a distance.

Now the president stared straight at me: fancy glasses in glinting frames, a long nose that seemed to have a life of its own, and the smell of expensive cologne that hit Ella and I like a wave.

The rector adjusted his glasses, muttered "What is this anyway?" under his breath and stalked out of the dean's office.

"Mr. Severyanov, are you here to see me?" the dean peeked out through the partially open door.

Dr. Stepan Petrovich Ivantsov PhD was a great guy, something the university top brass didn't really appreciate. He wore a worn-out jacket over a checkered shirt and his gray hair stuck out in a cheerful tuft. People like him are often called "eternal students." A battered camping kettle stood on his desk amid folders, schedules, and reports. Bags with tents were piled up in the corner: camping trips, hiking, campfires and folk songs on the guitar. The dean wasn't an "efficient manager," and as a result, neither he nor the school he headed inside the university could escape poverty.

"Mr. Severyanov..." the dean shook his head with a mix of reproach and guilt, as if he felt embarrassed to say what he had to say out loud.

Not only did he know all of his students by

name, but he was also aware of all our problems.

"Dr. Ivantsov, my dad's paycheck got delayed. He works for a private company, and they don't pay him regularly. My mom and I will take out a loan and I'll pay the tuition I owe by the end of the month," I began to wheedle, knowing full well that there would be no money, and I was just haggling for more time.

"We've already received a summons for you from the army enlistment office," the dean rummaged through a stack of papers on his desk, hoping to find the document to show me. Failing to find it, he just tapped the pile meaningfully. "What am I supposed to tell them?"

"That I'm still a registered student..."

A chill ran through me. I wasn't afraid of the army. In fact, until the seventh grade, I had been actively training for it. I ran cross country and did pull ups. Now, though, I didn't want to be anything like my father. Not even in that respect.

"You have to understand, Mr. Severyanov," the dean slumped, seeming to age suddenly. "I know you're a smart guy. All the professors speak highly of you. In the past, I would have transferred you to the state-funded program and given you a scholarship. But now, well, you saw it yourself," Dr. Ivantsov gestured towards the door, "Money... money... money... According to policy, I should have expelled you two weeks ago. You owe 30,000 for the first semester! And it's already time to make a down payment for the second!"

"What if I join the academy?" I proposed a

desperate option.

"The academy?" the dean said thoughtfully. "I could keep you on the academy's rolls for a year, in which case the military won't be able to touch you... Ella!" he called out.

"Yes, Dr. Ivantsov?" the secretary didn't fully enter the room, merely sticking her head through the door.

"Can we send this eagle to the academy?"

"If the eagle can take care of what he owes for the semester, then... retroactively..."

"You'll take care of it, won't you?" the dean looked at me.

"I'll take care of it," I nodded, avoiding eye contact.

And where, I wondered, would I get the money? I remembered the beta testing earlier that day and the thick, crisp envelopes handed out in the lobby. "Starting from a thousand rubles..." A couple of grand for half an hour in the VR pod. "*Idiot*," whispered my nasty inner voice. "*Moron! You just had to be a white knight and help that busty muppet! And now what? It's Simba who's got a shot with her. He's the one who passed the test, got the money, and the girl...*"

I strangled the voice right there. I had no one to blame but myself. Everyone is the gravedigger to their own happiness.

Should I beg the dean on my knees? He seemed like a decent guy. Maybe he'd give me a second chance? I didn't know him that well, but it was clear that he wasn't from the wealthiest background and the poor are seldom too proud to help.

"Are you daydreaming, Mr. Severyanov?" the dean asked.

I had forgotten where I was. I had completely disconnected from reality.

"Sorry, Dr. Ivantsov. I got lost in my thoughts."

"Go on now, Mr. Severyanov... Don't let me down," the dean suddenly extended his hand towards me.

A little taken aback, I shook it and left the office.

This time, I didn't try to hide. If Sullen crosses my path now, I'll beat his ass and his street punks. Sure, I might seem brave until someone knocks me off my feet and starts kicking my ribs, but right now, that was my mood. To my fortune or misfortune, we didn't cross paths that day.

However, a car I hadn't seen before was waiting for me at my building's driveway. A white Toyota Camry, the luxury version. The rear windows were heavily tinted. The chauffeur looked bored behind the wheel. You can easily tell a chauffeur from an owner. The owner always boasts, "Look at my ride... My whip... My beater..." But a chauffeur, well, he looks perpetually bored and restricted. He can't drink or smoke in his client's vehicle. He just sits there, chewing gum with a dull expression on his face.

Is this for Olga again? Seems like she's managed to snag herself a bona fide sugar daddy.

First a Land Cruiser, now a Camry. Switching cars midstride. Or is she switching sugar daddies midstride? Quite the hot commodity... a prostitute.

Realizing suddenly that I sounded like an old gossip at church, I snorted at myself. Getting old is no fun. I climbed up the stairs, laughing out loud with a strange strained laughter as I skipped two steps at a time up to my floor.

My apartment's door wasn't locked. Strange.

"Wash your hands!" called my mom from the kitchen. "We have visitors, Andryusha!"

Who would pay a visit to our place? Since my dad began getting in trouble, all the family friends had gradually drifted away. No one said anything, they just called less often, stopped visiting, and eventually forgot the way to our house.

Lathering my palms with tiny pink soap bubbles, I felt a mix of curiosity and irritation. "Andryusha" sounded so forced, like from a TV show about a perfect family.

None of my guesses hit the mark, not even the most absurd one. In the kitchen, sitting on a stool with long legs clad in thin black stockings, was the same office chick whom I'd seen greet Lance that morning.

"Would you like some more tea, Marina?" my mom fussed around her. "And here he is, my Andrysha!"

"Thank you, Mrs. Severyanova. I won't say no to another cup!" The chick beamed at my mom and then turned her gaze towards me.

Seeing both women, I fought the urge to rub my eyes. My mom had dressed up on account of the guest. She wore her blue dress for special occasions. Over the past few years, my mom had lost a lot of weight, and the dress didn't fit her properly. She had thrown a colorful scarf over her shoulders, even though it was sweltering in the kitchen. We had to keep the windows open all the time because it was so hot. Mom had even managed to fashion some sort of hairdo on her head.

I don't know what she had in mind, but she was looking at the girl as if she were my future wife and the mother of her grandchildren.

The girl, on the other hand, looked like she was posing for a commercial: "Having a tough time in life? Take out a loan!" Her modest white blouse was bursting at the seams, and the top buttons looked like they were about to pop off like bullets. Her full lips pouted as she blew on the hot tea, and I felt something stir in my pants.

This posh creature looked wholly out of place in our shabby kitchen with the cheap plastic tablecloth that didn't need washing, curtains with a big burn hole from when my dad smoked secretly and a cupboard with one door hanging on a single hinge that I had promised to fix a month ago.

It's like someone cut a picture out of a glossy magazine and pasted it over a photo of their shabby abode: "Kendall Jenner and I in my hovel: A family portrait." Or maybe I was going crazy? Maybe some circuit had blown in the VR pod, and

I'm actually lying in a coma, while my brain feeds me images to keep me amused?

"Hello, Andrew," said the girl. "My name is Marina. I'd like to speak with you!"

Mom folded her hands on her chest with a blissful smile. Fuck it all.

Did I screw something up during their stupid beta, and now she's come to sue us for millions? Or did Lance complain about being bullied, and now they're going to try to get me to apologize? All sorts of fears flooded my mind, each less likely than the last. There was definitely nothing good to expect from this visit.

A plate with yesterday's pancakes, some honey, some jam, and an open pack of assorted candies was arranged on the table. There were hardly any candies left. Knowing my mom, almost all of them had been offered to her guest. So, they've been sitting here for quite a while. She'd been waiting for me all this time?

"So speak then," I muttered.

It came out a bit rough. Mom even shook her head disapprovingly. At least she didn't make a remark too.

"Preferably alone," Marina looked at my mom almost apologetically.

"Of course, of course," Mom waved her hands. "I'll step out now."

"In another room would be better," the girl specified for some reason.

"We could go to mine," I shrugged.

I didn't really want to invite her in. It wasn't

like it was a mess in there, but there were a couple of t-shirts lying on my bed as well as yesterday's socks. I wasn't expecting guests. Besides, it's my personal space, my den.

There were children's trophies and medals for swimming on my shelves, an award for a half marathon I had run, as well as my prizes for the Gladiator Games. Posters of top games and esports champions adorned the walls. I had even found a spot for old Lance — he was a fellow countryman, after all. My old PC stood with its side panel removed — its guts on display to keep it from overheating.

"Let's go to your room," the girl nodded.

Marina had seemed taller that morning. Now barefoot, she barely reached my shoulder. She had refused the slippers my mom had offered her, and her feet looked delicate and cute in their stockings. I even repented a bit for thinking she looked bitchy earlier.

I led the way, although there was no getting lost. One room, the "big" one, belonged to my parents, the other "small" one was mine.

Marina followed me inside and shut the door behind her. Then she noticed the latch and locked it too. I noticed that she was just as nervous as I was.

"Andrew, on behalf of our management... and personally... I apologize..." she said with some difficulty. "I apologize deeply."

"Understood... okay..." I nodded, not sure how to respond.

What do I need these apologies for if I got kicked out of the beta test?

"We experienced a technical glitch," Marina continued. "The results of the first round of the beta were declared invalid. I'd like to ask you to return to our project."

I don't know what came over me. Just half an hour ago, I was agonizing over where to get money for my tuition. I was ready to go back to the office complex, sign up for an appointment and beg them if necessary.

Now, however, looking at this well-groomed corporate toady, I understood that she didn't give a damn about my mom or me. She had made this visit out of courtesy, just so I wouldn't trash her game on social media and ruin her company's reputation.

She sat there, waiting. Sipping cheap tea from tea bags, pursing her plump, pampered lips into a polite smile. All to gain our trust, elicit our sympathy so that we — who spend in a month on groceries what she spends on a manicure — would feel sorry for her technical glitch.

"No, thanks," I said, shaking my head. "You can go on without me."

That's right! Take your offer and shove it! Standing in front of Marina now, I tried my best to show that I didn't need her pity.

"What?!" Her eyes widened in surprise, like a doll's — the kind that have mechanical eyes: You lift them up and their eyes flap open, you put them down and their eyes flap shut. Lay them on their back and... Where is my mind wandering off to?!

"I have finals coming up," I said as calmly as possible. "I tried out for your project. It didn't work out. I guess I'm not a good fit for your company."

I noticed that Marina was getting nervous. Too nervous for mere politeness: Her cheeks suddenly flushed as if I had said something obscene, and her eyelids turned red. She looked like she might burst into tears at any moment.

"You don't understand..." she mumbled, slipping out of her customary PR tone. "It is critical that I... that I bring you back to the project... I am under direct orders from senior management to..."

A goatish stubbornness came over me. It had hurt me before. How many times had my parents been called to school, how many girls had walked away because of my whims, how many times had I gotten punched in the face or punched in the back.

"Unfortunately," I shrugged, "that's your senior management's problem, not mine."

Marina gave me a look that was both doomed and desperate, and suddenly, she dropped to her knees and reached for my zipper.

"What the hell are you doing?!" I cried out dumbfounded.

"I'm bringing you back to the project, by whatever means necessary," Marina replied, avoiding eye contact and staring at the floor.

CHAPTER 07

I JUMPED BACK like I'd touched a live wire. My shoulder slammed into the shelf, scattering my trophies on the floor. Marina crawled after me on her knees, tears welling up in the corners of her eyes. Her hairdo seemed to come undone on its own. Her plump lips clenched resolutely. She looked helpless, making her even more adorable. I backed away from her, not knowing what I feared more: her grabbing me or bursting into tears. My back hit the wardrobe, cutting off further retreat.

"Marina... What are you doing? You can't... you just can't," my voice suddenly went hoarse.

"I have a mortgage..." she sobbed, "and car payments for my Mazda... And they, well you saw for yourself, how they fired the head of security just like that..."

There was no arguing there. I had had front row seats to that episode.

"So what?!" I almost yelled at her, "What did they tell you to do?!"

"If you refuse..." Marina hesitated, embarrassed, until her fear of her boss overcame her embarrassment, "I have to suck you off until you change your mind."

My eyes nearly popped out of my head. Talk about corporate policies. I've heard of team-building exercises and always doing what your boss tells you — but this?

At the same time, judging by what I had seen of Marina, giving a blowjob to a stranger was simpler for her than parting with a cushy job.

Marina looked at me with pleading eyes. Despite her tears, her mascara didn't run. Must be expensive makeup. The lipstick smudged slightly, adding to her charm. A very beautiful girl was now kneeling before me, waiting for my response. Any response. A very beautiful and evidently expensive girl. Wasn't this what I was fantasizing about just yesterday?

The vision, however, brought me no joy now. To the opposite, I felt only deep embarrassment.

"Marina... You can't do this," I said again, realizing that repeating the same thing was pointless.

For some reason, no other words came to mind.

"Yes I do," Marina said firmly, moving even closer.

"Alright! Fine! I give up!" I said, unable to hold back. "I'll come back to your beta test."

Something clicked inside Marina. I could almost hear it in the room's silence. She stood up, efficiently fixed her blouse and wiped the invisible tears from the corners of her eyes.

"Do you have a mirror?" she demanded without looking at me.

"What?" I was taken aback by such a sudden change.

"A mirror, I said. Do you have one?" Marina repeated, a tinge of demand sounding in her voice.

"Oh, yes, of course."

I opened the door to the wardrobe, an old one from the Soviet era, made of heavy lacquered wood. There was a mirror on the inside. Marina snorted at the sight of my heaps of clothing. She took a lipstick from her tiny purse and started touching up her makeup.

"I need to get back to the office," she said without looking at me. "And you're coming with me."

"What? Why?"

"The Master wants to see you." Marina examined herself carefully in the mirror until she was satisfied.

She pronounced the word "Master" in a way that immediately made it clear — it was capitalized. I remembered the morning clash in the lobby: "It's an honor to serve you, Master." It was the grizzled man, the only one in that entire company who had seemed likable to me.

"We never discussed that," I stubbornly replied.

"Oh, stop being difficult!" the girl sneered bitchily, "You already said yes, why kick up a fuss now?"

"What about payment?" I suddenly realized.

Not long ago, money problems were my top concern. But as soon as I saw Marina on her knees, everything had flown out of my head. What a ninny!

"You can ask the Master about that," she snapped the latch open and opened the door.

In the hallway, I put on my jacket and shoes. Marina turned her back to me and patiently waited for me to hand her her fur coat. There must be some special system of rituals among women that makes men feel dumb.

I tried to convince myself that I had done the noble thing, but deep down, I knew I had been played.

In the Camry's rear seat, Marina leaned against her window. She had clearly expected me to sit in the front with the chauffeur and now radiated her displeasure with her entire demeanor. First, she scrolled through her smartphone, then she filed her immaculate designer nails, and eventually began to puff on an IQOS nervously.

I also stared out the window. We drove in silence. Some song played from the speakers, the chauffeur turned it up, and I plugged in my earphones.

Though the car was warm, I felt a chill creeping in. Who is this Master character? Just because he seemed normal to me didn't mean anything. He beat his own employees — skillfully and professionally. He gave them strange orders. And now, they're taking me straight to him. The nervous breakdown I had earlier was affecting me oddly. I almost fell asleep on the way and got out of the car feeling moody and disheveled.

Marina walked into the building with the confidence of a hostess. The guards straightened up at her passage. What happened in my bedroom so recently felt like a dream now.

Maybe I really was starting to lose the plot? Maybe I spent too long staring at her legs and now I was seeing things? But then how the hell did I end up in this car at all? None of this added up.

Marina called the elevator. She greeted people passing by in the hallway and they politely nodded back. I was witnessing an office life that was foreign to me. Businesslike guys and sharply dressed girls were scurrying about, carrying individual papers and stacks of folders, talking on the phone while walking, greeting and chatting with each other, studying something on their tablets' screens. When they did notice me, they looked at me with such surprise that Marina even stepped away as if to say, "He's not with me."

The elevator chimed melodically. We entered to soft music. I could see our reflections in the polished steel doors. The triangle on the display blinked, and the numbers changed: 1... 2... 3...

"Marina, who is the Master?" I asked.

She glanced at me as if she'd already

forgotten I was there. It seemed like she wanted to respond brusquely but held back at the last moment. Maybe she realized we were in the same boat.

"He's a very serious person," she said.

"So, you don't really know who he is?" I said in a friendlier tone of voice.

Strict formality has its limits too.

"All I know is that everyone in the company waits on him hand and foot," she replied pensively.

It was dawning on her that this scary Master had summoned me to see him, so she had better stay on my good side.

"It's like that, huh?"

"Will you let me know how your meeting goes?" Marina decided to suck up to me. "I'll buy you a coffee…"

I shrugged silently. I had no idea how things would go or even why these people were so interested me in the first place.

The elevator stopped on the ninth floor. The doors opened on an enormous office suite with soft beige carpeting. There were several doors and the space was flooded with sunlight from the large windows with breathtaking views of the skyline. That was all.

Marina headed towards one of the doors, adjusting her skirt on the way. She seemed nervous now.

We entered and found ourselves in a reception room, which was quite ordinary aside from the nondescript, middle-aged man in a black suit sitting at the desk instead of the customary office secretary.

"We have an appointment," Marina told the receptionist.

He fixed us with a gaze that resembled an X-ray and nodded.

The Master's office was divided in two parts. One was a standard office with a desk, computer, and a large display on the wall, as well as soft couches for visitors.

The second half was separated from the first by a half-opened glass partition. It resembled a greenhouse or a conservatory. Plants with large lush leaves were arranged in a way that the pots were hidden from view. It looked like they just brought a piece of the tropical forest here. I could even hear a waterfall murmuring in one corner. The water cascaded over pebbles, gurgling and shimmering, on its way to a small pool. I couldn't help imagine koi swimming in it.

A colorful rug covered the floor. A coffee table stood in the center. The Master was sitting behind a computer, typing something slowly with one finger, making long pauses and puffing his cheeks thoughtfully. He seemed not to notice us.

"I have brought him, Master," said Marina.

The older man smiled, jumped up from the computer, and approached us warmly.

He was dressed very differently from last time — and entirely unsuitably for an office setting. The Master wore a black silk robe with gold embroidery and black slippers. As he approached, he spread his arms as if he wanted to embrace me.

"Hello, Andrew! We already met each other earlier today but didn't get a chance to introduce ourselves." He ignored Marina entirely. "Call me Master. Let's have a talk," he motioned towards the table. "I'm eager to hear your opinion."

I recalled what the Master had said to the security guard the first time I met him: "*I'm not your master and you're not my student.*"

"About what?" I wondered.

"About the game," the Master said as if it were self-evident. "More precisely, about what you consider to be a game."

I didn't understand the Master's last words, and my excitement from the unexpected meeting turned to curiosity.

"Is it so urgent?" I couldn't help asking.

"When I want something," the Master raised his finger importantly, "it immediately becomes the most important thing in the world. I advise you to act accordingly. It's more convenient that way for everyone involved."

"May I be excused?" Marina interjected.

"Bring us some tea," the Master said.

"I'll have the assistant make some..."

"You. Will. Bring. Us. Some. Tea." The older man enunciated each word slowly.

"Yes, Master."

If cats could smile, the Master smiled like a satisfied cat.

"Come in," he headed towards the conservatory.

I reached the carpet and hesitated. The light snow on my shoes had melted, leaving wet marks. Leaning down, I untied my shoes and stepped onto the carpet in my socks.

Balancing with the tray in her hands, Marina took off her shoes. She stepped silently on the carpet and placed the tray before us. Besides the tea, it had nuts, dried fruits, and Eastern sweets covered in powdered sugar.

The Master poured himself some green tea.

"Help yourself," he said. "But first, tell me, why didn't you sleep with her?"

"What?!" I couldn't hold back and looked at Marina. She stood beside us like a piece of furniture, not saying a word and looking down.

"Why? Was she rude? Or do you simply not like her?"

"I like her, of course. It's just… it's wrong! She didn't want to!" I protested.

"How so?" The Master gave me a cunning look. "She offered herself. She had a choice, and she chose to be a good, obedient girl."

"And besides, why do you assume I refused?!" I challenged him.

"Because I can see it in her," the Master pointed at Marina, who stood next to us like a statue. "You think you did the noble thing, but she thought you were weak. That's how it works." He took a sip of tea and closed his eyes in pleasure. "Help yourself. Don't just sit there."

My ears grew hot. To avoid giving myself away, I grabbed a handful of nuts from the plate, my mouth watering instantly. I hadn't eaten since morning. First there was the cafeteria brawl, then Marina's visit... I had missed lunch twice.

"Uh-huh," I managed to say.

"As for you, you owe him," the Master said to the girl. "And Andrew can get it from you whenever he pleases, got it?" He waited until she nodded. "Now, you're dismissed."

"Understood, Master," Marina picked up her shoes and left the office barefoot.

"Do you have a father?" the Master suddenly asked.

"I do."

"Does he drink?"

"Yeah, so what?"

The old man nodded understandingly.

"You were brought up by your mom then."

"Is that so bad?" I challenged him. I loved my mom.

"Imagine, that you were taken prisoner in early childhood, Andrew." The Master took another sip of tea, this time without grimacing. He seemed much calmer with Marina gone. "In days of yore, captive children weren't killed typically. Everyone needed workers and servants. So, they raised you to be calm and obedient. They taught you never to raise a hand against your owners, nor even to argue with them because that would be 'undignified.' They taught you to work for them and provide for them. They taught you that their desires must be fulfilled immediately, while your desires mean nothing. You DON'T have desires, only duties. And they turned you into a good, hardworking, and harmless slave! So any piece of trash like this Marina girl takes advantage of you. You're not even a person to her, more like a racehorse. Whoever wants to ride you, does. That's what you boys who have been raised by women are like."

"But what about social norms? Ethics?" The sociology student inside me rebelled.

"Ethics?" the old man laughed. "Prince Vladimir Sviatoslavich raped his older brother's fiancée, Rogneda, right in front of her parents, and then killed them. And it was no big deal. She married him and bore him six children. And he had eight LEGAL wives and over a thousand concubines! He had a harem in every city! He slept with half of Russia! And you know what they called him? You think they called him 'murderer' or 'rapist?'"

"They called him a saint." I knew the history.

"A saint," the Master drawled. "And where's your ethics, where's your morality? Morality was invented to rule. A true warrior is beyond morality. He only has a goal." He suddenly jumped up from his seat. "Follow me!"

"Where to?" I said, following.

"Come on, come on!" The Master had swiftly crossed the office and was already at the door.

I stuffed my feet into my shoes and ran after him without lacing them. We passed through the reception area, crossed the corridor and entered another VR room. There were only ten pods here.

This had to be like a VIP VR lounge.

At our arrival, the technician on duty jumped up and rushed over. The Master approached one of the VR pods like a pilot approaching his jet: confidently and matter-of-factly, as if this wasn't his first or even tenth flight today.

"Prepare two for us," the old man said.

"Yes, Master."

He turned his back and dropped his robe. It made sense to me now why he dressed so oddly. From a virtual reality standpoint, it was very practical. It took me much longer to undress.

The Hypnotoad spiral from earlier in the day appeared before me... There was a sudden jerk...

I am standing in the same alley again. The same fence with the same boulder at its foot. I'm wearing the same trousers and shirt as this morning. I look around. The Master is beside me, wearing his silk robe and slippers, as if he had stepped right in, seamlessly from meatspace. It's good to be the king. You get to wear whatever clothes you like.

"Do you recognize it?" The Master points to the boulder.

"Yes, I saw it this morning," I nod.

"Look closer."

I squint. Something has indeed changed. The boulder has "sunk" slightly into the ground — as if rain had softened the soil and the boulder had settled under its own weight. Where do rains come from in the virtual world? An advanced physics engine?

There's moss now on the boulder too. A gray crust of it covers the part that's in the shadow of the fence. A small patch of moss, still tiny, but it seems to be growing. Blades of grass are sprouting from under the boulder. It looks much more real than a few hours ago. Now an ant even runs along it and now another one. They carry something in their mandibles, hurrying.

"I see," I think I understand what the Master wants to show me.

"Let's go," he calls me.

We step out to the town square. The exclamation mark above the mayor is gone. Now I can examine the NPC better. I didn't have time for that this morning.

He is a middle-aged man in a luxurious medieval tunic, with finely waxed whiskers and a Spanish-style goatee. He stands there and shifts his weight from foot to foot.

The program doesn't allow him to move. And he's bored! He takes out a flask from somewhere, puts it to his lips, and drinks. The goatee twitches, counting the gulps. Something alcoholic. A satisfied smile appears on his face, and his nose reddens slightly. He hides the flask and starts whistling a cheerful tune.

"What's with him?" I ask. "Is his AI developing?"

"That's the Neural Network," the Master says. "It's not just developing. It's learning."

"Learning what?" I inquire.

"The same thing all living beings learn. It's

learning to kill better."

I look at the mayor. He takes off his tunic, folds it into a cushion, and places it on the ground. Then he takes a seat on it with a contented look and takes another swig from the flask.

When I turn away, the Master's fist comes flying into my face.

CHAPTER 08

I BARELY DODGE in time. A knuckle grazes my cheek.

-4 HP: 96/100

The numbers flash at the bottom of my field of vision. Once my HP reaches zero, I'm dead meat.

The Master steps forward, pressing the attack. I block his blows stiffly, stepping back under the onslaught. In real life, he would just overwhelm me, cornering me against the ropes in a ring or against some wall and punching until I get tired and open up. But not here. Different rules apply here.

My health drops with each hit. -2... -5... -3... Judging by the damage he's doing, the Master is just as much of a noob as I am.

"Hey, you two!" the mayor suddenly shouts. "Halt! The both of you!" He hops in place, clearly agitated. "I'll call the guards! Guards! Guards!"

Predictably, the guards do not appear. In fact, I doubt there are any other NPCs here besides the mayor and the merchant.

-1 REPUTATION WITH THE MAYOR.

CURRENT STATUS: 0/10 (INDIFFERENCE).

What are you doing, you bastard? You're ruining my reputation! It suddenly dawns on me that the Master knows nothing about the game mechanics. For him, this is all just puppets and scenery — an ordinary world, but virtual. This gives me a chance.

I block and wait. Just a little more... come on...

The Master freezes and stares at his hands in amazement. They've gone limp — unable to strike or block. That's Stamina, my friend. In meatspace, a fight will last 2–3 minutes, but in cyberspace, players of equal strength and level can battle for hours. Only a noob would waste their Stamina attacking without restraint.

I do a spinning kick and strike him in the head. This is called a "tornado" in taekwondo and is usually performed for showmanship.

In esports, this kind of move is called a "FATALITY" and is performed to win ovations and entertain the audience.

The Master keels over like a felled tree. His body remains however, without respawning, so he probably doesn't have much health left. After a kick like that, he might have a few HP left, no more.

I approach cautiously to finish him off...

It feels kind of awkward standing over the big boss. He's supposed to be a big deal and here I just knocked him out. I wonder if he'll take offense.

I hesitate for a mere second or two, and suddenly I find myself face down in the dust. The Master cleverly entangles my legs with his own, and I lose my balance. I realize that he was playing possum lying on the ground, gathering Stamina to counterattack.

My neck is caught in a tight grip. I try to get up, but the Master pushes me into the ground with his knee, wedged between my shoulder blades. I scrape my hands on the ground, trying to throw him off, but I have nothing to prop myself up against.

"You little pup," the Master says to me, "you dared to bite?!"

I wheeze in response. My HP keeps dwindling in his iron grip. A choke sure does take a long time in this place. I wonder what'll run out first, my HP or my Stamina?

It seems he realizes it too. I hear a sharp crack, momentarily drowning out all sound, and then feel an explosion of excruciating pain in the back of my head.

YOU HAVE DIED.

The white pod lid appears before my eyes. The solution flushes away with a sucking sound. The only sound is the blood pounding in my ears. *Thump... thump... thump...* I can hear my own pulse. It's racing after that beating, racing at a breakneck pace. Especially since I'm not used to this. I've grown unaccustomed to fighting in the arena — unaccustomed to the sour taste of adrenaline in my mouth.

My lips stretch into a smile. I almost got him! I know it doesn't count, but having seen what the Master can do in a real fight, I'm pleased with myself.

The VR pod's lid opens with a satisfying hiss. A technician hands me a robe. I look around, searching for the grizzled man.

"The Master has already left," the technician explains.

My feeling of triumph gives way to anxiety. What was all that about?! A test? In that case, did I pass or not?

I hadn't had time to think in the heat of battle. I only wanted to win. And also there was this feeling of tranquility that came over me, as if, for the first time in a while, I knew exactly what I was doing.

I guess I expected to talk about it, some analysis like "you really got me..." or "you just got lucky..." The only thing I didn't expect was this nothing.

The technicians are no longer paying attention to me, busy with their work. They sterilize the pods and tinker with the equipment.

Missing my opportunity is becoming a habit for me.

Hunching my shoulders, I shuffle for the exit in my slippers. If anything gets in my way, like say a robot vacuum, I'm sure I'll kick it, but the floor is spotless and sterile like the rest of the place.

In the locker room, I find Marina waiting for me.

* * *

I was scared at first when I saw her. I assumed that she had come to carry out the Master's orders then and there. After the recent duel and the desolation that followed, sex seemed like a laborious and pointless task. I already felt drained, empty.

At the sight of her, I flinched enough for her to notice.

"What's wrong?" Marina asked, surprised.

"I didn't expect anyone to be here," I lied.

"How sensitive of you," she snorted, but then caught herself, "I promised you coffee…"

I was incredibly hungry. I only managed to eat a handful of nuts back in the Master's office. Nothing was going well for me today — neither women, nor food, nor money. Would I finally catch a break or what?

"If you get me a pastry along with it, I'll be grateful," I grumbled.

"I'll buy you a pastry," Marina smiled.

When she smiled, she looked like a girl my age. A cute girl without all the corporate bells and whistles.

"I need to take a shower," I said.

"I'll wait," she agreed obediently.

"Right here?"

"Are you shy?"

"Not a bit."

The truth was that, of course, I was shy. And not about my body, which was perfectly fine. I didn't go to the gym or anything, but I regularly lifted weight at the warehouse. No, it was simply that I was afraid of looking silly. I was sure that Marina was much more experienced when it came to sex than I was. Girls don't fall for guys without a fancy car, a house, or a wealthy father. And I don't even have an ugly car. I don't even have enough money to go to the movies. All I have is a tiny room with my mom and dad on the other side of the wall!

Naturally, I had had my share of hookups at parties when we were all wasted. But that was whatever... third-rate stuff. In the morning, you don't even remember it, and if you do, the last thing you want is to call her again.

But now, it was like I was playing the lead role in the plot of a high-budget porn movie!

The changing room was small. Right in front of the entrance, a row of metal seats were joined into a single structure resembling a bench. That's where Marina was sitting. There were lockers for personal belongings along one wall and a huge mirror covering the entire surface of the other wall. Two shower stalls at the far end of the room with transparent doors.

Feigning indifference, I walked to the stall, turned my back to Marina, dropped my robe right on the floor and stepped inside.

There were so many thoughts spinning

through my mind that not even a cold shower could wash them away. Where would I get money to pay my university tuition? What did the Master want from me? Had I passed his test? All of these questions, however, were overshadowed by another, new one: What the fuck am I supposed to do in the current scenario?

I'll have to come out of the shower at some point... Naked... Well, not totally naked, but wrapped in a towel... Water droplets trickling down my shoulders... Who am I kidding? I'll be completely soaked... Sloshing my wet feet along the floor... Sexy as hell... Okay, I'll put on my slippers at least...

Then I'll walk up to her and I'll say... or maybe I won't say anything at all... I'll just place my hand on her waist, pull her close, and kiss her... Or better not on the waist, but on her tit and give it a squeeze... Yeah... And instantly soak her blouse with my wet hand... Or maybe instead of kissing her, I'll spin her around and set her doggy style... She's pretty bitchy, isn't she? Bitches like it rough.

Oh damn, I forgot that she was sitting down! I'll have to ask her to stand up, and then turn her around...

I stepped out of the shower, not entirely sure what to do, but feeling quite determined. I looked around. Marina wasn't in the locker room.

She was waiting for me outside in the lobby.

"I decided not to embarrass you," Marina said with a serious expression and a glint of mischief dancing in her eyes.

"It doesn't matter," I feigned nonchalance. What else could I do?

Instead of taking me to the cafeteria on the first floor, where I'd been before, she led me to another café on the fourth floor, much smaller and cozier.

"Here, help yourself," Marina placed a big dish with pastries, éclairs, and cakes on the table. The whole thing was crowned with a basket topped with creamy custard. "I cleared out their entire display case for you."

"Thanks!"

The conversation paused for about five minutes. I simply chewed, devouring one pastry after another and washing it down with tea. Marina fidgeted impatiently but stayed silent, earning a few bonus points in my eyes. I was starting to get used to her.

"So, tell me already, what did you and the Master talk about?"

"You," I said through my mouthful. "About you, I mean."

"Come on, stop messing around!" Marina tensed visibly.

She took a sip from her huge cappuccino mug, leaving a funny mustache of foam above her upper lip. I grabbed a napkin from the table and reached out to wipe it off.

It was a cool move. I had seen it in some movie. It seemed very intimate at the time. Deep down, I decided that if she let me do it, I'd definitely bang her. Marina yielded, even leaning in a bit.

"I'm not messing around," I replied with a straight face. "He asked me how you had done on the special assignment he gave you."

"And what did you say?!"

A feeling of bitterness swept over me, more so than before. Here's this cool, interesting girl who is genuinely interested in me. She waits for me, buys me pastries, and we sit here chatting it up. Passersby are even looking over at us as if we're a real couple.

Yet the second I tell her the gist of my conversation with the Master, it will all be over. Vanished in a puff of smoke. And she'll become cold and distant again, like during our ride over here in the Camry, when I was as good as any other simp riding the same bus with her.

What the hell for? I don't want that! Take Lance for instance — it's definitely not his charming personality that everyone loves him for. Maybe inside, he's a total jerk. The reason people like him are his achievements, his victories and popularity. So, what's stopping me from playing my cards right too? The ones that life dealt me?

"I told him that you were bad. That you didn't put any effort into it."

"Are you serious?!" Marina's initial reaction was outrage, but upon further reflection she punched me flirtatiously on the shoulder.

She seemed so completely normal in that instant. There was not even a whiff of her typical aloofness about her.

"If you want the truth, the Master needs a person of his own in the beta test," I said, spinning my own web of lies. "So this will hardly be the last time you and I will work together."

Well why not? There's no way to check this lie of mine. Marina won't dare to ask the Master herself, and he wouldn't ever tell her anything.

"Why you?" the girl asked with a look of surprise.

"You should ask the Master about that," I replied, my bravado growing. I even gave her a debonair smile, feeling like a regular James Bond.

"And what did you talk about today?" Marina persisted.

"We took a look at the game from inside. Together."

Again, I wasn't entirely lying. I had been racking my brain about what the Master had wanted with me, and now I fed Marina the most appealing fantasy that had occurred to me.

"Did he say anything about me?" she asked eagerly.

"He said to keep an eye on you," I squinted slyly.

"Damn, and then what?!" Marina's anxiety made her less coherent.

"Look Marina, we're allies, remember?" I took her hand for emphasis. "I can help you, and you can help me."

She nodded and didn't pull her hand away, so I decided to press on.

"Tell me, what do you know about this beta

test? What's this game even about?" I leaned in to whisper the last words.

Marina looked around cautiously. The café was tiny, only five tables. Surely it served only senior personnel. Right now, we were completely alone. Even the waitress had disappeared somewhere behind the counter.

"I know that four people are in charge of everything," Marina brought her face closer to mine, and I caught a whiff of her perfume. Very pleasant, fresh, floral. "The Master is one of them. He's from the military. He used to head up a project related to national security. Later he found a way to privatize it and turned it into a business. Supposedly the authorities tried to pressure him, but he didn't give in. Then there's Doc, or Dr. Dmitry Kotov. He used to be the head of the research institute that developed virtual reality. Now, he's the CEO of MosTech Corporation. He's on Forbes' wealthiest people list — and he's currently going through a divorce..." Marina's voice took on a dreamy tone.

I recalled the company's banner. The slogan was "*Reality Virtualized. MosTech.*"

"You know him personally?" I asked to steer the conversation back on track.

Marina nodded, blushing for some reason, and continued, "The third one is Sergei Zvyagin, a mathematician who won the Nobel Prize and died a month later." Marina's eyes widened, and it was clear that the mathematician's death was no accident. "His son, Benjamin Zvyagin, now runs the technology division. He's a complete jerk, take it from me."

"And the fourth?"

I thought that the trio would be enough to handle anything and everything: The Muscle, the Brain, and the Coder. A classic team.

"The fourth one," Marina grimaced, "is Dr. Irina Vladimirovna Skuratova. A psychologist and psychiatrist, a doctor of sciences. A specialist in advanced neural activity." It sounded like the girl was quoting some presentation. "They say she raised it. Became like a foster mother to it."

"Raised who?" I didn't understand.

"The Neural Network."

Marina said it in a way that sent shivers down my spine, as if she was talking about something living and sinister.

"Why would you raise a neural network?"

"Our corporation deals with self-learning applications: voice assistants, navigators, smart homes, quality control systems. At the core of everything is a neural network. It doesn't work based on pre-programmed scripts; it learns to execute commands, continually improving its functional efficiency."

"You sound like you know what you're talking about," I said, truly impressed.

"Well, I am the one in charge of marketing around here." Marina raised her nose slightly. "I edit all the texts, making them more human-readable. You should see the reports the scientists bring me. 'Formation of conditioned reflexes based on the reflex arc,'" she aped. "Who would want to buy that? So, I have to explain it in normal language. As for your question, to put it simply, a neural network is like a puppy. You can teach it to give you its paw or fetch your slippers. And with each repetition, it does it better and better. It learns your preferences, desires, and adapts to you."

"And does it sell?"

Due to my financial situation, I had fallen a bit behind on my high-tech purchases. My ancient smartphone couldn't handle such things. If Simba were here, he would understand Marina much better. But I could only focus and listen.

"Definitely!" replied Marina with a bit of irritation. "For instance, one of our offerings is MovieBuddy. You decide to go to the movies, so you choose the theater, the movie, and the seats yourself. But the buddy learns, so the next time you go, it gets you the seats on its own, and the tenth time you go, it already has tickets picked out for when you have leisure time and even orders your favorite drink in advance. All you have to do is click 'Accept.' It's a complete package. Four hundred thousand units sold in the first month!"

"Awesome," I agreed. I would never install such crap in my life. I hate it when others think for me.

"But it's a very basic neural network," Marina continued, "to handle that tiny VR testing ground, we needed a network a thousand times more powerful. Or a million, I'm not sure. Are you done?

Let's go, I'll show you!"

She finished her cappuccino in one gulp and stood up from the table. I grabbed a couple of éclairs and downed them on the go. They were delicious — airy and supple, the cream melting on my tongue.

"And it can learn too, the network?" I asked when I finished chewing.

"Rapidly," Marina boasted.

I recall the Master's words: *"It's learning to kill better."*

We walked through several corridors and then took the elevator. Marina swiped her badge on an electronic lock, and a thick, heavy door opened in front of us. It may have even been bulletproof. The room clearly wasn't meant for ordinary mortals.

When I saw it, the words that came to mind were "flight control center." It was smaller of course than the other hall. There were no fewer than a hundred screens glowing in the semi-darkness and manned by about ten operators. Some of the operators turned our way when we entered and quickly returned their attention to their screens.

The screens were tracking different parts of the game. Most of them showed empty streets. Some even showed the outskirts of the town. Among them, I spotted a meadow, a small grove, and some fluffy creatures rutting around the trees.

There were familiar places too. In the town square, the mayor was drinking with the merchant. The latter had brought a table and two chairs, and they were now engrossed in a dice game, by turns taking swigs from a large straw-encased bottle.

The spiders meanwhile had spread out some more and started scouting the neighboring houses. In one of them, the spider web had covered the pink bushes and some of the trees. In another, the windows on the ground floor had been shattered, and the building had acquired a typical abandoned look.

And then, on one of the screens, I saw something that blew my mind.

CHAPTER 09

TWO SPIDERS, WHO HAD BEEN peacefully minding their own business, happened to collide. This happened all the time, but for whatever reason, these two didn't go on their ways peacefully. Instead, they squared off and began to shuffle in place, waving their front legs at each other menacingly. Suddenly, one of them pounced.

It pressed its victim to the ground, drove its short curved jaws into its body and injected its venom. The other one initially wriggled, trying to break free, but its movements became weaker and weaker. Finally, it went still and crumbled to the ground.

The victor proudly stomped in place, then shook itself like a dog — and suddenly grew larger.

Its legs lengthened a bit, its fangs split apart and turned into small pincers and the green fuzz at the jointed segments thickened, forming a noticeable cross on its back.

The mobs were gaining experience! I had just watched one LEVEL UP! I looked around the room, but the others couldn't care less. Two of the operators were chatting, another one was engrossed in his phone, a fourth managed to bite into his sandwich without spilling any of the mustard on the desk. They were all busy. Marina was the only one who noticed my astonishment.

"What's wrong?" she asked.

"What a place you got here!" I feigned excitement. "Could you watch me in there too?"

"Of course!" Marina said, as proud as if she had personally made it all happen. "Remember that when you're in there. I'll be watching."

"I'll make sure to send you a signal!" I chuckled. "Just for you!"

"A signal?" Marina asked flirtatiously. "What'll it be?"

She looked incredibly cute with her lips slightly parted like that.

"You'll see! So when's the next round?"

"Come with me," the PR girl glanced distrustfully at the operators as if they might eavesdrop on us. She opened the door and pulled me along.

We returned to the ground floor, not far from the entrance lobby. Marina dashed into one of the offices and came back with a bright flyer.

"Here!" She practically stuffed it into my hand. "A VIP invitation for tomorrow at 9 a.m. You'll be able to go straight in, so you don't have to wait in line."

"There'll be two of us," I insisted. I wasn't going to ditch Simba, even if he had no idea that they had called me back to rejoin the beta.

Marina frowned slightly but didn't object. She disappeared again for a minute and brought out a second VIP pass.

She didn't even ask who it was for. What if it was for the girl? And why did I assume she wouldn't care? Uncertainty washed over me again, along with anger.

Perhaps sensing my irritation, the PR girl became afraid that I might change my mind and decided to wrap up our conversation.

"I'll meet you at the entrance tomorrow. Make sure you come, and remember, you promised!"

"Promised what?"

"The signal!" She smiled.

I couldn't resist and smiled back. I had no illusions about this girl, she was as out of reach for me as the moon itself. However, a little daydreaming couldn't hurt, right?

*   *   *

"How long have you known her, Andryusha? What does she do for a living? Tell her we're always happy to see her..." My mom buzzed around me, moving from one side to another as I ate. Usually, she left me alone and went into the other room, but she was straightening the tablecloth now, slicing hot dogs and more bread.

I deliberately ignored her prying. I ate steadily in silence, although the sweet pastries had ruined my appetite. I had wanted to call Simba but then decided to surprise him the next day. After all, it was a VIP invitation. Besides, he was probably wooing that new girl at the moment, so there was no point in distracting him.

What was her name again? AngelCake, I think. No matter how hard I tried, I couldn't recall anything beyond the curves jutting out of her shirt. That's when my mom noticed the flyer.

For whatever reason, I had got it out of my jacket, intending on taking it to my room, but I accidentally took it with me to eat dinner instead. I thought it would fit in my pocket, but that was dumb of me.

With the agility of a magpie stealing a shiny trinket, my mom snatched the flyer and stepped back.

"What's this?" She snapped her glasses down from her forehead to her nose. "Online testing... a virtual multiplayer game..." she asked, her voice growing shrill. "More of your toys again?!"

"Mom, calm down," I tried to reassure her.

"Don't you 'mom' me!" She had already switched to the nagging tone I'd hated and feared since early childhood. "More fights, more weapons... Did you not see how that turned out for your father?! You want to end up the same way?! We got you into university! We paid for your education so that you can study and be a decent person! And you're getting involved in this trash again?!"

"What university, mom? What money?" I couldn't hold back and stood up too, almost knocking the plate over. "There is no more money! And there won't be a university soon! I was trying to do something for you..."

I realized I couldn't tell her anything specific. They hadn't paid me for the testing, and I had no idea how much they would pay me if they did. Besides, she wouldn't believe me. Her mind refused to accept that games could be a job or a sport.

"Over my dead body!" My mom folded the flyers and started tearing them into tiny pieces. The thin paper tore easily. She opened the window and threw the scraps outside. The small colorful bits fell tumbling in the wind like confetti.

"Well that Marina you're so enamored with is involved in games too!" I yelled. "She's the one who invited me to work there! In the game!"

My mom stood in an inflexible pose, arms folded across her chest, eyes flashing. Talking to her was pointless. I left the table without finishing my meal, went to my room and locked my door.

It was all just too much for one day! Lance... Yumi... The game... Lance and Yumi together... The brawl... The Academy... Marina's sexual advances... The Master... The game again... Marina again... Gaaah!

It felt like my head was going to explode. Putting on my headphones, I collapsed on the bed and shut my eyes.

I thought about Marina. About the moments when she dropped the pretense. Her bare feet in black stockings, her lip with a strip of coffee foam above it. Then my thoughts drifted to Yumi's belly, twitching under my touch, the playful nurses, and eventually, it was all overshadowed by AngelCake's voluptuous and perky breasts. I fell asleep.

I dreamed of the Gladiator Games. The final. Eight people entered the arena, but now only two remained. Lance versus Ratmir. Lance was taller and stronger. I was faster and more agile. He pressed and I dodged and counterattacked. Everyone said Lance dyed his hair. I knew he was an albino. Completely white hair and light blue eyes with a reddish pupil. Like a vampire. Undead.

For the final, Lance chose his favorite weapons — dual Katzbalgers, the swords of German landsknechts. Lance loved close combat, and his short cat-gutters inflicted tremendous damage. Perfect for group fights. At first, Lance was wary of my katana, but then he realized I had to avoid direct confrontation.

Broken in half, my wakizashi was proof that grace sometimes yields to brute force. I begin getting tired, making mistakes. He stays a step ahead of me in almost everything. I search desperately for any weak spot in his defense but can't find a single opening. Dammit! Come on! Show me something, anything! You're not AI! You must make mistakes. Give me a single chance!

I strike. Lance traps my blade with his

swords, crossed like scissors. I watch the grin on his face. With a peal, my katana snaps like glass.

Rage engulfs me. Dammit! While he's breaking my sword, I kick him in the knee as hard as I can. A strike of the street, bearing no relation to the refined art of fencing.

Lance stumbles back and falls onto his back, awkwardly, like a turtle, trying to get up. I leap onto him, pressing him to the ground, not letting him escape. I pin his right arm with my elbow, but his left arm is free.

A hit! I feel pain in my side. My HP drops into the red. One of Lance's short blades is in my abdomen. He twists it, releasing blood... in the message log, my HP gushes out of me in strings of digits.

I look straight into his eyes. He could play an undead character in a movie without makeup. I look at him and jam a fragment of my katana directly into his throat. Critical hit! More and more! Critical hit! Critical hit!!! I strike like a maniac, sprawled out on my victim, until I find myself alone on the arena sand. Lance is gone. I'm victorious.

* * *

I was running late in the morning. Slipping on frozen puddles and shivering from the cold, I approached the bus stop and spied Simba from afar. In his vibrant jacket, he was lighting up the chilly gray morning like a beacon.

"Hey there! Isn't the university that way?"

Simba said teasingly.

"Well, I'll just tell them that I'm you," I replied emotionlessly. "I need the money more, you know."

Simba laughed and slapped me on the shoulder.

"You gonna grovel?" he said sympathetically. "It's unlikely to work, but you can try."

"They reset the results," I lied, playing it off like it wasn't a big deal. "They called yesterday. They had some sort of glitch. The count was off."

"Ho-ho! Super!" Simba rejoiced. "The champion is back!"

An electric bus pulled up. We squeezed through the crowd of stern old ladies and gloomy workers and found two free seats at the back.

"Why are you alone?" I asked, curious. "I thought you'd show up with your buxom girl."

"We'll meet there," my buddy waved his hand. "Plus, she's not mine. All day yesterday it was, 'Andryusha this... Andryusha that... Oh, maybe Andryusha is mad at me...'"

"Well she's not mine either," I distanced myself. "I haven't seen her in the flesh even once."

"You're missing out man!" Simba's eyes lit up. "Her boobs, bro! We were at the coffee shop and I didn't know where to look. Like it or not, your gaze just slips on down!"

"So, make a move."

"Nah," Simba grew sad again. "It looks like she's from the country. She lives in a dorm. Give her the slightest excuse and she'll get all wifey. Never get rid of her then."

My friend jealously guarded his future living space from any invaders. A marriage prospect was his greatest nightmare.

AngelCake was already waiting for us at the bus stop. Her lilac tracksuit and light jacket hugged her figure so snugly that I gulped.

"Hello!" she waved at us cheerfully.

"Hello," Simba grumbled.

From his mood, I understood that his fixation on having a bachelor pad of his own had prevailed over all other temptations.

"I'm Anastasia, but you can just call me Stacy." AngelCake didn't seem to notice. "I know your name is Andrew! Please forgive me! I really didn't mean to frag you yesterday! I hope everything will be okay for you? Since you came back, everything must be fine, right?"

She prattled rapidly in a tinkling voice and it actually cheered me up. She was all lively, spirited, and positive. A bright teenager's backpack in the shape of a rabbit bounced on her back. Whenever she turned to Simba, the bunny winked at me.

"Hey," I smiled, "Yeah, everything's okay."

"Then let's go! There's already a bunch of people over there!"

Without waiting for us, she turned around and trotted up the steps. Her well-rounded buttocks rolled beneath the soft fabric of her sports pants. Up and down... up and down... Simba nudged me with his elbow, signaling with his gaze, and I nodded in approval.

The VIP passes were gone and I didn't want to

look like an idiot in front of Marina. So, we headed towards the long line and joined at the very end.

"Andreeew!" a voice came from above.

"Andryusha, looks like it's for you!" Simba nudged me.

There was no point in hiding anymore. I sighed and ascended the stairs. Simba followed in astonishment and naturally, AngelCake tagged along too.

Marina was waving from the VIP doors. The line stared at us with curiosity, whispering and discussing. Some had already decided that we must be renowned esports pros, and of course most of their curiosity fell to Simba. He did look the more presentable among our group.

"Did you get lost there, Andrew?" Marina was stomping in place at the doors, blowing on her hands.

She looked like she was freezing. Her trendy boots were totally unsuitable for the winter weather. Simba meanwhile was devouring her with his gaze. He liked her kind of girls — posh and status-driven — the kind you could show off with.

"Top o' the morning to you, m'lady! Allow me to introduce myself. Simon's my name!"

Marina looked him up and down, smiled politely and turned back to me.

"I'm freezing," she complained, slipping her fingers into my hand. Her fingers were truly icy. "Why didn't you come earlier?"

"I forgot the passes..."

"Nonsense," Marina laughed. "I'm the one handing them out. Are there two of you?"

She completely ignored AngelCake.

"Three."

"Three," Marina pulled her fingers back and made a note in her tablet. "Go ahead!"

Finally, she looked at Stacy and smirked. Stacy responded by raising her head haughtily. The guard preemptively opened the door for us, and I slipped inside past Marina. I really didn't need any more girl problems here.

The door led to the same lobby, but the two paths were divided by a stretch of red tape. The attendants, with polite smiles, directed us to another hallway, up the stairs, and to the second floor.

"Wow!" Simba couldn't get over Marina. "You two know each other?!"

"It turns out we do," I didn't know what to say, and I didn't want to tell the truth in front of Stacy. She was an outsider in all of this.

"No, seriously?! Did you see her?! She's got this air about her! And those lips... Those lips!" My buddy was ecstatic about Marina. "So who is she here?"

"The head of the PR department."

"Damn!" Simba chuckled. "We've got some connections!"

He gave a royal nod, gracefully acknowledging the guards lining our way. They politely nodded back.

With stylish Marina in the picture, AngelCake

completely faded from my friend's mind. She didn't seem to care much however. She caught up with me and accidentally brushed against my thigh a couple of times. Her thigh was firm and warm.

VIP players got their own individual changing rooms located on the second floor. We were handed electronic keys with room numbers. Mine was at one end of the hallway, while Simba's and Stacy's were further down.

My changing room was modest, yet somehow cozy. The room was tiny, but it had a separate shower cabin — wide and tall and installed snugly against the wall. There was also something between a bench and a couch, a small table for belongings, and a hanger with a lonely robe hanging from it.

A small screen hung on one of the walls. Right now, it displayed the word "wait" in red. Unexpectedly, on the other wall, there was a painting. It depicted a somewhat strange, abstract landscape. Part ruins, part city in the clouds.

The ubiquitous soft electronica emanated from hidden speakers. I changed into my robe and slippers, sat on the couch, and shut my eyes. I was trembling again. Now that I was alone with my thoughts, my trembling only grew stronger.

Destiny had given me a second chance. And not just for today's test. I had been certain I would never enter virtual reality again. It was too late to return to esports. That career started at 10–12 years old. At 14, talented boys and girls were recruited by scouts for professional fights. By my age, they would either reach the peak of their careers or fade into obscurity.

Buying or renting my own VR pod was as unrealistic as buying an airplane. They were available for purchase, but they cost as much as a luxury car. Plus, they constantly required upgrades and technical maintenance.

I knew this was my only chance, and I was determined to latch onto it with all my might. No nonsense, no experiments, no saving young girls or clashing with the organizers and security. From here on out, I'd be a boring and predictable beta tester, a middle-of-the-road guy who collected his paycheck and pulled his weight. And no girls — they were only trouble.

And yet... Why did the Master bring me into the game? What did he want to show me? If I could understand, I would become more useful: a person to be reckoned with, someone you can't just take and throw out the door.

The screen blinked, snapping me out of my reverie. Green letters appeared on it: "The next round of the beta is about to begin."

No sooner had I stood up than a knocking came on my door. I went to open it, my mind ticking through various possibilities: Simba... AngelCake... Marina dropping by to wish me luck... The Master coming in to offer tea and nuts...

I was expecting anyone but the person standing there.

"Hey, Ratmir," he said.

Chapter 10

"CAN I COME IN?" Lance pushed me aside without waiting for a reply and stepped inside.

I shrugged: "You already have."

Lance was clearly coming from his changing room but hadn't bothered to prepare for the game. He was wearing a black tank top and baggy black trousers with plenty of pockets. I was certain they were considered terribly fashionable.

Since I first met him years ago, Lance had transformed from a lanky, gangling teenager into a jacked bro. You couldn't build muscles in a VR pod, so I guess he was hitting the gym regularly. Eating salads, drinking protein shakes and going to the gym. Just the thought of it cracked me up.

"What are you grinning about?" Lance stood in the middle of the room, his legs planted wide apart. "Thought I wouldn't recognize you?"

"I couldn't care less, actually."

"You're here on purpose, aren't you?" Lance persisted. "Plotting something against me?"

"Lance…" I didn't even feel like lying. His sudden entrance had thrown me off completely, and that greatly irritated me. "You're delusional if you think the whole world revolves around you. I'm here for the cash. I didn't even know you'd be here. It's just a beta test, it's not some championship, or a cup, or an exhibition for sponsors. I mean, I should be the one asking you — what are *you* doing here?"

"Oh sure," Lance smirked. "Don't play innocent. I know you'd kill your own mom to win!"

"Hey, leave my mom out of this!" I couldn't hold back. "And cut the whole celebrity shtick. It's been a while since someone smacked you in your gob, eh?!"

"Come on and try it then — what are you waiting for?" Lance stepped up to me. "Chicken?"

I realized he was trying to provoke me. It was so blatant and childish. He was still hung up on yesterday's scrap and just wanted a pretext to get me in trouble. My anger gave way to a cold, crystal-clear appraisal of the situation.

"Get lost," I replied without malice. "You're holding me up. And by the way, I'm not your rival. As I recall it, some girl wiped the floor with you yesterday. Seems like she has bigger balls than you do."

Lance started.

"She'll wipe the floor with you too, you pup. Don't get involved with Anna, she's a nutjob."

"Then go annoy her, maybe she'll take pity on you," I turned away from Lance, who was still standing there like a monument to himself, and walked towards the door. "Lance, you were a whiner before and you're a whiner now. If you're not gonna leave, then I will. I gotta go anyway. Make yourself at home."

And I walked out, leaving Lance standing there in my changing room. He can change my towels if he likes. I only hope he won't be there when I come back. In-game is the only place I wanna see that crybaby ever again.

*   *   *

The alley. The fence. The boulder. The fence had aged some more and begun to rot in places. The paint had peeled off some of the pickets. It was clear that there was no one to mend it. One of the pickets had come loose and was hanging on by a single nail. It wouldn't be long till the local kids start squeezing through the gap to pick cherries in the garden on the other side. That is if there even were any kids in this place.

That there was a cherry tree on the other side, I didn't doubt for a second. The fence reminded me of my childhood, of the endless summers at my grandma's place when my buddies and I used to sneak into the neighbor's garden. I had my own cherry tree in my backyard, but the ones from the neighbor's garden tasted better. This virtual fence here now looked very similar. No, actually, it was

EXACTLY THE SAME. I noticed a nail near the gap, crooked and rusty. Ten years ago I tore my shirt on the same nail and lost my phone privileges for a week.

I even had to shake my head a bit to drive away the reverie. It's just a nail, dummy, a simple nail. It's easy for memories to play tricks on your mind. I can't even properly remember that summer; too much time has passed. I can only remember bits and pieces anyway.

This game had misled me again, confused me. I wonder if I'm the only one it affects like this?

I instinctively checked my character screen. I was a lowly Level 0, with all my Stats at 1 and a blinking envelope next to the quest log.

EARN EXPERIENCE AND LEVEL UP!

Below was that countdown timer again: 59:22... 59:21...

I heard the sound of footsteps. Someone hurried past out on the street. People were running to the town square to talk to the mayor and get their quest. There weren't many options for earning XP — you could either do the quest or try and grind mobs. The latter of the two seemed more reliable to me. I'd find Simba and we'd go wipe out the spiders.

And there'd be no showing off after that. I'd take my money and go home. There were too many things going on in my life right now. Everyone seemed to want something from me, and not one of them was offering anything in return.

I peeked out of the alley. Beta testers were

crowding the square. They looked surprised for the most part.

"Are you sure he was standing here?"

"Yes, right in front of the tower! I even thought maybe he came out from there?"

"Stop making shit up. He never came out of anywhere! He never moved from that spot."

"I've checked everywhere... He's not here!"

"Hey... don't grab my ass!"

"It wasn't me... Oops!... It wasn't me again!"

The mayor was missing! The drunk had probably wandered off somewhere to sleep off his hangover. Or maybe he went to the tavern with his buddy from the weapons shop. Or maybe he went home to his family. To his wife and kids.

I had seen what no one else had. And now the others were stunned.

No mayor, no sword. The merchant only responded to players who had quests last time, and no one had any coins to buy weapons outright. Money didn't grow on any tree I'd seen here.

I recalled the two meter picket hanging onto the fence for dear life. If you're given a chance to arm yourself, you'd better take it.

The picket resisted. I pulled it towards me, rocked it, even tried to twist it, but the lone nail held it firmly fast. Twice, I drained my Stamina to zero and and, heaving, had to sit on the boulder to rest.

Yelling came from the town square, first joyful, then frightened. People were running around the town. And I had my own battle to fight. Just a slight turn... hook it with my fingers... yank it towards me... and again... and again...

Pause. Rest. Another quarter inch of the rusty thick nail sticking out. They gave me an hour. An hour is a lot. I'll make it in time.

Bam! Suddenly, I found myself on my ass, holding a long and sturdy picket in my hands.

The interface suddenly flashed urgently. I glanced over the icons and saw a message:

NEW WEAPON ACQUIRED: FENCE PICKET.

TYPE: BLUNT.

DAMAGE: 8–10.

DURABILITY: 94/100.

NEW WEAPON ACQUIRED: RUSTY NAIL.

TYPE: PIERCING.

DAMAGE: 3–5.

ADDITIONAL DAMAGE: TETANUS (POISON) 1–2 DMG/MIN.

DURABILITY: 497/500.

Here's a brilliant idea — I can scratch someone with the nail, then just run away. In half an hour to an hour, the enemy is sure to kick the bucket. Just kidding. It's hard to come up with a more useless ability for a weapon.

Holding the picket like a quarterstaff, I headed for the best place to earn XP around here: I was going to pay the spiders a visit.

I remembered the direction to go in and decided to cut through the alleyways. The town was arranged like a sun — a central square with streets radiating in all directions like rays. The alleyways linked the radiating streets at set intervals... Only now did it occur to me that from above, the place looked like a spiderweb. Gah!

I was a few blocks away from the spiders' nests when I heard a voice begging, "No, no... please, don't! No! Ahhh! Noooo!!!"

The begging gradually turned into a screaming. *"Had the spiders advanced so much from their nests?"* I wondered, as I ran in the direction of the sound.

The spiders weren't the issue, however. Right in the middle of the street, on the cobblestones, lay AngelCake, with two players standing over her with the firm intention of having their way with her.

I couldn't see their faces, but I recognized Stacy by her voice. She was screaming the way she had when she realized that she would have to get the spiders' green blood on her. One assailant was practically sitting on her head, pinning her arms with his knees. He had pulled up AngelCake's short top and was fondling her ample breasts. The second was trying to pull off her skirt and panties.

The girl struggled, but the odds were against her. The rapists were applying the same principle we had discovered on the square. Two units of force working together were twice as effective as one.

And that meant that in a few more minutes, AngelCake would be raped. Most likely, twice over.

Oh but why the hell did I deiced to go this way? Didn't I tell myself I'd keep my head low and avoid girls? I can't... I need to pay for my tuition... I need to get some money for my mom...

And anyway, there's two of them and only one of me. The busty girl wouldn't be much help, so they would overpower me too. What could be simpler... You can go your own way...

"You motherfuuuckers..." Stacy's prolonged scream erupted behind me. "I fucking haaate you..."

I turned around. The one pulling on her skirt had put his hand between AngelCake's legs and was roughly rummaging in there, pressing down with his fingers.

Thunk! The hardwood fence picket slammed into the base of the bastard's skull, a juicy, hollow sound.

CRITICAL HIT! -28 HP (STUN 4s...).

The wretch slumped aside like a sack of potatoes. Without wasting time on a wind-up, I kicked the second one in the jaw, knocking him off the girl.

"Quick pin him down, Stacy! Just hold him!"

AngelCake was batting her eyes senselessly and trying to cover herself with her hands.

"Pin the rapist, you pinhead!"

She jerked as if I'd slapped her, understanding dawning in her eyes. Turning, she latched onto her assailant's leg with all her might.

Meanwhile, the first one I'd hit was shaking his head, recovering from the stun, so wasting no time, I grabbed the picket closer to one end and teed off on his head.

What's that? You thought I'd fight fairly? No such thing as a fair fight. Blood sprayed in an arc around us. My blow only dealt did 15 damage and dropped the wretch's health to yellow, but more importantly he was stunned again.

I stood over him and methodically began to pound his head into the cobblestones like I was driving a pile. Only now did I have the time to examine him. Scrawny, not tall, clearly below average height. He looked like an ordinary street punk. You couldn't make out his face — I'd already beaten it to a bloody pulp.

Somewhere behind me, his partner was yelling, and Stacy was screaming. I couldn't make out a single word, and it didn't matter. The important thing was that they were both still there.

Strike... another strike... Finally, the stun effect wore off. Not every hit dealt a stun, not even the most successful ones. The freak was trying to crawl away. I stepped on his hand. I was tired. My worst enemy — my lack of Stamina — again reared its ugly head. I finished the job though. One last blow, and his empty clothes crumpled in a heap on the cobblestones.

In the next instant I collapsed right there beside him. Convulsions wracked my body and limbs. An unheralded, unbelievable sensation grew somewhere in my loins, sprouting and spreading up to my heart and then through my arteries to every organ, muscle and ligament, a warmth intensifying into a burning... becoming unbearable...

"AAAHHH!" I scream, riding the incredible rush.

This is a pleasure I have never even suspected exists before. It's as if every one of my million nerve endings has had an orgasm. As if I've risen at dawn of creation itself and the nubile sun has warmed every cell of my body. As if a cool stream has washed away all my doubts and fears. As if I've been reborn and the world is new and wonderful again.

And then everything turned ordinary and gray again. I almost howled from disappointment when the magical sensation abruptly left me.

This is nature at work in VR: carrot and stick. Want to experience a rush? Level up and get hooked on the game's needle.

YOU HAVE LEVELED UP! YOU ARE NOW LEVEL 1!

YOU HAVE EARNED 5 STAT POINTS!

ALLOCATE STAT POINTS WISELY. THESE CHANGES ARE PERMANENT!

I allocate my free stat points without giving it much thought: +2 to Strength, +3 to Dexterity. Then I walk over to AngelCake.

"Oh! It's you!" AngelCake exclaims in surprise, releasing her captive and covering her luscious breasts with her hands.

Her prisoner tries to run but I sweep him with my picket and he keels over like a bowling pin.

"Please... let me go... please..." he whimpers.

"Angel_o_Death," I read above his head. Pretentious and sophomoric. Pal, you're just a frag to me now.

I yank him up and make him kneel. Our difference in strength allows me to do as I please with him now.

"Come here Stacy!"

"Hang on!" Stacy stands with her back turned, pulling up her skirt. Unhindered, I admire her voluptuous ass. "Hey, no peeking!"

"I've already seen all there is to see!"

I don't have time to act embarrassed or courteous in the heat of battle. Stacy blushes and, tugging her tank top, comes over to me.

"That didn't count," she tries to argue. She's embarrassed and generally behaving as if nothing at all happened.

Hoping I'm distracted, Angel_o_Death makes a run for it. I trip him again, pressing his head to the ground with my knee.

"Stay down, jerk!"

I'm still weak and all, but with 3 Strength, I'm three times stronger than him. Which means he's a goner if he moves.

"Oh!" Stacy covers her mouth, shocked. "You're hurting him!"

A little more and she'll start feeling sorry for this perv. How did she even end up in this beta test? Was she passing by when she saw a line of people waiting for something and decided she'd better get a spot before it was too late?

"Did you forget what these two tried to do to you?" I yell at her. "They were going to tear you apart and have their way with every hole! Do you think they would have spared you?! Neither your mother nor the police would have saved you!"

AngelCake blushes and pouts but seems to understand. Her lips tighten sternly, her gaze hardens. I offer her the nail. It's come in handy after all.

"What's this?!" Stacy recoils. "Why?"

The nail does look rather ominous. It's long, crooked, and rusty. Probably a good six inches in length. Or maybe not, I don't know what six inches looks like.

Seeing the nail, my prisoner's eyes widen in terror and he begins to whimper. He sure is a pitiful bastard.

"Take it, I said! Goddamn…"

She takes the nail hesitantly, looks down at it and then at me.

"Strike him!" I say, stepping back a bit and pushing his throat towards Stacy.

The poor fucker's Adam's apple throbs in his throat.

"No!" Stacy's eyes widen in horror.

"Aren't you a country girl?"

"Yeah…" she nods, puzzled.

"You ever chopped off chicken heads?"

"But that's different! This is a human!"

"Of course, it's different, you idiot!" I explode. "Because for the chickens, that's it — it's game over! But this asshole will wake up in his VR pod, go home and jerk off! He's not a human in this game. He's just a frag!"

AngelCake squints and stabs almost at

random. The victim wheezes, splattering blood over my arm. What the hell is with this gruesome realism? Why is it in the game, even if it's rated 18+?! Who the hell needs this game to be so graphic...?

"...*what you think is a game...*" the Master's words echo in my mind.

My prisoner's clothes crumple into a heap and my foot drops through them to the cobblestones. I feel around where his body had been. AngelCake had a sword, and weapons drop when you die, which means one of these two took it from her.

Meanwhile it's AngelCake's turn to feel the ecstasy of a new level. She nearly collapses, but luckily, I catch her. She struggles in my arms, a daft and happy smile on her lips.

"What was that?" she asks, slowly coming to her senses.

"You leveled up," I let her go as soon as she can stand on her own. "Congratulations, you're Level 1 now!"

"And why did... Why did it feel like that?" AngelCake is at a loss for words. She seems more intrigued as she looks at me.

"So that you'll want more."

Stacy laughs, thinking I'm joking, but there's no joke about it. What else could make a spider attack its own kind? Only pleasure. People eat, drink, have sex... for pleasure. If the spider can feel even a fraction of what I felt, it will happily kill whatever to experience that feeling again.

"What are you looking for?" Stacy sees me rummaging through the wannabe rapist's clothing.

"The sword that you had."

"I still have it," Stacy raises her hand, and I see a thin strip of steel, "I put it in my inventory so they wouldn't take it from me."

I smack myself on the forehead. Why did I assume they robbed her first? There's nothing to take from her but what nature gave her.

"Do you mind trading?" I ask cautiously, worried that she no longer trusts any men at all like a character in a Hollywood movie.

"No problem!" Stacy takes my fence picket. "This seems more convenient."

Looking at her with her new weapon, I couldn't help but be impressed. The Russian countryside has some impressive women after all. This one looked like she could take out a horse's legs midstride.

I still had a ways to go to feel comfortable with this sword. That ease when the weapon became an extension of the hand, when I could wield it as if it were a continuation of my thought, remained far off.

The sword was heavy, not very comfortable and terribly balanced. But at least it didn't slip from my hand, making it possible to hit a target.

"You have to make a choice, Stacy," I said firmly, "either you come with me, but then you ask no questions, you just listen and follow. Or you stay here. You've already completed the quest and you can fend off any Level 0 on your own now."

"I'm coming with you!" Stacy replied without a second thought. "That's the second time you saved me. I won't leave your side now."

"Then let's go!" I said and hurried in the direction of the spider nests.

Time was already slipping away. A half hour had elapsed on the timer. I knew we had to use our advantage of being one level higher here and now. Both the other players and the mobs would catch up soon enough, so this was our chance to grind as much as we could.

A few minutes later we were approaching one of the spider-infested houses. As I looked around, I froze where I stood: Just ahead a large pile of spiders had formed — and I could see Simba's legs sticking out from beneath it.

CHAPTER 11

WHY IS IT THAT I COULD identify my friend by his feet alone? Firstly, because Simba's feet were huge. Even a size 12 shoe didn't always fit his paws, making finding footwear a serious challenge for him at times.

Secondly, when you've known someone since they were three years old, when you've done everything together, from playing in the sandbox to camping by the river, you won't mistake his feet for anyone else's.

"He's still alive!" was the first thought that flashed through my mind. If the spiders had finished him, his body would be a cocoon by now. I remembered from the first encounter that the spiders were repulsive and aggressive, but the damage they did wasn't too high.

"Leeroy Jenkins!" I yelled to boost my morale, rushing towards the writhing pile.

Striking a spider on its arched armored back, I made a long gash, but the creature didn't even respond to my blow. That hit didn't do anything? There goes being Level 1! I had hoped I would be knocking down mobs in batches now.

"Andrew?!" a muffled voice came from under the crawling mass.

"Hold on! We'll save you!" I encouraged him, though I wasn't feeling so confident anymore.

Bam! Stacy entered the fray. She felt much more confident with her new quarterstaff than with an edged weapon. Perhaps it was the length of the picket, which allowed her to strike from a distance, making the whole business less revolting.

AngelCake smacked a spider forcefully, knocking it aside. The creature lay for a bit, then rose unsteadily to its legs and wobbled away.

I decided to change tactics. Taking aim, I began to lop off the spiders' legs right at the base. This worked better, but it was slow going. In the time it took me to disable one spider's legs, Stacy managed to knock away four.

"Andrew, I'm down to 10% HP!" Panic sounded in my friend's voice.

What to do?! I stashed the stubborn sword in my inventory and started tossing the spiders away, grabbing them by the legs. I quickly got the hang of it. The spiders flew like medicine balls in gym. I even got carried away a bit.

"Hey jackass, watch where you throw those!"

"Ouch! Get this bug off of me!"

"Hey, be careful over there!"

The players around us began to complain and fight off the spiders I had thrown in their direction. Others began to flee. One even thought about getting on our case about it, but thought better of it upon seeing the very serious expressions on our faces.

Freeing our friend at last, we took up positions next to him in a defensive circle. The spiders seemed intent on finishing what they started — maybe they'd liked the taste of Simba — they weren't scary individually, however.

I got into the groove, hewing the creatures' front legs, and when they stumbled with their chitinous faces into the pavement, I plunged the sword into the gap between the head and thorax. This blow counted as a critical hit, and the spiders died instantly.

Stacy's approach was simpler: Cheering herself on with loud whoops and exclamations, she hammered the creatures with her quarterstaff until they succumbed. This time around, her attempts were much more effective. What a difference the right mindset makes!

Simba struggled to get to his feet but only managed to sit up.

"How much HP do you have left?!" I yelled without pausing.

"Seven percent... Ooof..." He shook his head like a circus bear. "Everything's throbbing red and the fog won't go away. Is that Stacy there with you? How did you two find each other?"

"Stacy here, checking in," AngelCake rejoined crisply, even a bit provocatively. "While you were being overrun here, I almost got..."

"Let's discuss it later!" I interrupted, unwilling to let her air our business. "Stacy and I ran into each other by chance on the way over here. How did you end up like this?"

"Dunno..." my friend shrugged. "Everyone took off running this way, so I followed them."

That was Simba's entire approach to strategy and tactics in a nutshell. He was indispensable in any fight. But more often than not, he was the one that started it too.

The spiders' onslaught now ebbed and I got a moment to look around. The spiders' part of town now included three houses. The initial ruins where they had started their conquest were now so covered in webs that they no longer looked like ruins at all, but rather like a massive gray cocoon, with the trees and bushes around it encased in smaller cocoons.

The eight-legged tenants had moved into two additional houses. They occasionally darted out to the porch or the lawn, busily mending broken windows with their webs.

The spiders' main line of defense ran along where the fences to these properties had once stood. They didn't let players approach their houses, but they didn't wander far themselves either. They just raised their legs and clicked their jaws menacingly. It was an intimidating sight.

I noticed that only small spiders occupied the

front ranks. The Level 0s. Their larger kin could be seen closer to the houses. They differed not only in size but also in their brighter green bristles.

If I hadn't seen for myself how the spiders leveled up, I wouldn't have noticed anything strange. I would have thought they were elite mobs, and I bet I was an elite mob for them too. I wonder if this scared them or made them aggro me? Would they level up faster fighting someone like me too?

"Wow!" Simba was coming to his senses and simultaneously recovering his usual chattiness. "We're forming a pretty good party here! I'll tank, Andrew can dps, and Stacy... Stacy can be our priestess! She can motivate us before battle!"

"I'll tell you what: I'll give you a smack upside the head with this staff!" Stacy brandished the picket at Simba, who was still sitting, recovering. "That should motivate you."

"Really. You're not much of a tank, Simba," I chimed in. "You'll dissolve from a single bite. Especially since you're still in the red."

"When did you two level up anyway?"

"When the spiders were giving you a full body massage!" Stacy joked, and the three of us burst out laughing.

It was easy to see what level someone was: Each creature's level was displayed in parentheses after their name. So Simon was Simba (Level 0), Stacy was AngelCake (Level 1) and the spider over there was Spiderling (Level 0).

Meanwhile, a pitched battle between the beta

testers and the spiders had unfolded right beside us. We stood at its very edge. The main fighting was taking place in the middle of the street. Players armed with swords, either individually or in groups, were attacking the ranks of spiders. Most of them were already at Level 1.

Not everyone was lucky. Diligent worker spiders were already dragging away several elongated cocoons with players' bodies and stacking them on the lawn in front of a house, probably to demoralize the surviving players.

Those without weapons or those simply standing bewildered on the sidelines were trying to help by throwing stones and sticks at the spiders, albeit without much effect.

"Do you have a sword?" I asked, wanting to test a hunch I had.

"Yeah, it was in my inventory from the start," Simba confirmed.

So, yesterday's round of the beta had counted after all. And if you had acquired a weapon and didn't lose it in battle like I had, it was waiting for you in your inventory for subsequent quests. Those who had died and gotten a second chance, like me, still had to pick one up in battle.

"The usual tactics won't work here," I said. "Maybe in the future, tanks will have some buff that lowers their pain threshold. But for now, you want to just stand there and endure getting slashed and bitten? You'd have to be a masochist."

"What about you, AngelCake? Don't you like it rough?!" Simba grinned.

"That's it! I'mma let you have it now! Back off! Back off! Andrew, let me hit him!"

"QUIET EVERYONE!" I yelled, unable to control myself. "This is like kindergarten all over again! Time is running out, we have twenty minutes left, and you two are just messing around!"

I knew we had to act. While we were waffling, our competitors were leveling up, and Simba was still in danger of failing his quest and being eliminated from the beta test.

"Listen up. I'll grab a spider and flip it on its back, Stacy will hit it with her staff, and Simba will finish it off. You got that, Stacy?"

"I got it!" AngelCake nodded vigorously the way a teacher's pet nods at her favorite teacher.

"If you hit me again, I'll find you in meatspace and pay you back in kind, got it?"

"I got it," said Stacy, blushing and biting her lip.

The plan worked out nicely. We flanked the spiders from the house they had most recently taken over — where their defenses were thinner. I quickly grabbed one of the monsters by its front leg, pulled it towards me, and swung it against the cobblestones.

"Now! Get it! Get it!"

Stacy diligently clubbed the spider, dazing it, so that all Simba had to do was finish it off. Gripping the sword with both hands like a cleaver, he struck the creature's head with several blows. And voila!

"Order up!" Simba announced.

We hit our stride and the fight went like clockwork. Toss a spider, stun it, a few finishing blows, and the little spider dissolves into a handful of dust. It took Simba ten spiders to earn his first level, but it took fifty to get to the second one.

"Simba, hold on!" I needed to collect my thoughts.

It took us about half a minute to kill one mob. For any one of us to reach Level 2, it would take 25 minutes. And we only had fifteen minutes left until the end of the round. There wasn't enough time.

I couldn't get the elite spiders out of my mind. They had to be worth more XP. In any case, we had already completed the assigned quest and could afford to take a risk now.

"I propose storming one of the houses," I announced.

"What do you mean storming?" AngelCake rounded her enormous... eyes.

That's right, I was looking right into her eyes and not at whatever was heaving below.

"We'll go in and slash 'em all to hell!" Simba blustered. "I'm in!"

Stacy nodded along, looking at me trustingly. Damn, somehow Simba had managed to become the leader.

Forming a wedge, with Simba and I on the flanks and Stacy in its center, we easily breached the weak screen of Level 0 Spiderlings. Stacy wielded her staff from the rear, dishing out the majority of the dps, and stomping like horses, we dashed through a hole in the fence and burst into the yard. As I expected, the elite spiders were already waiting for us.

"Let go, you bastard! Give it here!"

The nearest large spider lunged at Stacy, and she thought of nothing better than to shove her staff into its mouth. The spider snapped its jaws down on the fence picket, latching onto it like a bulldog. Unlike your ordinary bulldog, however, this spider was bigger than we were.

"Simba! Together!"

We went to work with our swords, wielding them like butcher's cleavers to dismantle the spider. I delivered the final blow, and the XP bar immediately jumped by 10%. With the progress I had already made, I had 40% left to the next level. Four elites. We're in business!

"Stacy, you're our tank!" Simba declared.

"What an idea!" AngelCake pouted and rejoiced at the same time.

She seemed flattered, yet resented the comparison.

"Look!" she squealed. "Oh, crap!"

It was indeed an oh crap moment to say the least. Elites were converging on us from all sides of the small yard. There were about twenty or thirty of them — the exact number didn't matter. We'd have had our hands full with ten if they attacked all at once. I looked around.

"Make for the house!" I called an audible.

Who knows what awaited us inside. But at

least there would be hallways and doors and therefore chokes. We'd stand a slim chance in there, but a chance nonetheless.

We rushed inside just as the first spiders were skittering onto the porch. I slammed the door right on their noses — and wondered whether spiders even have noses. The door trembled and shook. Down below, I spotted a sturdy iron bolt, exactly as I had imagined it. A click, and we were safe, relatively, of course.

"Die, you fiend! Die! Die!!!" AngelCake was screaming behind me.

Spiders were descending the stairs from the second floor. There were many of them, but the narrow staircase prevented them from fanning out and surrounding us.

"Cut them off! Cut their legs from under them!"

The railing was in the way. Simba shoved a table, I jumped onto it in a leap, and found myself level with the steps. The spider spun around in place, hissed, and clicked its jaws. It got whacked in the side by AngelCake's staff, then lunged at her, positioning itself for a strike. Raising my arm high, I drove my sword precisely between its head and the raised part of its thorax where the green cross was.

A crit! I nearly yelp from the rush of wild, adrenaline-fueled excitement. Another spider takes its fellow's place. I lop off its front legs, causing it to stumble and tumble — right into Simba's attack. The third one backs off, blocking the passage, raising its front legs as a warning. It's almost like it's guarding something.

"The window!" notices Simba. "Stacy, they're coming in from there!"

Black legs are visible in the window. Stacy swipes at them with her staff, crushing one of the limbs and making it ooze a green liquid and breaking off the other limb.

Simba and I make our way upstairs. It feels like I've been bitten. There's a venom effect on me, and my health bar is slowly dropping. Will I make it or not? I haven't seen any potions or antidotes around here. This definitely doesn't feel like a tutorial quest. Reminds me more of a hardcore speedrun.

The second floor is dark. I expected more light here, but it's as dark as a cellar. The windows, walls, and the vaulted ceiling, like you'd find in an attic, are all covered in cobwebs. They're everywhere. The whole room is cluttered with junk beneath the cobwebs. Its outlines are blurred beneath the white, dense layers of spider silk.

Two elites stand at the edge of the staircase. They're retreating, waving their legs and emitting a strange chittering. Whether they're trying to scare us off or calling for help is unclear. It's steel versus chitinous feelers. The spiders aren't attacking; they're defending themselves. But steel is far harder.

My body recalls the Gladiator Games, the wild dance of arms and armor. Strikes... blocks... feints... combos... A surge of delight washes over me, almost like I've leveled up again.

But it's not the real thing this time. It's just a memory. I refocus on what I was doing. I pass Simba, vault over the railing, and land two-footed on the back of one of the spiders. Its carapace crunches, and I drive my sword into its open jaws with both hands.

We corner the last one against the wall, sever its legs, and finish it off together. I have 10% of my XP bar left until I hit the next level.

"Simba, how much XP do you have?"

"Twenty percent to the next level."

The upper floor is divided into several rooms as well. Right by the stairs, there's a wall with a closed door, and we find ourselves in a dimly lit hall.

AngelCake shouts menacingly from below. I'm about to go down to help her and get the XP I need while I'm at it, when I notice movement deep within the cobwebs.

I come closer and realize that what I mistook for random junk is actually masses of spider eggs — grape clusters of small round cocoons, the size of a fist, each containing trembling baby spiders.

They are still a light gray color because their armor hasn't had time to harden and darken. The revolting sight makes me shudder with disgust. Grossed out, I stomp the egg cluster with my foot and my XP bar jumps noticeably. It seems that each cocoon is worth about 1% XP, but there are hundreds of them!

I start stomping left and right until a warm

wave engulfs me. Hitting Level 2 doesn't feel as amazing as Level 1 did; I don't collapse and writhe on the ground, but a pleasant shiver still runs through me, reaching beneath my skull.

"Crush the cocoons, Simba! They're easy XP!"

He doesn't need to be told twice. Gleefully stomping away, Simba soon earns his second level too.

I walk over to the stairs and shout to the floor below, "Stacy, drop everything and come up here!"

And that's when the closed door swings open. I see a girl standing in the doorway. At first, I think she's naked. Then it dawns on me that she's simply not wearing a skirt. Her bronzed skin contrasts sharply against the bright white of her thong. Her cropped top is cut high and only covers her nipples, baring most of her ample breasts.

She's covered in green spider blood from head to toe, as if she just took a bath in it. Her long black hair is knotted high on her head. Her dark eyes squint with malice. The handle above her head reads: "Anna (Level 15)." She holds a sword in each hand.

Simba and I are stunned by her sudden and strange appearance. My best friend comes to his senses before me, but this time his senses mislead him.

"'Tis a pleasure to make your acquaintance, m'lady! Simon's my name and slayin's my game..."

The girl takes a swift step forward and the next thing I see is Simba's head separate from his body. We trade looks of surprise as his face sails past me.

I raise my sword to strike and feel her heel smash into my chest. She kicks like a horse, at least that's how it feels, and I go tumbling down the stairs.

YOU ARE STUNNED (10s... 9... 8...).

I lie there dazed, helpless as the Fury strides past me.

Seeing what's happened to me, AngelCake emits a squeak of horror. She hurls her staff at Anna to at least slow her down a bit, then dashes for the door. The spiders must seem much less scary juxtaposed with this oncoming vision of death.

Anna overtakes her victim in two steps and shoves her to the ground. She could kill AngelCake right away but she savors her pleasure. Sitting on top of her, pressing her down, Anna lays her bloodied sword nearby. Then, with a quick movement, she grabs Stacy by the hair, tilts her head back, and slits her throat.

CHAPTER 12

THREE... TWO... ONE!

The stun fades away and the instant it's gone I spring into action like a coiled spring and take off running. Even while lying on the ground, I had a chance to think. Maybe just a few seconds, but time behaves oddly in battle. Sometimes an hour will fly by in an instant; other times a minute will go on for an eternity.

There's only one option when facing this monster — to run. I don't stand a chance against a Level 15. Not a sliver of a chance.

And I really don't want to die now. I barely gained any XP after reaching Level 2, but losing it would be a pity. The further I go, the harder it will be to get it. But that's not even the main thing. I just don't want to die. I've had enough of that. What kind of champion is constantly getting killed by chicks?

So I take off running — but not away from her. No, I spring at her as fast as I can.

Anna is sitting on the floor, where AngelCake's body just was. I grab the fence picket (our Excalibur for all the times it saved us) mid-stride and with all my strength clobber Anna on the back of the head with it.

The picket snaps with a crack. It feels like I hit the Terminator. A short useless fragment with sharp splinters remains in my hands, while the monster before me seems unaffected.

But no — she rocks forward, supporting herself with her hands. Damage is damage, but you can't ignore a status effect. Stunned, Anna shakes her head, her elbow propped on her knee.

She's not bad looking actually... Real skinny, sure, but...

Damn, what am I thinking about? How much longer will she be stunned for? Five seconds? Three?

Whatever it is, that's the time I've got to live. I dash back upstairs to the second floor. It doesn't matter where, so long as I can buy myself time. The quest timer is already counting down the final seconds of this round of the beta.

54... 53... 52...

Never imagined I'd be spending it like this.

A crashing rises from the floor below. Sleeping beauty has awakened. Footsteps sound on the staircase, bounding my way three stairs at a time.

I come face to face with the door she emerged

from. I slam it shut and wedge the handle with the fragment of the fence picket I'm still holding. It proves useful one last time. What a great weapon that turned out to be!

It probably won't stop her for long. But the timer is down to seconds.

41… 40… 39…

I turn around. The room is a slaughterhouse. The cobwebs hang from the walls and ceiling in damp green icicles. It's as if a whole barrel of spider blood exploded in here.

There are bits of cocoon and pieces of tough chitinous armor strewn around the floor. It seems that some massive creature was in here earlier, and now it's dead. In fact, this is the first time I've detected any trace of a dead mob in this game. Even the spiders don't drop any loot, which is pretty odd actually.

Taking advantage of a moment's respite, I shove a piece of what looks like the creature's carapace into my inventory. Once in, the carapace immediately expands, taking up almost all my available slots.

I guess I'll sort it out later. If there is a "later" — if I don't die and leave all my belongings here.

The door shudders from a heavy blow. Here's Anna! It seems like she kicked it with half her strength, hoping it was open.

24… 23… 22…

The door flies inward taking the frame with it. Her silhouette stands in the doorway. I turn the other way and barge through the window, crashing through it. A brief tumble from the second floor, and I find myself lying on the lawn.

I feel like a bulldozer ran over me. And yet, there's no real pain. It's just a sense of utter helplessness.

Now I understand what Simba meant when he was blathering about the red fog. Everything is swimming, I can't see anything except the interface. HP: 3% — I'm down to 3%! If some passing spider even sneezes next to me, I'm done for.

Anna appears in the window, a bright spot framed against the dark background. Without much thought, she leaps forward, feet-first aiming to land right on me.

3... 2... 1...

Instinctively, I throw up my hands to protect myself. They hit something solid. Motherfu–! Am I in a grave? I'm alive, damn it! The monster didn't get to me!

"Sergio!" I hear a muffled cry. "Come over here! This one's wigging out! I think he thinks he's drowning!"

"What is wrong with them today?! Get the syringe!"

Pshhh... Light...

Two startled technicians are bending over me. I'm alive and the wall is just the lid of the VR pod. I'm lying in a pod... It was all a game. Just a game, damn it.

"Guys, I'm okay," I try to say, but my vocal cords aren't cooperating. The words come out in a weak whisper.

"What?" they exchange glances. "What's he hissing about?"

"I'm fine!" I say. It comes out better the second time. "Put away that syringe. Everything's fine."

I straighten up in my pod causing the technicians to stagger back warily. It seems that I'm not the first beta tester who's confused reality with the game today. I notice that one of the men has a scrape on his chin and that there's a fresh scratch on the other's cheek. I guess if you come out of the game swinging, their job is to give you a shot of some sedative and knock you out for the rest of the day.

I try not to make any sudden movements and smile. It doesn't really earn me much trust, but at least they aren't taking emergency measures.

"Can I put on my robe?" I slowly reach for the hanger.

"Yeah," one of them replies. "Have you come to your senses?"

"Yes." I nod amicably. "I couldn't snap out of it. I thought I was still in the game. It looks like I'm not the only one this has happened to?"

Both technicians relax visibly. One even reaches into his jumpsuit pocket, probably for cigarettes, then catches himself and pulls his hand back.

"One guy lunged at me today, tried to strangle me," he nods towards his coworker. "Luckily, Sergio was nearby, and we subdued him."

Suddenly, I recognize the technician who helped me out during the first round of the beta. Nothing shocking about that. There probably isn't that many of these guys around in general.

"Hey," I nod at him. "Remember the first time you helped me? In the basement?"

"Hey there!" Sergio seems to recognize me, or at least pretends to.

"They say that a girl broke loose in the basement today," continues the first guy. "Took off running naked down the hallway, screaming. They had to chase her down." He chuckles.

"Was she good-looking at least?" I ask, trying to keep the conversation going.

"I didn't see her," the tech says disappointed, "but they did say she was quite a looker."

Tough break for this guy. The other techs got to chase a naked girl, while all he got was a punch to the face and someone trying to strangle him. Something was off with today's beta overall. Last time I felt drained; now it was the opposite. I was filled with energy. It actually took a lot of effort not to run down the hallway, jumping and swatting at the ceiling as I went.

I burst into my changing room, dropped my robe to the floor and hopped into the shower. I turned the heat up as high as I could bear, then switched the faucet to cold, then hot again. The shower beat down on me like a waterfall. It was clearly a luxury setup, not some cheap shower head from the flea market.

I relished it, completely detaching from

reality, washing off not only the pod's saline solution but also all thoughts of today's beta. I'll think about it all later, once it settles in my head. But for now I needed rest. I was proud of myself today. I did well.

I stepped out of the shower, feeling for the towel with my bare feet and letting the water run off my body. When I opened my eyes, I realized I wasn't alone in the room.

"Oh, I brought you some pastries," said AngelCake. "You'll want to eat after the game! You men are always so hungry!"

"Damn it, Stacy!"

AngelCake was busy pulling out packages from her backpack, which turned out to be surprisingly roomy, and arranging them on the couch. As she did so, she leaned forward, enticingly sticking out her ass, clad in purple jogging pants.

Hearing me, she turned around.

"Oh! I'm not looking, I'm not looking!" Instead of turning away, she covered her eyes with her hands, while spreading her fingers, the better to peek through them.

All the blood in my brain drained into my groin. To hide my reaction, I bent down to grab my robe and wrapped myself in it.

The pastries smelled intoxicating, and I hadn't any strength left to be angry with Stacy, who kept smiling boisterously.

"You baked those yourself?" I asked, surprised.

"Of course! These aren't store-bought!" Stacy even seemed a little offended. "These here have a savory filling, and those have an apple filling…"

I grabbed a savory pastry just to distract myself from staring on Stacy's ass. My body seemed intent on betraying me. I pulled the sash of my robe tighter so as not to give away the plot and sat down on the couch.

"Stacy, do you remember how you died in the game?" I tried to change the subject.

"Nope…" AngelCake shook her head frivolously. "Something pushed me in the back. I fell and died. Why?"

"Nothing," I decided not to spoil AngelCake's mood. "I'll tell you later."

"Here, try this curry one!" Stacy came up to me. "It's nice and spicy!"

I looked up to look at her and encountered her prominent breasts at eye level. They heaved deeply with excitement. The zipper on her sports cardigan was half undone, and if there was a T-shirt underneath somewhere, I couldn't see where it began.

In that moment, all the tension of the day spilled out of me. I grabbed her by her pliant ass and pulled her towards me. Her skin smelled of fresh blackberry. At that moment I didn't even think much about what I wanted. I just loved squeezing and squeezing her luscious, supple body, stroking the velvety soft fabric of her tracksuit and her cool, smooth skin.

It was the first time that I was alone with a

girl and I wasn't worrying about how I looked or what I needed to do. I was thrilled by her softness, by my strength, by the fact that everything would now go exactly the way I wanted.

I pressed lightly on her shoulders, and Stacy knelt down willingly. She untied the belt of my robe and gaped, her eyes wide.

"Oh, look at him!"

"Who?"

"This handsome fellow..."

I have no idea what was handsome about what she encountered down there and I didn't care. Stacy's simpleminded babble and moaning were only turning me on more.

I ran my fingers through her hair and pressed. AngelCake deftly licked the head and placed her plump lips on my penis.

"Mmm," she smacked her lips carefully, "mmm-yum..."

She definitely knew what she was doing. I did not expect such skill from this flirtatious, but otherwise modest-seeming girl. AngelCake sucked deftly, skillfully and with great eagerness.

Her lips slid back and forth along my penis, taking it deeper and deeper. Without pausing, she took off her blouse to reveal a tight sports top, from which her big tits almost jumped out.

What a buzz. Never in my life have I gotten so much pleasure from a blowjob. From the tension, I began to thrust my hips, fucking her mouth. AngelCake opened her eyes wide, but managed to cope — though she did let slip something between a moan and a hum through her taut lips.

This completely blew my mind. I let go of her hair, allowed my penis to slip out of her mouth, then jumped up and tossed the compliant girl tits-down on the couch.

Her plump ass was stuck up and out. I quickly pulled off her pants along with her panties and ran my hand between her legs. Wet. Fuck, I used to think that the word "gushing" only ever came up in dirty jokes.

But Stacy was gushing so much that even her inner thighs were wet. I stroked her with my fingers, spreading her legs wider, while she arched like a cat and began to rub her tits against the couch.

"Andrew... please... take me... Andrew... I want to feel you inside of me."

She no longer smelled like blackberries. Her smell was that of desire now, the smell of a soft, pliant female giving herself to her male.

I slipped into her completely without any resistance. It was intoxicating, unexpected, savage sex. I drove down on her, growling with rage and delight, driving my dick into her over and over again, as she whined from beneath me, sticking out her ass and pressing her cheeks against my thighs.

"Yesss... Ooohhh...Yesss... Oh, goddamn, that's sooo goood..."

Stacy suddenly tensed up with her whole body, even squeezing my penis inside of her, then began trembling, then shaking, and then relaxed all at once.

"Rrrraaaah!"

I think I forgot what words even were as I pulled out and began to cum onto her plump ass.

Knock... knock... knock...

The sound of knocking gradually branched from the beating pulse in my head. Not now... Later... I just want to lie here a bit longer... just a little bit... the tiniest bit more...

Knock-knock-knock!

I think that's the door. Someone's knocking at the door!

"Stacy, did you lock the door?"

Stacy looks blankly somewhere past me and smiles.

"What?"

"The door!"

"No... Does it lock?"

Damn it... What the heck?! Is this a public street or is it a changing room? I may as well put up a sign with visiting hours.

As I walk over, I quickly tie my robe closed. Then I crack open the door and peek out. Marina is standing there, looking displeased.

"What took you so long, Andrew?"

"I was in the shower... didn't hear you knock..."

She looks at me suspiciously. Maybe I'm too dry for someone who was just in the shower, I don't know. Damn! What if they have cameras in here? But then again, why do I care? Is she my wife or fiancée? Why should I explain myself to her? A magnificent wave of fuck-all suddenly washes over me.

"Is everything okay?" Marina tries to peek past me into the changing room.

"Yeah, why?"

"I thought I heard a noise..."

"I was singing in the shower."

Marina is stumped, unsure how to respond. It sounds like nonsense, but she can't really argue. Why did she even come here? I cast her the look of a contented cat, which makes her even more uneasy.

"Actually, I came here on business," Marina starts adjusting the collar of my robe.

She smells just like yesterday... pleasant... floral... expensive... I think she's trying to sniff me too. Why? Or is this some female intuition thing?

"Want to make me some coffee?" I ask cheekily.

"Later," she replies, without declining outright. "At the moment, Benjamin Zvyagin wants to see you."

"*A complete jerk*," my memory helpfully supplies Marina's earlier introduction.

"To what do I owe the honor?" I wonder.

"The Master asked him to," Marina replies, as if that explains everything.

My mind slowly emerges from its relaxed state. Talking to Zvyagin could be interesting. This guy must know more about the game than anyone else. Yes, this is a golden opportunity. Plus, it means the Master hasn't written me off, and I didn't fail his test.

"Shall I go like this?" I curtsy in my robe before her.

"No, of course not," Marina snorts with a short laugh. "Get dressed. I'll wait."

I shut the door and look around. AngelCake's gone! I find her in the shower stall without panties, but in a cardigan and with the rest of her clothes in her arms. I put my finger to my lips, indicating that we need to be quiet. She widens her eyes in fear and nods. I don't know if she heard our conversation, but she is clearly afraid of Marina.

In a strange way, this gives the office blonde a few points in my eyes. It takes a couple of minutes to get dressed, but Marina is already impatient, tapping her toe in the corridor. Then again, her renewed interest in me requires little explanation.

"Will you tell me what you'll talk about?" she asks as we ride the elevator.

"What if it's confidential?" I tease.

"Oh, stop it!" Marina swats at me playfully.

Suddenly, I catch her wrist and pull her close. We're inches apart and I can feel her heart racing. I'm acting as uninhibited as if I'm drunk, though it's been ages since I've had a drink.

Ding! The elevator announces our floor and the doors slide open. Marina pulls away and walks to the office in total silence, glancing my way now and then. Something's different between us, though I'm not sure what.

Zvyagin's secretary, a curvy brunette with

curls, starts to say something. Marina just cuts her off with "He's expecting us," but stays behind in the waiting room once I enter.

"Hello…" I realize I don't know how to address him. Using his first name might be too casual, but I don't want to be too formal with someone so young either.

"Hello, TargetAi," Zvyagin greets me, clearly not thrilled to be interrupted yet being cordial. "Do you like to read?" he inquires a bit pompously.

"I do."

"Me too, sometimes," he says, sounding a bit defensive. "I've been too busy lately."

"Mmm," I hum, sensing the conversation isn't going so smoothly.

Zvyagin sighs, takes off his glasses, and meets my gaze with his kind, nearsighted eyes.

"You think we're a bunch of morons around here, don't you, TargetAi?"

"Eh? What makes you think that?"

"'Basic quest giver', 'weak scripts', 'shallow plot'… Wasn't that your feedback for the first round of our beta?"

"It was," I say stubbornly.

"Well, we *would* be a bunch of morons," Zvyagin concedes, "if we were making a game. The only problem with that is that this isn't a game."

CHAPTER 13

"WHAT DO YOU MEAN, 'this isn't a game?' What are we testing then?" It sounded like Zvyagin was just being enigmatic for the sake of it.

I had just played it myself, slaying mobs and earning XP... If it looks like a game and plays like a game, then it is a *game* — regardless of what this pompous ass wants me to believe.

I kind of get why Marina called him "a complete jerk." At least when it came to my interactions with the Master, I felt like an equal: His different experiences and knowledge didn't automatically make him superior or make me a loser.

This Zvyagin character, however, spoke gently and with a smile, yet something in his tone told me that he thought I was just a naive kid, and it was only the Master's orders that compelled him to talk to me at all.

"Of course you understand that everything

said here in this office is confidential," Zvyagin says with a frown, as if stating the obvious. "We won't make you sign an NDA, but leaking details would complicate your life."

I wanted to leave right then and there. This felt like the start of a bad spy thriller, and it usually went downhill for the MC from here on out. There were too many things keeping me here, however: the money; the desire to prove myself to Lance and that sadistic Anna chick. And above all, my own curiosity.

"I understand," I nodded curtly.

Zvyagin approved of my response.

"I don't know what the Master sees in any of you, but he has a knack for picking good people." Zvyagin leaned back, choosing his words carefully. "Listen here. Initially, this was a combat simulator for the army. The armed forces first ventured into VR thirty years ago. Back in the Soviet days, they were the only ones with the resources to do it. The whole tech industry was at their beck and call. Flight simulators... Tank simulators... Then they began using them to train soldiers. The best of the best: the Spetsnaz, special forces. The programmers created jungles, cities, and deserts for them. When the army asked for Washington, D.C., they made it for them."

Zvyagin grinned and went on, "And when the soldiers tried it out, their feedback was that it was 'garbage.' Why do you think that was?"

"They were fighting bots?" I ventured.

I was intrigued. And as Zvyagin loosened up

and kept talking, he didn't seem so bad. I realized he was only a bit older than me — maybe 25 at most. He had grown a beard and wore glasses to seem older. His plaid button-down had a T-shirt beneath it — with a glimpse of Bart Simpson and a ketchup stain. On the whole, he had the air of a very intelligent slacker.

If Marina was on the outs with Zvyagin, she was in for a bumpy ride. People like him usually held grudges. And she definitely missed out on this conversation. It's confidential, after all!

"Precisely!" Zvyagin exclaimed, his eyes asparkle with interest. "You get it! The bots were too predictable. They had weapon stats, tactics for different units, and still, the Spetsnaz took them down effortlessly."

"Well, what about without the bots? What about PvP?" I wondered.

"That didn't work either. All the Spetsnaz guys shared the same training, same tactics, same instructors. They'd react the same way in any given situation. They were too logical, too deliberate. In real life, however, they could encounter a jihadist with explosives, a neo-Nazi with a knife, or a kid starting another Columbine. An opponent could be tweaking on meth today, and blazed on dabbs tomorrow," said Zvyagin, slapping his desk with his hand. "And that's when dad suggested they use neural networks."

He said it so casually — "dad." Not "Professor Zvyagin" or "my father" — just "dad." I suddenly realized how deeply personal this was for him.

There was a long silence and I sensed an opportunity to ask a question and get a truthful answer. But what to ask? What would help me understand my current situation and maybe even give me an edge?

"What's a neural network?"

"I thought everyone knew that," Zvyagin grumbled, glancing at me like I was an idiot.

"I don't mean what the marketing department tells me it is…" I clarified, "What is it really?"

Zvyagin glanced around the room, seemingly lost for words.

"Do you know how the human brain works?" he asked, then went on without awaiting a reply. "We used to think that a human brain was superior to any computer. Why? The brain consists of thin microscopic threads — synapses. When it faces some new task, it grows new synapses. It adapts. It learns. We used to think that computers couldn't do that since they weren't living things. And so it was, until we came up with neural networks. Neural networks can form new connections, enhancing their abilities and transcending their limitations. They're like humans. Only better."

"So then they integrated one into the combat simulator?" A chill ran down my spine as images of Skynet and *The Matrix* flashed through my mind.

"It *became* the combat simulator," Zvyagin continued. "A semi-conscious entity that's constantly under attack."

"Did it work?"

"At first, yes. The military loved it. But then a new problem arose. The combat sim became unbeatable. The Neural Network created bots so advanced they could defeat any Spetznaz or private military contractor. They would reset the network, but it would level up again."

"That's when my father came up with what's now called 'Zvyagin's crutch.' A temporary fix to control the Neural Network's development, to slow its growth. You start the Neural Network at a very, very simple level. Like an infant that can't walk or talk. You give it basic functions. An exclamation point above the head for a quest. Exchange weapons for money — a merchant. The less data you feed it initially, the more time you have. The better your chances of beating it."

"But why are you testing it if you already know all this?"

"What makes you think we're testing it?" Zvyagin smirked. "We're testing you."

*　*　*

Our conversation went on for a long while. I lost track of time, but when I emerged from Zvyagin's office, Marina was no longer in the waiting room.

"Where's... Marina?" I asked.

The receptionist just shrugged and pursed her lips as if to say, "It's no surprise a busy lady like that didn't wait for someone like you."

Exiting into the empty hallway, I tried to

remember the way out: straight... then the elevator... left... or right?

Speaking with the game's chief tech guru had raised more questions than answers. I understood why they had turned their combat sim into a game for the public — to make money. But the whole beta test part was like a deep dark forest. Who are they testing and why? We're like rats in a maze. Guinea pigs in their lab.

The changing room was empty too. Only the lingering scent of pastries reminded me of AngelCake. I wish she had left some for me! I hadn't even finished the first savory one because we... The sudden, visceral memory gave me goosebumps. Stacy sure was a fine girl, not just as a baker, but in other areas too. Simba had missed out. He liked flashy girls like Marina too much.

Grabbing my jacket, I made my way through the building lobby, headed for the doors.

"Mr. Severyanov!" A loud female voice resounded through the empty hall. "Young man! Are you Mr. Severyanov?"

"That's me."

"Come over here, please!"

The tables for paying the beta testers were set up in the same spot as yesterday. A young brunette, probably not much older than me, sat at one with an annoyed look on her face.

"What do you think you're doing, Mr. Severyanov?!" she began to scold me. "Where were you? How long do I have to wait for you? I've been here for an hour!"

"I... I was busy," I mumbled, taken aback by her anger.

Probably wouldn't be a great idea to tell her I was talking with one of the board members. She wouldn't believe me and might get upset, thinking I'm mocking her. I decided to let her get to the point.

"Do you have your ID, Mr. Severyanov?"

"Here," I handed her my passport.

She took it with repulsion, as if it were something dirty, and began entering my data into her laptop. Her long manicured nails, adorned with rhinestones and little hearts, clicked against the keys. How does she type with those?

"Your tester ID number?"

"Two hundred fifteen... no, two hundred twelve," I tried to recall.

Or wait, was that for the first round? I didn't get a number for the second one. Damn, what should I say?

"That doesn't match," she said suspiciously. "There's another name listed here."

"That was my ID during the first round," I explained. "They didn't give me a number for the second one."

"That can't be!" she retorted. "You have to remember your ID number, or I can't help you! You beta testers! First you go missing and then you can't remember your own ID number!"

"Bravo!" rang Marina's cheerful voice from the doorway. "I've recorded this whole scene and I'll make sure to share it in our company chat so your boss can see why she's getting penalized. Customer service indeed!"

"Ms. Marina..." The girl turned as pale as if she were seeing death incarnate. All her pride vanished at once.

"I was waiting for him, and here he is, fighting harpies like an ancient hero," Marina remarked, showing off her knowledge.

She approached me, her heels clicking sharply, and stopped beside me.

"Ms. Marina, he doesn't remember his tester ID number... That's why I was helping... I didn't know he was with you... Who could tell by the look of him?"

"Shut your mouth, idiot, before you lose your severance!" Marina hissed like an irritated cat. "He's not with me. He's a VIP. It's your job to check the details and not his job to report to your stupid ass."

The girl lowered her eyes fearfully and rummaged through a desk drawer. She pulled out a thin envelope and placed it before me.

"Please sign here. I'll fill out the rest myself."

"Thank you," I took the money.

"I don't have time to deal with nuisances like you," Marina finished her off, "but you might as well start packing your things. Once she's reprimanded and finds out that she's lost her annual bonus, your boss, Ms. Neklyudova, will smear you across the lobby floor." Marina turned to me. "Allow me to personally apologize on behalf of the corporation to you, Mr. Severyanov. I will walk you out myself!"

Marina took my arm demonstratively and led me to the entrance. Only then did I begin to grasp Marina's status in this building. She may have been small fry for some of those who worked high above — people like the Master or Zvyagin — but for everyone else, she was a fierce beast shrouded in glitz and glam.

"You were a bit harsh on her, don't you think?"

"You can't deal with them any other way," Marina snapped, quickly changing the subject. "What took you so long? I've been waiting for you!"

I was amazed at how abruptly her mood could shift. She had just been an ice-cold witch, her eyes shooting lightning, and now she was as soft as a fluffy kitten.

"Were you really waiting for me?"

"Of course, I was! Who else would I wait for? Everyone else has left. Did Zvyagin hold you up this entire time? What were you two talking about for so long?"

She didn't even try to hide her interest in me. She had never even noticed Andrew before, the simple, kind-hearted guy in his prime. But now that her bosses were interested in him, she was interested in Andrew very much indeed. The only problem for her was that, I was beginning to catch on to the rules of her corporate game.

"I was told our conversation was strictly confidential," I stared at Marina sternly, "I could tell you, but I'd have to kill you."

"Oh, stop it! That doesn't apply to me. I'm senior management!" Marina stamped her foot impatiently. "Give me a general idea at least!"

Well, I wasn't going to tell her that at the end of our conversation, Zvyagin had said, "Not a word to anyone, especially that chick from advertising."

I had to make something up, but my brain was completely blank at the moment.

"Not here!" I said, looking around dramatically.

We stood at the building's entrance. The outside air was chilly, a light November sleet fell from the sky, and a bone-chilling wind collected it into a thin layer of frost.

"Need a lift?" Without waiting for my reply, Marina beeped her key fob, and a brand-new red Mazda-3 beeped back from the parking lot.

Inside the car, it was warm, cozy, and smelled of flowers and cinnamon cookies. A funny, furry little devil with bright red horns and a plush pitchfork dangled from the rear view mirror. Club music played softly from the speakers, which Marina immediately turned down.

"Are you heading home? I still remember your address."

I nodded, and Marina skillfully pulled out of the parking lot and merged into traffic. I used the opportunity to open the envelope I had been holding.

"Holy cow! Are these euros?!"

It was a thin envelope, so I didn't expect much. But pulling out ten bright hundred-euro bills was a shock.

"We're a transnational company," Marina proudly explained. "We don't deal in rubles."

"Is this the typical pay?" I couldn't hide my surprise.

"Not everyone cleared the second round. Plus, you got certain bonuses…"

A lure, I realized. Not all testers got a thousand euros for an hour's work. They wanted to keep me invested. They needed a rat that could run their maze better than the others. Well, for this kind of money, I could keep running as long as they kept paying.

"Could you drop me off at my university?" I asked suddenly.

The cash was burning a hole in my pocket. It had been a while since I had held more than a measly five or ten ruble note. I wanted to settle some debts quickly.

"The one on Kutuzovskaya Street?" Marina nodded. "Okay, I'll turn around."

"And maybe a quick stop at a currency exchange?"

"Really?!" Marina laughed. "Do I look like a taxi driver to you?"

"Why kick up a fuss?" I replied with the same phrase she'd used in my room yesterday. "You already said yes, don't be difficult."

"Why the cheek of you!" She tried to sound annoyed, but I could tell she was amused. It felt like my audacity had broken through her icy exterior, making her respond genuinely for once.

"Which currency exchange do you want?"

"You should know better than me. You're the one working for a transnational!"

We popped into an exchange that offered the best rates ever, nearly got into an accident on Vernadskogo Ave., had a shouting match with an SUV, and finally reached the university, adding a few more gray hairs to my head in the process. For some reason, Marina decided to follow me inside and was currently admiring the plain interior of my faculty building with surprise.

"Is Dr. Ivantsov in his office... alone?"

Ella, the graduate student, nodded twice and stared inquisitively at Marina, who returned the favor. Leaving them to their staring contest, I slipped into the office.

"Mr. Severyanov!" The dean brightened up. "What brings you here?"

"I brought the money, Dr. Ivantsov," I laid the envelope, which was now substantially thicker after our stop at the currency exchange, in front of him. "Cash is okay, right? There's thirty thousand there. To lift the academic hold."

The dean seemed startled. "You didn't rob anyone, did you, Mr. Severyanov?"

"Of course not," I replied innocently. "Just earned it. Got lucky."

"Sure sure," the dean said skeptically.

He got up abruptly, took my envelope, and stepped out of his office.

"Ella, record this tuition payment and remove the academic hold right away," I overheard him say.

Returning to his desk, he shut the door firmly, looked at me and whispered, "Is that your fiancée outside?"

"No," I said, surprised. "She's just a coworker."

"I know all about 'coworkers' like that," he replied with a hint of warning. "You should be careful. You're smart. She's not your type. Trust me, I have a knack for reading people."

"Don't worry, Dr. Ivantsov," I chuckled, "It's not what you think."

"Sure sure," he said again. "Come by tomorrow to sign the paperwork."

Then he shook my hand firmly in parting.

"Done? Then let's go," Marina, who was playing on her phone, adjusted her skirt and briskly headed to the exit.

I turned to say goodbye to Ella. She was smiling, making heart symbols with her hands. What was going on?

The conversation about Zvyagin got postponed again. Marina didn't press too hard, and the ride was short. Instead, we decided to meet in the evening "to celebrate the first win." I had a plan in mind that I wasn't ready to share with her yet.

As we pulled up to my building, I said, "Here's good Marina, you don't have to take me right up to the front door. The people in my building, they like to throw... stuff from their balconies here. They might dent your roof."

"Sure," she agreed. "I'll call you at six. And don't even think of bailing. If you stand me up, my revenge will be swift and cruel!"

I nodded and headed towards the building entrance. I made up the bit about the balconies. If mom saw me with Marina, there would no end to her questions. Meanwhile, the fifty thousand rubles in my pocket felt reassuring. Finally, I could show mom that gaming wasn't just child's play.

"Why look at this sweet, defenseless, little chick!" Sullen appeared before me, moving to cut me off. "What's up, Drone?"

His clique of braindead street punks came fast on his heels, surrounding me from all sides: five of them... no, six... seven...

"You think you're too good for your old friends? Not even a hello?" Sullen drawled. "Are we beneath you now?"

Crap! Why did it have to be today of all days? Getting into a fight now would mean not only risking a fractured rib or two, but risking the money in my pocket. They'll stomp me into the ground and take all my loot. The smartest thing to do is push Sullen away and run for it... Why doesn't Marina drive off already? Running in front of her felt weird and cowardly....

"Are you all right, Andrew? Can I help?" I heard Marina's anxious voice behind me.

"Whoa!" Sullen stopped, his gaze locking onto the girl getting out of her car behind me. "Look at this bimbo!"

Goddamn it, Marina! Why didn't you just go?!

CHAPTER 14

"ARE YOU ALL RIGHT, Andrew? Can I help?" I hear Marina's anxious voice behind me.

"Whoa!" Sullen stops, his gaze locking onto the girl getting out of her car behind me. "Look at this bimbo!"

Goddamn it, Marina! Why didn't you just go?!

"Marina, get out of here! Go now. I've got this!" I bark without turning to look at her, but it's already too late.

"Who are these guys, Andrew? Hey! Get your hands off me, creep!"

She sure is dumb and fearless. I realize that the time for talking is past, and I swing — not at Sullen but at the guy next to him. His name's Nikolai, aka Hammer. I remember him from school. He took boxing and is the toughest fighter in Sullen's crew. Next is Sullen himself and then Zheka, a lanky dude who's completely unhinged when it comes to fighting. He'll hit you with a brick, a bottle, or whatever's at hand. I don't see him anywhere at the moment, and that's a bad thing. The rest are just high school punks — dangerous only as a collective. If they all have a go at me at once, they're sure to knock me over and kick the crap out of me.

Nikolai slumps to the ground, knocked out cold. One down.

"The fuck, brah?!" Sullen gasps, enraged. "You asked for it, jerk!"

I kick him in the kneecap and drop him to all fours. Not a bad start — that's two down, I think. But then something thumps the back of my head and everything goes black.

I come to on the ground, the back of my head pounding like crazy, but it feels like my skull's intact. Must've been a fist, not brass knuckles, otherwise I'd be down for longer, or even dead. Maybe ten seconds now that I've been out.

Marina saved me — or, more accurately, her being there did. If she hadn't been there, they would have finished me off on the ground. But with her there, the punks figured that she was their prize. Even Sullen began limping her way, dragging his injured leg. Only Hammer remained sitting on his ass, looking dazed and shaking his head.

Coming to behind them, I scan around for a weapon before getting up. I spot an empty bottle, a couple of broken bricks, and a big two-by-four that's about a yard long. That seems like a good sign.

Pshhh! I hear a sharp sound followed by a scream:

"Ah! Mah eyes! Ya feckin' bish! It burns like hell!"

Marina's packing pepper spray and she knows how to use it. It's not the perfect weapon though: A cryin' dick can still be a dick.

Marina's shriek sounds high and loud... Who needs a siren? I leap to my feet and grab the two-by-four. Hope you're ready, dipshits!

"I'm gonna tear you apart, ya fucks!" I roar with all my might.

They turn to face me — one of them charges — some little guy I don't recognize. He gets my two-by-four's other end right in his gob and drops. Another's doubled over, rubbing his eyes. I finish him off with a whack to the back of the head.

The street punks hesitate. They're stunned, unaccustomed to having their victims fight back. While I have a moment, I turn and deal a coup de grace to Hammer's head. I don't want any surprise comebacks later.

"You've gone and fucked up now, Drone!" Sullen hisses at me. "You know I'll find you and when I find you, I'll cut you up... You're as good as dead."

That's when I snap. Not earlier when I took the first hit, and not even when Marina screamed. Back then, I only felt fear, anger and rage.

This, now, however, is pure, unbridled fury. I relish the feeling of it coursing through me.

"You're all just frags to me now," I announce and then repeat it for emphasis. "YOU'RE. ALL. JUST. FRAGS!"

I snap the two-by-four across my knee, a piece of it for each hand.

Lanky and dead-eyed, Zheka steps from among the street punks and gets into some sort of fighting stance. What a joke. Knee... arm... neck... head...

"Raaah!"

"Andrew! He's got a knife!"

Sullen lunges at me, switchblade in hand. The steel point traces an arc in the air before me.

I strike his forearm, breaking my right club on it. Then I hit his wrist with the left half of the two-by-four to knock the knife out of it, and sweep him, taking his legs out from under him.

Sullen lands on his back and I pin him down with my knee. All that's left is to stick him with this jagged shard of wood in my hand. From the look in his eyes, he knows what's coming too.

"Raaah!" I yell in his face. "RAAAHHH!"

As if in reply, an acrid, unpleasant stench wafts up at me. Sullen's pissed himself. I hear footsteps running away behind us.

"He's gone mental, my bros! Let's bail!"

The stench brings me back to reality. Marina's sobbing by her car. Her blouse is torn, her hair a mess. She rushes over when she sees me.

"Andrew, you're bleeding!" She touches my neck and shows me my blood on her finger. "Your collar's soaked in blood."

"It's just a scratch," I brush her off. "I'm going home, Marina. Will you get out of here now, please?"

"What do you mean 'you're going home?' You need to go to a doctor," she insists. "Don't argue with me. I can see that you do."

She practically shoves me back into her Mazda. That's when it sinks in: I just took on seven guys all by myself. Well, two ran off, and Marina helped some. But still, not bad.

I hope I didn't hurt any of them too severely. I don't want what happened to my dad to happen to me. I recall my mom saying, "Your toys are nothing but trouble," and "all you think about is fighting and violence." Maybe she's right? Don't most folks solve things peacefully? Negotiate? Yet here I am, ready to throw down at a moment's notice.

Marina doesn't take me to the public ER, but to some private medical center. The nurses start working on me, looking me over and doing bloodwork. Despite my protests they stick me into an MRI to make sure I don't have a concussion. Then, a trio of doctors inspect the cut on my head and deliberate over whether to give me stitches or a band-aid.

I try to argue at first, but they pop some pills into me, and everything turns warm and mellow. It feels like I'm watching some goofy movie.

Meanwhile, Marina is busy making calls, even ringing my mom.

"Don't worry, Mrs. Severyanova. Andrew had a small fall at work while changing a light bulb. He's okay, there's no concussion... Yes, I'm with him at the medical center. We'll bring him home, don't worry about a thing."

"How did you get my mom's number?" I ask.

"It came up on your phone," she explains. "She called you, and I answered. I had to tell her something, right? So, I made up a story."

"Thanks."

I genuinely did appreciate it. My mom worries too much as it is. It'd be nice to come home with a wad of cash, but a wad of cash and a bandaged head? She'd immediately assume I had joined a gang. And the worst part is that I wouldn't be able to convince her otherwise. However, Marina had built up so much rapport with my mom, that even her ridiculous explanation was accepted without a second thought.

Then, a man in a sharp suit showed up. I recognized him as the security guard who refused to fight the Master in the lobby on the first day of the beta test. He introduced himself, though I forgot his name almost instantly, and handed me a business card "in case I had any further trouble."

Trouble was inevitable. I didn't need a crystal ball to know that. Sullen wasn't going to let this slide. For him, it was a matter of pride. But I decided I'd deal with that matter when the time came.

They drove me home in a boxy black Yukon. Massive, like a bus, it barely squeezed into the apartment building's courtyard. Two security guards in black suits escorted me to my apartment. I felt like 007. Stunned by their appearance, my mom didn't bother asking any questions. I slipped into my room and finally fell asleep without even changing.

* * *

The ringing had drilled deep into my brain by the time I realized that I was already awake. My phone was blaring above my head. The clock read 8 p.m. The call was from an unknown number. Who the hell was trying to reach me at this time of day?!

"Good evening, Andrew," Marina purred over the line. "How are you feeling? I got a bit worried and decided to call."

Damn it! She had me doxxed: my phone number, my address. I wanted to send her packing but realized I was fully awake. Also, I was famished.

"I'm feeling fine. Weren't you supposed to treat me to dinner?" I teased.

Just how curious are you, Marina? I don't believe in your gratitude, but your curiosity about my conversation with Zvyagin must be consuming you. That's why you called — couldn't wait until tomorrow.

"I haven't changed my mind!" Marina chirped. "What would you like?"

"I want beer and meat!"

"Are you sure you're allowed?" she hesitated.

"I don't have a concussion, so not only can I, but I should. Need to replenish my energy."

"Let's meet at the Spitzberg Brathaus in an hour then," Marina suggested. "My treat!"

I agreed and hung up. The Spitzberg Brathaus was a beer restaurant downtown. I'd never been there. A liter of beer from a local brewery cost as much as our family's weekly grocery bill. Marina's "treat" was timely — I didn't plan on blowing what was left of my earnings on such an outing.

Damn, what am I supposed to wear to a place like that? It's a restaurant, after all. A suit? I hadn't worn mine since graduation, and I had bulked up quite a bit since. Irritated, I remembered Lance's outfit from earlier. He always knew what to wear for what occasion. In the end, I put on jeans and a black turtleneck. I checked myself in the mirror and nodded, satisfied. I was going to drink beer, after all, not attend a ball.

Not wanting to skimp on transportation, I hailed a taxi. Why not? I'm rich now. But my nerves started coming back to me during the ride. I was feeling like I was headed to a date. I had felt so casual with Marina during the day, like she was a fellow student. But now, my anxiety was coming back.

An intoxicating aroma of fresh grilled meat wafted into my face as I walked into the Spitzberg. The smell was so rich and delicious that it staggered me a bit. The place was full of lively music reminiscent of German and Austrian folk tunes, laughter, clinking beer steins — an endless feast for the moneyed class.

"Do you have a reservation?" A guy in a white shirt and colorful apron practically jumped in my path. "We only seat with reservations." He eyed me skeptically from head to toe.

"Andrew!" Marina waved from a table in the center of the dining hall. "I'm here!"

"I'm with that lady over there."

"May I take your jacket?" The waiter quickly changed his tune.

"No, I'm good… Where's the coat check?"

"Don't worry about anything… We will take care of everything. Please enjoy yourself…"

Reluctantly, I handed over my jacket and made my way through the dining hall. I needn't have worried about dressing up. The clientele here wore whatever they felt like: suits with loosened ties, bright plaid shirts, tank tops. I even spotted a table of bikers in eclectic, stylish outfits.

"Hey, I ordered you some beer and ribs!" Marina informed me. "They make them really good here. I haven't asked for a menu yet."

It was strange seeing Marina in something other than her office attire. She was wearing a burgundy dress with a bright floral pattern, a generous neckline, and playful, puffed sleeves. It fit the atmosphere perfectly: cheerful yet chic. And Marina looked incredible in it.

She may not have had AngelCake's chest size, but her figure was sleek and striking. Men from neighboring tables were glancing her way, and I felt flattered. The waiter brought our beers: a liter for me, half a liter for Marina.

"A toast to you, my knight!" Marina raised her beer stein.

I thought she was joking, but she looked dead serious.

"Aye, to the Lancelot of the Slums," I played along.

"Well, they aren't exactly slums..." Marina pondered. "Maybe... Lancelot of the Neighborhood?" She clearly emphasized the "hood" part.

"No objections, Dame Marina," I clinked my stein against hers and took a sip.

The cool, slightly bitter ale flowed down my throat, and for a moment, I forgot about everything. I just drank and drank, unable to stop.

"Whew," I finally said, having drained half the mug. "This is so good."

"Really?" A pleased Marina looked me in my eyes. "I knew you'd like it. So, before our ribs arrive, tell me about Zvyagin."

I felt her leg touch mine under the table. The heavy artillery had been deployed. Luckily, I'd rehearsed this conversation at home. The cavalry was coming, and I just had to hold out a bit longer.

"I don't think he likes you," I said sympathetically.

"Why?" Marina looked worried but not surprised, suggesting that I had hit the mark. "What made you think that?"

"He asked a lot of questions about how the

beta test was organized, about the first round..." I made up whatever seemed plausible, blending truth with utter lies. "He even quoted answers from my feedback..."

"And what did you say?" I noticed Marina's fingers gripping the table edge, turning white.

"Well, to be completely honest, I told him that the way the whole thing was organized was utter crap..." I paused, savoring the panic in Marina's eyes. It seemed she was ready to kill me and only had to hear the end of my sentence first. "*BUT...* that it wasn't your fault at all!"

"What do you mean?" Marina stared at me, totally lost.

"Why just that — that's what I mean," I took another sip, relishing the moment. "They set you up to fail. The never briefed you. They had you go in blind. I told him you're smart and know plenty about online games. They need to trust you more, that's what I said!"

I finished my speech and leaned back in my chair.

"But I don't know a damn thing about online games!" Marina snapped, still failing to catch on.

"Well, yeah, but I do."

"Oh..." was all Marina could muster. "Ohhh..."

"And Zvyagin also told me..." I began, knowing I wouldn't get a chance to finish.

"Andrew! Hey hey!" Simba's voice boomed from the entrance.

The host from before was trying to block his

way, as my buddy tried to get my attention. Next to Simba, I could make out AngelCake's supple silhouette.

"Since, we decided to celebrate our victory," I said. "You don't mind that I invited my friends, do you?"

CHAPTER 15

TO MARINA'S CREDIT, she knew how to roll with the punches. Her face twitched in irritation for just a moment, but almost immediately, she masked it with a serene smile.

"Your friend… Sergio, was it?"

"Simon."

"Right, Simon. Is he…?" Marina glanced at me pointedly. "And his girlfriend?"

"It's complicated," I didn't clarify further. "Why? You fancy him?"

Marina only snorted in reply. Simba was squeezing our way among the tables, a task made challenging by his bulk. He had worn a hoodie with a print of a sad bulldog in sunglasses for the occasion, and he was beaming. I knew that his smile was meant for Marina.

By contrast, AngelCake had dressed for "a final showdown." She wore short denim shorts, fishnet tights, and a cropped shirt tied flirtatiously just below her chest. A ruby glinted from her navel.

Marina clearly had her outclassed in terms of elegance, but Stacy's raw sexual energy was overpowering. I quickly looked away and downed another half glass of beer to cool off.

The tables in the Spitzberg were broad, thick, and low. Ours could easily fit six people comfortably. Simba sat down across from Marina, while AngelCake sat down across from me. Even outside the game, I thought of her more by her gaming nickname. She was so sweet and irresistible that it suited her well.

"Marina, it's such a pleasure that you invited us," Simba began ceremoniously. "I had no idea this goofball was friends with such gorgeous girls."

"This goofball has many hidden talents," Marina said, placing her hand on mine while glancing strangely at AngelCake.

"Could we get some beers too?" Stacy asked, unfazed.

Suddenly, I felt a dainty foot creeping up my thigh… AngelCake glanced at the ceiling, a mischievous smile curling her lips. Damn! When did she take off her shoes? It seems like I was in for a fun night.

"Of course!" Marina snapped her fingers in the air, and a waiter appeared at our table. "Another round for us and the same for them. You want half a liter, Stacy?"

"I'll have a liter please," Stacy replied proudly.

"Shall we split the bill?" I offered Marina,

leaning towards her.

"Don't worry about it," she said, dismissively. "I'll write it off as a business expense."

"Speak up you two. We can't hear you over here," Stacy teased in a sing-song voice. "What are you whispering about?"

"They're talking about how fine you look," Simba jumped in, causing Stacy to blush.

The beers arrived. I raised my stein and tapped it with a fork, calling for silence.

"Friends," I surveyed everyone at the table. "First, I want to introduce you to Marina. She's an influential figure in the MosTech Corporation, which is running our beta test. We all know what a trade secret is, but any advice — a hint or a tip that we get before the other players — can give us a serious edge. I don't need to explain to you how much we value your friendship." Saying this, I shot a pointed glance at AngelCake, who nodded grudgingly.

"To friendship!" Simba announced, reaching across the table with his stein.

Marina smiled at each one of us in turn regally. The beer was having its effect and she seemed to be relaxing more and more. My friends' sudden appearance didn't seem to bother her as much. After the toast, I took the floor again.

"Since we did so well together, I propose that we continue working as a group. If everyone agrees, we can discuss our strategy for tomorrow's test in advance. There is another round tomorrow, right?" I asked Marina.

"Sure, but it's going to last longer," she nodded.

"How much longer?" I asked with interest.

"The first quest was half an hour, today's was an hour. Tomorrow will be an hour and a half," Marina explained. "Don't even ask me why. It's all cooked up by the techies. My job is to make it happen the way it was planned." She sighed, as if to emphasize just how tough this "making it happen" was.

"Andrew, I nominate you to be our party leader!" Simba declared.

Typical of him. Always passing the buck. I didn't expect anything less.

"I second that," squeaked AngelCake.

"A toast then to our new leader!" Simba quickly downed his liter and snapped his fingers in the air, signaling the waiter. "Another round!"

Everyone ordered another round except for Stacy, who hadn't finished her first yet. My head was buzzing quite a bit. At this rate, we might not even get to any strategizing.

Then the ribs showed up and conversation ceased for a moment. We just savored and sucked on the tender meat. The girls did it especially sensually. It was almost like they were competing with each other.

"All we need to do now is get Marina drunk and find out about tomorrow's quest objectives," I joked, but the hint was clear.

"You'll never succeed!" Marina cheerfully responded. "No one knows what the objectives will be tomorrow."

"But the techies know, right?" I pressed.

"Nope! No one knows what that crazy system will come up with next! Haven't you figured that out yet? Didn't Zvyagin tell you?"

I realized that Marina was already tipsy. I glanced at my friends, but they weren't following our conversation. Simba was engrossed in his plate of ribs, momentarily lost to the world, and AngelCake was battling with her liter, her victory imminent.

"What didn't he tell me?"

"So you really were talking about me," Marina nodded, "I thought you might be bluffing. No, he definitely would have told you."

"Told me what?"

"That thing creates objectives on its own! It creates monsters..."

"Mobs," I corrected.

"Same difference," Marina agreed, "It invents quests. Ever since we launched it, no one can influence it. Sometimes, I'm really scared of it. I look at the screens, and it's there, building, creating, thinking..."

"Wow," was all I could muster.

I had hoped to get some inside information from Marina: quests, tasks, class assignments. But what she told me now came as a complete curve ball.

"Where does it get it all from though?" I tried to wrap my head around it.

"Get what?"

"The information."

"It studies you," Marina gestured over the table, "the players. You're digitized. You live inside it. For a while, you become part of it. And it reads all your thoughts. It learns, fulfills your wishes, shows you the world as you want to see it."

I recalled the fence. It had been exactly how I remembered it from childhood. That whole alley where I kept spawning was so similar to the village where I spent my summers during childhood staying with my grandma. It had been exactly during the second round. Even the nail was in the same place.

And I had been so sure that I had seen the bolt on the door when we hid from spiders somewhere before. It was exactly how I imagined it. I wonder whether the neural net knew about door bolts at all before scanning my mind?

"I need a drink," Marina said. "Whenever I think about that crap, I just want to knock one back. Listen," her face lit up, "they've got some amazing horseradish vodka here. You in?"

"I'm in!" Stacy chimed in.

"We'll have a yardstick of the horseradish vodka," Marina ordered the waiter. "Some more meat for everyone, and an assortment of snacks — you know, mushrooms... pickles... you'll figure it out..."

To my surprise, the waiter nodded understandingly. The table began to fill up with various bowls, dishes, and plates of sundry delicacies. The yardstick of horseradish vodka looked like a long, narrow wooden plank exactly a yard long, lined with shot glasses of the slightly cloudy, sharply scented spirit.

Even from my manly vantage, it seemed like an awful lot, but Marina seemed confident, like she knew what she was doing, and I trusted her. As I found out later, this was a big mistake.

After the first shot, all serious conversation ceased. The horseradish vodka turned out to be insanely strong, yet it went down smoothly without requiring a chaser. Soon, the music shifted to upbeat country, and people began to dance. A portly biker invited Stacy to dance, and she went with him, shooting me playful glances.

Meanwhile, Marina and I drank toasts to each other. Later, I danced with Stacy. We weren't quite in sync, but it was loads of fun. Then Stacy and Marina took turns feeding me sauerkraut and pickles. Someone ordered steaks, which seemed utterly unnecessary at that point. Simba was the only one excited about them and hogged all the plates to himself.

Later, I remember making out with someone in a dimly lit hallway near the restrooms, but I can't recall who. I think it might've been Marina.

* * *

"Are you up, champ?!" a cheerful voice roused me. "Didn't I tell you to eat something with your drinks!"

I tried to lift my head from the pillow, but a

sharp pain in my head forced me to lay it back down.

"There's some Alka-Seltzer on the nightstand next to you. Take it. You'll suffer less," Marina said.

MARINA?! WHAT THE HELL!

Marina stood in the doorway wearing a silky pajama set that was both alluring and modest. I quickly looked under the blanket. I was fully dressed, right down to my socks.

I sighed in relief. So, nothing had happened. After all, if something had happened, and I didn't even remember it, that would've been twice as frustrating.

"What time is it?" was the most intelligent thing I could think to ask.

"It's already 5:30." Marina looked as if she hadn't had a drop to drink the night before, "Time to get ready for work. I have to be in by seven, so you'll have to hurry too."

We sat in the kitchen, drinking coffee in silence. Or rather, Marina drank while I stared glumly at my mug. My headache had somewhat subsided, but my stomach was a rollercoaster on repeat.

Marina's kitchen looked like it was straight out of a glossy magazine. A bar counter, tall chairs, lots of high-tech appliances. A large, almost panoramic window yielded a view onto the riverbank. The street lights along the boardwalk were still on, their weak lights making the winter frost dance in the air.

Marina's two-bedroom apartment was at least three times larger than ours. Just yesterday, my testing fee seemed substantial. Now, I couldn't even guess how much this woman made.

"Do you live here alone?" I asked, trying to break the silence.

"Well, yeah. Who else would there be?"

"Well... I thought maybe you had a husband," I blurted out, "or a boyfriend..."

"Everyone thinks that," Marina snapped back unexpectedly. "You're all so scared of being rejected you don't even try. If you're not gonna drink it, don't torture yourself..." She took the cup from my hands and dumped it in the sink. "Let's go."

Outside in the cold, I felt a bit better, but back in the car, the nausea came back. Marina drove more carefully this time, maybe feeling sorry for me. We reached our destination in about ten minutes. There was no one outside the entrance. It was 7 a.m. for crying out loud — and still dark as hell!

The lobby was also empty: no ribbons, no counters, or registration desks. The security guards nodded at Marina and me. It seemed like I'd become a familiar face here.

Marina disappeared inside the dimly lit lobby, taking charge and shouting at someone. Her voice faded. I found a comfy sofa in the corner, sat down, and curled up in an almost fetal position.

"Dum-de-di-di-dum!" A sung jingle echoed through the quiet, empty lobby. It reminded me of an old cartoon tune from Winnie the Pooh: meaningless but upbeat. The entrance door shut almost silently as a short, lively figure appeared in its frame. The Master brushed the snow off himself, looked around and began walking, either mumbling or snorting something to himself like a big hedgehog. Suddenly he stopped, sniffed the air, and headed straight for me.

"Andrew?!" His gray eyebrows shot up, looking both surprised and pleased. "You're an early bird."

"It's just how things worked out," I managed, "Good morning."

"Not such a good morning for everyone is it?" the Master observed me closely. "You look rough… Come with me… I'll make you some tea…"

"Oh, that's all right," I said, feeling incredibly awkward. Not only did I reek of booze, but I hadn't showered since yesterday.

"Don't argue. No one argues with me in this building," the Master admonished me. "You don't want to try it, trust me."

Mustering all my willpower, I followed him. In the reception area outside the Master's office, a nondescript secretary was bustling around, arranging something on a tray. The Master nodded at him and dragged me inside.

"Stand over here," he ordered as soon as I entered the office, "Take off your jacket, and maybe your sweater too… put them right on the chair, they'll be fine… now, spread your arms and take a deep breath…"

I breathed.

"Phew," the Master said, "don't breathe on me, just try to take a few deep breaths."

It wasn't as easy as it sounded. My stomach lurched every time I took a slightly deeper breath. The Master watched my struggle, as if admiring a sculpture in a museum. He circled me, stood behind me, then suddenly placed his hands on my shoulders, pressed just below the nape of my neck, once below my shoulder blade, and then, moving quickly around, poked my forehead.

"How about now?"

"Ahhh!" I inhaled the cool, fresh office air like a whale surfacing from the deep.

The pain subsided, my stomach settled. Only a slight lightheadedness reminded me of moments ago when death was all I wished for.

"How did you do that?!" I asked, flabbergasted.

"Do what?! I didn't do anything... Now, the tea!" The Master clapped his hands, and the secretary brought in a tray, then quietly retreated.

Remembering my first visit, I took off my shoes, earning a smile of approval from the Master. He served the green tea into the cups and squinted as he took the first sip.

The pause lingered, but oddly, it didn't feel awkward. In fact, it was chit-chat that would seem like a distraction here. The tea smelled of herbs, honey, and a hint of smoke. It was as if it had been brewed by a campfire.

"What if they had injured you?" The Master

asked suddenly, "Or if they'd killed you... Why didn't you run?"

"I couldn't," I replied.

"Nonsense." The Master frowned as if I'd said something foolish. "People always have a choice. You could've run. That would've been the smart thing to do."

"Marina was still there..."

"So what?" He looked genuinely incredulous. "Who asked her to get involved? Her own fault if you ask me."

He squinted slyly at me.

"She's a girl... a woman..." I struggled to phrase it.

"But she's not your woman!" He retorted.

"But she's not theirs either!" The answer came to me suddenly. "If I stayed, it means she's mine!"

The Master looked at me, amused, as if I were a toddler who'd just used the potty for the first time.

"And what if they had injured you?"

Suddenly, I remembered that feeling from yesterday. I wasn't just "putting in my time." I stepped in because I had to. I had to win or die... Although, a better way to put it, is I had to simply win.

"We sure do have many guests this morning," the Master said suddenly, turning to the door. "Come on in, we're just having some tea..."

I looked up and jumped in place, nearly flipping the table. Instinct told me to run or strike

— and it took a few deep breaths to calm down. Thankfully, no one noticed my idiotic reaction.

"I don't like tea, you know that," the visitor responded.

Her dark, almost black eyes were studying me. A disdainful smirk played on her lips. She was clad in black leather motorbike gear with protective pads on her elbows and knees. She held a helmet in her hand, her dark hair tied in a high ponytail.

Anna stood in the doorway.

"Oh, we'll make you some coffee!" The Master cheerfully replied. "Even a blackberry latte if you like!"

Anna eyed the Master warily, as if he'd promised her a cup of poison, instead of coffee. She carefully placed her helmet on a chair next to my jacket, took off her heavy boots, and joined us.

She moved just like in the game — restrained, calculated. It felt as if I was sitting next to a large predatory cat, not a person.

"Great, then, I'll go sort out the coffee!" The Master seemed very amused by our meeting. "You two chat... Get to know each other..."

And before either one of us could say another word, he darted out of his own office like a mischievous schoolboy.

CHAPTER 16

MORE THAN ANYTHING in the world, Marina Skvortsova despised poverty. And although she could forgive a woman for being poor, a man who wasn't well-off simply wasn't a man to her. This seemed so natural to her, that she had no sympathy for women who were maintained and yet felt burdened by their status. "Spoiled by luxury," she'd scoff, reading about them in books or seeing them on TV.

She was drawn to men with money or power, preferably both, from back when she was in high school. Age or appearance didn't matter much to her.

In her senior year, Marina, a young woman in full bloom, so dazzled a young assistant principal at her school that unsavory rumors began to circulate. But we shouldn't believe rumors, right?

Thanks to him, Marina graduated on the

honors list and was admitted to a prestigious university on a full ride. The assistant principal had connections and he ensured her admission, not realizing that he was setting the stage for his own demise. In college, Marina no longer had to be discreet. She had an affair with the dean, later switching to the vice-president. She excelled academically, passing exams effortlessly, and soon added a summa cum laude diploma to her resume.

She even felt something like affection for the former regional VP of MosTech. He was a generous and gentle man who provided Marina with a lavish "comfort zone." She passed all the tedious and challenging assignments on to her subordinates, only making corporate appearances at award presentations, charity events, and TV shows.

Over time, Marina began to believe in her own brilliance, thinking she was paid a hefty salary for her bright ideas, not her knack for being available to the management anytime, anywhere. And the VP — wary of rumors and bridled by a jealous wife — primarily used Marina as a status symbol to flaunt before his coworkers.

The new senior executives who now occupied her office were both rich and powerful, which caused a whirlwind of emotions in Marina's heart. But there was one problem — they weren't interested in her.

To stay afloat and avoid the humiliation of poverty, Marina now had to work her tail off and serve them as loyally as a puppy.

And now, before another meeting, Marina

stood in the hallway, meek and quiet, trembling as if before an exam, waiting for her turn to be called.

Four people had gathered once again in the small conference room. On the screen was a chart. The names Xavier, Lancer, T-Rex, TargetAi and about ten others were written over the columns. Benjamin Zvyagin hovered over them with his mouse, the others nodding thoughtfully.

"Oh!" the Master greeted Marina cheerfully. "Come on in! That move you pulled yesterday? Did you ad lib that on the spot?"

"She took a risk," Doc interrupted. "The conflict was planned for that evening. She was supposed to start a fight with the bikers at the restaurant. Dance with one of them, play the victim, trigger TargetAi's insecurities..."

"What a brawl that would've been!" The Master grinned. "He was there with a friend, a big guy... what's his name?"

"Simon," Marina offered, sensing that a storm had passed her by, but still unsure why.

"Exactly!" The Master chuckled. "They would've taken down your bikers with their bare hands."

"My people are professionals," Doc huffed. "They would've faked it. We just wanted to trigger spontaneous aggression in the subject..."

"Or maybe he wouldn't have taken the bait at the restaurant," the Master continued, ignoring Dr. Kotov, "She's a tramp after all. Why defend her?"

Marina blushed.

"So why'd you instigate the fight outside his apartment building then?" Dr. Skuratova chimed in, "Look me in the eyes as you answer and don't even think about lying."

"I saw a two-by-four lying on the ground," Marina blurted out.

She didn't really know why she had left her car or why she had called out to Andrew. At first, she just didn't grasp the situation and wanted to intervene. Then... then she realized that the scene at the restaurant that evening would be staged, an act, whereas what was happening then and there was an opportunity for her to earn praise, redeem herself and restore her honor and respect.

She wanted to tell them how scared she had been, seeing him lying on the ground — not for him, but for herself. The thought of being fired overpowered her survival instinct, and she screamed like a madwoman, hosing the punks' nasty mugs down with pepper spray. Dr. Skuratova's eyes were drilling into her so intensely, that she felt like they were tickling the back of her skull.

"A two-by-four?! What two-by-four?"

"Like in the game during the beta test," Marina couldn't explain where the feeling had come from. But she had felt like she was in the right place at the right time. "I saw the two-by-four and realized he wouldn't stop and would prevail."

"She's an idiot," Benjamin chimed in.

"Don't be so sure," Dr. Skuratova shook her head, "This girl has potential. Of course, she's no

Sofia Kovalevskaya... but people like her... their instincts are highly developed, which means their intuition is too. I think I'll take you under my wing. For now, you're dismissed." And she cast Marina a look that made her heart drop.

"Can we get a sitrep for Lance's team?" Marina heard behind her as she closed the door. There had been enough secrets for one day.

* * *

"What's this nonsense about the two-by-four?" Dr. Kotov didn't want to drop the subject. "Complete idiocy. And you all support her..."

"Don't take it personally, Doc, but subtleties aren't your forte," the Master interrupted. "You just worry about the investments. If you must know, I'm sure Dr. Skuratova could explain it to you."

"In the game, Andrew encountered a situation where he used a picket to kill two other players and save a girl," Dr. Skuratova began patiently. "The picket in this case is a trigger, a reminder of a scenario that played out positively. It worked then, it'll work now. The boy has great potential, but it's almost ruined by his poor upbringing."

"So, you want to manipulate him into no longer being able to tell reality from the game?" Doc asked. "Why?"

"Because soon there won't be any reality for him, Doc," the Master said somberly. "The game will become more real than any ordinary reality.

And the barriers holding him here will hinder him there! He's a good boy! He helps old ladies cross the street, saves girls from thugs! But I need a ruthless guy! I need... What is it the kids call them these days?"

"An Alpha," Benjamin offered.

"What a... nice word," the Master mused. "An Alpha that will dominate everyone. Tell me, Benny, what's the easiest way to earn experience in the game?"

"Kill another player," Benjamin explained. "But we only had 5% beta testers try that. Only half a percent did it two or more times."

"And how many did our Anna take down?" the Master inquired with a sweet smile.

"Seventy-two," Benjamin's face grew serious.

"Why did you even let her into the beta?!" Doc exclaimed. "We had a deal!"

"How could you not let her in?" The Master shrugged. "She owns as many shares of MosTech as Benny here does. She could be sitting here with us right now."

"And why isn't she?" Doc wondered.

"Because she's sitting with someone else," the Master beamed.

*   *   *

"Did you swipe the carapace?"

I started. Just a moment ago, this girl was looking at me like I was invisible... Although, that's not right, no. People tend to look at empty space with indifference, whereas she was looking at me with unconcealed distaste, like at an insect, something akin to a cockroach. And then all of a sudden she even spoke to me. Hallelujah!

"What carapace?" was the best I could muster.

"You're TargetAi, right? I want that carapace back! I counted. Before you went in that room, there were eight pieces. After you left, there were seven. You took it. No one else could have! Hand it over!"

"Or what?" I chuckled.

She was a monster in the game, a nightmare, death incarnate. But here? Just a regular girl, maybe a bit older than me. Maybe not. She'd asked for blackberry cascara and was now sipping some from a paper cup. I don't even know what cascara is. Smells like coffee. A good smell.

"Or I'll make sure to frag you every time I run into you!" Her eyes narrowed menacingly.

"You'd do that anyway," I yawned, showing my indifference. "You're a PKer, it's obvious."

"Idiot, you can't play any other way in there," she huffed. "It's kill or die in there!"

"Okay, but what do you need with the carapace?"

"It's prime loot!" she exclaimed. "Don't you get it?"

"And so what?"

"Prime is the first drop. It's always valuable! It could be legendary or even..."

"So, you've played this game before?!" It was

my turn to be shocked.

She went silent, visibly irritated. Clearly, she'd said too much. She even gave up trying to get the carapace back.

"Can I try that?" I said after the pause drew on too long.

"Try what?"

"I've never tried blackberry cascara before."

My experience with Marina demonstrated to me that audacity works wonders on these arrogant types. An ordinary girl would be offended. But these kinds of girls? Quite the opposite.

"Here," she handed me the cup.

I took a sip and gave it back. "That is tasty, thanks."

It tasted like watered down coffee, but I said it was good so as not to offend her.

"You've really never tried cascara before?"

"Nope."

"Are you a caveman or something?" she wondered.

"*No, stupid, I'm just poor,*" I thought to myself but said nothing out loud, changing the topic instead: "And what do I get if I give you the carapace?"

"I won't kill you."

She calls me a caveman and all she can talk about is killing or not killing. What a little monster.

"That's not enough," I haggled. "Promise that you'll never kill me if we run into each other, no matter what."

"And then you'll give me the carapace?"

"I will."

"Just like that?" she was surprised.

"Take it!" I pulled out a clenched fist and offered it to her. "Here!"

She fell for it, lowered her eyes, and I burst out laughing.

"I'll give it back," I promised once I stopped laughing. "Where do you want to meet?"

"In that same house where we... where we met."

"Alright."

"And what if I lied to you?" she asked with a skeptical look.

"Then you lied," I shrugged.

"You're odd," Anna observed me with interest.

"You too."

She scoffed and turned away. Offended again.

"Anna, I couldn't find your blackberry cascara anywhere!" the Master announced from the doorway. "I checked all the coffee shops but they were all out! They probably only sell this cascara of yours to pretty young girls, not old men like me."

"Don't be silly, Uncle Eli!" Anna jumped up, approached the Master, and began to put on her shoes. "They brought me the cascara a long time ago! If you wanted an excuse to go deal with work, you should have just said so."

I just sat there — firstly, stunned that the Master had a regular human name — and secondly, that there was at least one living creature who called this odd man "uncle."

"Is this another one of your creatures?" Anna nodded towards me.

Definitely offended — she's calling me names and everything.

"This is a promising young man, Anna. What if I decide to marry you off to him?"

Anna snorted, giggling and covering her mouth with her fist in a girlish gesture.

"I've already kicked this suitor's ass. He'll have to learn to fight before he can propose."

Hearing this, the Master burst out laughing.

"You always know how to light up this old man's day! You should come visit more often!" he said, trying to look stern. "And don't call me 'uncle!'"

"Okay, Uncle Eli!" Her voice trailed from behind the door.

The Master sighed and shook his head.

"Did you two hit it off?" He walked to his desk and sat at the computer.

I took the hint and began to leave.

"Well... sort of..."

"Remember, Andrew," the Master dropped his playful demeanor and grew very serious. "Anna knows more about the Neural Network than anyone else. Whether she'll share that knowledge with you is a different story. She doesn't want to share it with me."

With that, the Master fully immersed himself in his computer screen, and I understood it was time for me to leave.

"Thanks for the tea!"

"*Por nada*," he muttered without looking up.

* * *

"I think they'll introduce character classes next," Simba said. "What's an RPG without classes? Just an FPS or a fighting game. What do you think, Stacy?"

"Uh-huh."

"I'll probably be a paladin... or a barbarian," Simba sipped his sparkling water, sighed deeply, and went on, "It's the life of a tank for me. I am sick and tired of dropping dead every time a spider sneezes my way. What about you, Stacy? What'll you choose?"

"Uh-huh."

The two of them had cornered me in my changing room, comfortably settled on the couch, and clearly had no intention of leaving. To get a good view of them, I had to perch on the edge of my own couch. Simba was doing all the talking, while AngelCake was conspicuously silent. At first, I thought she might be feeling ill from last night, but I soon realized that she was angry with me.

Although Simba still got some of her attention, she was pointedly ignoring me. And as my buddy began to pry about the details of the previous evening, her mood grew stormier.

"You know, I think Marina's got a thing for you, yeah?" Simba was never one for tact. "I've been wondering why she's giving you VIP passes and buying you dinners. Don't drop the ball, Andrew! She's awesome... rich... beautiful... and look at her position! Heyyy... maybe she can get me a job?! Why not? I can work security. Or in an office. I'll even wear a tie... Yes, Ms. Marina... May I check the report?... How's Andrew doing?... Is he going fishing anytime soon?' You just make sure you do well there, Andrew! Keep her happy! Don't let us down!"

Thump! Dropping her backpack, Stacy jumped to her feet, snatched it up off the floor and stormed for the door.

"Stacy?" Simba too leapt to his feet. "What's going on?!"

She seemed to be waiting for this, pausing at the door without turning. It all felt so rehearsed. She was clearly expecting to be chased and apologized to.

"Simba, hang on," I restrained my friend.

"You seeing this, Andrew? What's with her?"

"Listen, Stacy," I said calmly, "If you walk out that door, you're never coming back."

AngelCake turned and glared at me.

"No one's keeping you here," I went on. "And I'll also point out that no one invited you. The VIP passes and the separate changing rooms ere provided by Marina for Simba and me. So go ahead and walk out if you feel so strongly about it all... But tomorrow you'll be waiting in line with everyone else. And in the game, it's every man for himself. No one will come running to save you, got it? Now, think about it, how far would you have gotten in the first two rounds of the beta without our help?”

Simba tried to interject, but I silenced him with a look. Stacy stood there, sniffling, on the verge of tears. But she didn’t leave. I too remained silent. At last, Stacy wiped her nose with her sleeve and sat back down.

“Do we understand each other?”

“Uh-huh...”

“What’s that?” I raised my voice slightly. “I didn’t get that.”

“I understand,” Stacy mumbled.

“And another thing, I don’t care what you do in real life. But in the game, everyone listens to me. You two chose me as your leader, so now we’ll play as a team.”

Stacy nodded.

“There’s no argument here, Andrew,” Simba slapped my back. “You’ve pulled us through twice. So you lead the way.”

“Alright, I’m glad everything’s clear now. When we get into the game, we’ll immediately regroup. We’re heading...” I thought for a moment, “to the store. Everyone remembers where the store is?”

Two affirmative nods.

“We’ll meet outside the store. Do NOT wander off alone. Do NOT pick classes or skills on your own. Do NOT allocate stats points before we get to discuss it. Got it? Let’s go!”

* * *

Seeing me, Sergio the VR pod technician waves at me: "Gonna wreak some havoc today?"

"We'll see," I reply. "We'll see."

The spiral... The descent... The alley.

The hole in the fence has been mended. There's a new picket there now, fastened with fresh, shiny nails, as if they came straight out of the store. The picket is painted with fresh paint; even its shade is different. The boulder is half-buried in the ground. Now, even if you wanted to pick it up, you can't.

Maybe I could've boosted my strength like the legendary moon sculptor in the first two tests. Now that I've committed my initial stat points, it would be pointless.

As expected, there's a short sword and an unknown item in my inventory. That's why I decided to check the store first. Maybe the merchant could identify this so-called primal-loot carapace. And at the same time, I could take a look around.

I had no intention of reneging on my deal with Anna, but you'd have to be a complete fool to buy a cat in a bag and hand it over without taking a peek at the pussy. If this carapace really is valuable, maybe I could renegotiate terms in my favor.

With these thoughts, I tapped on the now familiar quest envelope.

XP SURE IS TASTY!

KILL AT LEAST ONE PLAYER TO SUCCESSFULLY COMPLETE THIS QUEST!

GG GL HF!

01:29:32... 01:29:31... 01:29:30...

CHAPTER 17

TOTAL CARNAGE HAD DESCENDED upon the town square. I peeked out of the alley and froze still, unable to look away. Screams of terror, shrill cries of horror, pleas and lamentations reached me, mingled with the killers' ferocious roars. It didn't take much to imagine the beta testers enter the game, pull up their quest log, read what was expected of them and immediately plunge their swords into their dithering neighbors.

Into their throats... their sides... their stomachs! Time and time again... the system tallied up the damage. At our levels a single hit wouldn't be enough. Clumsily with cutlery or as skillfully as butchers in a slaughterhouse, the players cut down their neighbors and anyone else within reach.

The unarmed, meanwhile, turned on each other barehanded. They punched... choked... bit...

I wasn't the only one who'd gotten a whiff of easy money. No one wanted to be left behind, to be the loser.

Some tried to flee, into alleys, gateways, courtyards — these were the game's future craftsmen, herbalists and alchemists. Casual gamers who'd only joined the beta to explore a new world.

Their murderous coworkers chased them, knocked them down and set upon them. It's always easier to cut down someone who doesn't resist.

But damn, what the hell are you cutthroats doing?! Who's going to forge your armor now? Fail this quest, and you're out of the beta. Here's the true fear of virtual death! An insurmountable barrier for those who couldn't bring themselves to kill.

If it weren't for Marina's drunken rant the night before, I would've thought the test creators were sick freaks. Now I only believed what she had said even more. The Neural Net had decided to thin out the players' ranks and arranged a good ol' free for all.

I run to hide, but not so scrupulously that I won't get spotted. A skinny bald guy with a thug's scowl, who's just taken out a brunette, locks eyes with me. He grins menacingly and strides my way. That's right, bud. Hurry up — come get your well-earned rest.

I quickly allocate the stat points I got from leveling up. Another five points. Another +2 to

Strength and +3 to Dexterity. I still only have one in Constitution. I'm easy to kill, but... You gotta hit me first!

I backtrack to avoid drawing attention, in case he has friends. But my worries are unfounded. He rounds the corner, panting heavily. Clearly, he's used up his Stamina trying to get to me. He looks around, spots me and notices that I'm Level 2. His eyes go wide. Dummy. His greed's his downfall.

I dodge to the right and lop off his hand, sword and all. Blood gushes from the wound. He screams, more from the shock than the pain. Pain in the game is weird in general: It's there and all, but it feels distant, like you're drugged and your severed hand is just kind of itchy.

My next strike lands on his throat with a crit — which he survives. He clutches the wound, blood gushing in spurts. Seems like a "bleeding" status effect, with rapidly dropping HP, which however still gives you a chance of surviving if there's a healer nearby. Or if there's a potion on your belt.

Actually, I hadn't seen any healing here at all. And AngelCake wouldn't make a good healer. Too hysterical. I wouldn't trust my life to someone like that; she'd lose her nerve and mess up when it mattered most. "Oh, I wasn't quick enough... Oh, my hand slipped... Sorry!" I've come across players like that plenty of times before in non-VR games. You always have to cover for their mistakes and watch what you say around them.

My would-be murderer crumpled less than a minute later. The bleeding effect did its job; he was writhing on the ground one moment, and the next, there was a neat bundle there for me. Loot! I touched it, and some novice's trousers, a novice's shirt, and a crude short sword appeared in my inventory.

I took it all because who knows what could come in handy, and I equipped the sword right away into my free hand. Dual-wielding felt awkward, as if my balance was off now. Makes sense though. It seems the game's mechanics penalized me for trying to exploit them: Two weapons meant double the damage. So, I'm sure I'll suffer a penalty to Dexterity until I acquire a specific dual-wielding skill. There's sure to be one down the line.

It's time to find my party members. I figured it'd be foolish to go to the town square. Even if I am Level 2 now, a cohesive pack of three or four Level 1s could easily take me down. With all this chaos, there are probably other Level 2s around, and maybe even Level 3s now too actually.

You only need a kill to reach Level 1. You'd need about five for Level 2. For Level 3, by my calculations, you'd need 20 frags. Not that much if your victims don't resist. What was happening in the town square at the moment was akin to a zombie apocalypse. Half were running and screaming in horror, while the other half were feeding on them.

I quickly planned my route in my head and

briskly wound through the alleys, saving my Stamina. There weren't many people around. The first I met was a burly, bearded man, as big as Simba or even bigger. Seeing me, he squatted on the ground and covered his head with his hands.

"Don't kill me... please... I won't harm you..."

"Close your eyes," I responded to his whining.

He shut them in fear. I circled behind and swiftly struck him three times below the shoulder blade. He just groaned and folded into a gray lump.

Sorry, man. You won't last long in here with this kind of attitude anyway and a swift death is as good as a gift right now.

"Stop, you fucker! Stop, you bastard... I'll catch you, you little rat!"

Two Level 1s were chasing a skinny, lanky guy with gusto. Surprisingly, the pursuers were a boy and a girl. The boy suddenly ran out of breath and stopped, gasping for air.

"Trip him up, Bella! Take him down, I'll catch up!"

The girl clumsily struck the runner in the shoulder area with her sword. She didn't kill him but slowed him down, then kept striking again and again. She swung from above, like she was beating a rug. Both were Level 1s, and their victim didn't even try to fight for his life, merely trying to limp away from the girl.

I jumped out in front of them. With the blade in my right hand, I blocked her clumsy strike, and with the left, I thrust into her side, almost to the hilt.

"Ya motherfu — !" she grunted, staring at me. "Ya a real fuggin' bitch you know that?"

She was kinda cute actually — a blonde with two peppy braids. Freckles dotted her cheeks.

"Hey you freak, get away from Bella!" yelled the boy as he rushed towards me. "I'll tear you apart, you freak!"

His Stamina was low as it was, so he only got a few steps in before he began limping, cursing and contorting his mouth like an idiot.

I twisted my blade in her wound. The bleeding effect set in and finished her off, and the blonde turned into another crumpled heap.

"No! Bella! You fugger... You're a dead fugger, you asshole!" the boy screamed.

Meanwhile, their victim stopped and backtracked, thinking I was his savior.

"Bro! Thanks, man, really that was..."

I cut him off with a blow to his neck — a crit. I was trying out various strikes while I had the chance. Learning to kill better.

He turned into a useless lump. Didn't even have a sword on him.

Bella's boyfriend had recovered somewhat and now lunged at me so furiously as if his beloved Bella wouldn't wake up in the pod next to him, but had gone to the afterlife for good. Either he was traumatized from something that had happened to him IRL, or he was talented, but I had to spend an entire two minutes on him. At last though I tripped him, disarmed him, and finished him on the ground.

I only took the swords from the loot now. Compact and, surely, worth more than the rags. I just hoped the shop was open. If there's loot to be picked up, there should be someone to buy it. Then again, there were lots of things in this game that didn't work as they did in others.

At this point I needed just three more kills to reach Level 3. I resisted the urge to go hunting in the alleys and headed to the meeting place. I wasn't too worried about my companions. Their current Level 2 would give them an edge over most players. And Simba was definitely neither a coward nor a fool, while Stacy…

Well, if she can't get away from some Level 1s as a Level 2, then she's dead weight and no good for our team.

My worries turned out in vain, however. Both of my team members were already standing near the store, waiting for me. Simba had managed to get a sword, while AngelCake stood by empty-handed, berating him with a pissy look on her face. *Probably going on about what a jerk I am.*

"Can you believe a Level 1 attacked me? Stubborn bastard. I had to take him down. But I got a sword out of it!"

"Simba, did you read the quest objective?" I exclaimed.

"Nope. You told us not to do anything but rendezvous at the store. The plan was to decide everything here."

"Well read it now!"

"Ah... oh... wow!" Simba reacted with shock as the gist of the current quest sunk in.

"What about you, Stacy, did you read it?"

"I did! But, uh, what am I supposed to kill people with? A nail?! And I don't even have that. I dropped it when I died last time! My inventory is empty!"

"You could smother them with your tits!" I couldn't resist, but then grew serious: "Let's not stand out here and go inside."

Surprisingly, the store was empty. The quest objectives didn't require anyone to come here and this place was off the beaten path. Also we were simply lucky.

The merchant, stood behind the counter, sorting various pieces of clothing.

"Sir, may I offer you some items?" I tried to get his attention.

"Go ahead," he grunted.

I placed two swords, a shirt, and some trousers on the counter before him.

"Simba, do you have anything?"

"I'm keeping the sword," Simba said stubbornly, "so just the clothes."

"Put them down."

The merchant glanced at our rather modest assortment and immediately named the price.

"Swords are two coins each, clothes are one coin per set. Total of six coins, okay?"

"Wait a minute," I said, puzzled, "if I buy a sword, it costs five coins."

"That's for one of my own house brand of

swords," the merchant said. "This one's different. What if it's made of shoddy steel?"

"Got it," I didn't argue."Can we also see what else you got?"

"What?"

"I mean, can we see the wares you have here for sale, my fine sir?"

I was expecting a window with all the items, their prices and stats to pop up before me, but the presentation here turned out to be more mundane.

The merchant laid out his wares one by one, and the buyer had to pick them up and try them out. Full on realism — except that all the clothes were magically one-size-fits-all to the ladies' delight!

We were out of luck, however. The most basic wooden shield cost 10 coins. A quilted armor which offered minimal armor, unlike the clothes on our backs, was 20 coins. Leather armor cost 50.

The cost of weapons was similar. I was thinking of leaving one of the swords for Stacy when I stumbled upon something interesting.

"Stacy, do you know how to use a slingshot?"

"Of course! I could shoot one as well as the boys when I was a kid."

"Here, take this!" I bought her a sturdy black slingshot with a thick rubber band for five coins and fifty stones worth of ammo for the remaining coin.

"Hey, boss, are you in?" a cheerful voice sounded from the doorway.

The newcomer was dressed... oddly. He wore a baggy gray cloak and held a long and heavy quarterstaff in his hands. Most importantly, he wore boots!

The inscription over his head read "Level 4." While Stacy blinked in surprise, Simba and I immediately drew our swords. Three against one... despite his advantage in stats, a fight between us could go any way.

The newcomer took off his hood, rubbed his shaved nape and — casting us a sidelong glance without saying anything — began to place his offer to the merchant on the counter. It was all swords... Ten swords... Fifteen... Simba counted twenty-seven, and counting was something he did well.

"Oh," Stacy said out loud when she realized that 27 swords implied at least 27 bodies... or kills, I guess. And perhaps even more if you counted his unarmed victims.

The merchant quickly gathered the swords from the counter and placed a dark brown leather armor before the buyer. It vanished in an instant and in the same instant the stranger stood clad before us in rigid, layered leather with copper rivets. The man smirked, gave us a pointed look, turned and went out of the store.

"Some find profit in war, others in peace," Simba remarked enviously. "While we hesitate, others grow wealthy."

"And stronger," I chimed in quietly.

One question remained. I produced the

massive piece of carapace from my inventory and asked the merchant:

"Can you identify this?"

He squinted, examining the item, all but biting it, and even tapping it with a tiny hammer.

"Unfortunately, I would need special equipment and chemicals to identify this," he replied. "But I'm willing to buy it from you for... 200 coins!"

As he said it, the merchant looked and sounded like a game show host: *"Come on down! Fabulous riches await!"*

"Take the money," Simba whispered. "It's just enough for all three of us to get leather armor. It'll give us the edge we need."

In a way, he was right. Good gear at the start mattered way more than later, when more levels and skills were available. We could each take on ten newbies if we had leather armor, if not more. But...

"Thanks, I'll wait." I placed the carapace back into my inventory. "I have a feeling I can get much more for this."

The merchant shrugged, and I received a disgruntled look from Simba, while a new note appeared in my inventory: "Unidentified Carapace Armor (Legendary)."

"So, where to, chief?" Simba scanned the empty street before us predatorily.

"Did you allocate your stat points for Level 2?" I remembered.

"No, we're waiting for your orders," Simba

smirked.

"Simba, you do +3 to Strength and +2 to Constitution. AngelCake, you do +3 to Dexterity and +2 to Constitution. You're gonna be our dps, Stacy."

"As long as she's not the healer, I'm happy," Simba laughed, earning a stern glare.

We spent a few more minutes in a quick huddle. Simba was going to take point. I planned to get him a shield and armor in the future. He'd be our tank. I would cover his right side. Why? Because his right would then be his opponent's left and most people are right-handed, leaving their left side more vulnerable. Stacy, on the other hand, would shoot from Simba's left side, so I wouldn't get in the way of her line of fire.

I made us drill our movements in the empty street before leading my squad towards the town square. If there were still any easy kills to be found around here, this is where they'd be.

A couple blocks up the street, we came across an alley that had been turned into a redoubt. A large party of ten or so had pushed together and overturned two carts, blocking the alley. They waved their swords at us, cursing fiercely, and ordering us to keep moving if we knew what was best for us. At least two of them were Level 2s and I decided it would be better to avoid them.

Further down, a melee was underway in an alleyway. Seven Level 2s had cornered two Level 3s. Good thing we heard them early on. I scouted out the situation, and then guided my party in a wide arc around it.

At this point, I began to understand that I'd made a mistake. We should have leveled up as soon as the slaughter began. Back then, being Level 2s gave us a significant edge. Now, we were just like all the other Level 2s running around.

Suddenly and out of nowhere, a frenzied Level 3 player attacked us. Simba and I engaged him, while Stacy calmly whittled him down from a distance. Ten stones gave AngelCake the kill she needed and brought her to Level 3.

A few more blocks and we arrived at the town square.

"Like a graveyard," Simba whistled. Impressionable AngelCake even sniffled slightly.

The square was indeed as empty as a graveyard, and its smooth cobblestones were dotted with small mounds. Upon closer inspection, I realized they were loot bundles. Only swords had been taken from the kills, leaving behind the cheap and bulky items. Some 200 players had been slaughtered here in the first minutes of the quest. Those who had managed to rack up a kill of their own before succumbing themselves, would return to the game.

"Think there's a Rat King running around here somewhere?" Simba asked me.

I nodded. If you ever have rats, catch and throw a few of them into a bucket. Once the hunger sets in, they'll start gnawing at each other, and the one that survives will be the strongest and most vicious of the lot, with a taste for rat meat to boot. That's the Rat King. Let him go and he just might take care of your rat problem for you.

"I wonder what level this many PKs would get you?" I mused aloud.

"Whatever it is, I wouldn't want to run into the Rat King," Simba replied.

Something was nagging me in the back of my mind, something I'd seen before...

"The barricade!" I remembered. "With Stacy's slingshot, we'll have a killer advantage there. If we can keep them from rushing us, Stacy has enough stones for at least five of them."

"You want to go and negotiate with them?" Stacy interjected. "It looked to me they were doing just fine without us."

"Negotiate?" I echoed, surprised. "I suggest we take their barricade for ourselves."

CHAPTER 18

IT HAD BECOME DANGEROUS to be out in the streets. The virtual town had turned into a jungle. The herbivores had been slaughtered, and now the larger predators were picking off the smaller ones. Or the smaller ones were banding together for survival, to gang up and pick off the larger loners.

Twice we stumbled across such bands: First, a party of eight eyed us for a while, deliberating whether to attack or to find easier prey. Caution won, even though Simba was itching for a fight and I didn't view them as much of a challenge. But in the end, they moved on.

The second time, we barely ducked down in time. My intuition saved us. Hearing a party approaching, I realized that only those who were fully confident of their strength would move so boldly and noisily. Without further hesitation, I dropped to the ground, pulling AngelCake down beside me. Even then, she resisted...

"What the — ?"

"*Shhh!* Be *quiet!*"

Simba caught on faster and dropped down beside us.

A raid of them jogged past along the parallel street a few houses away. Not some ordinary group or party — but a real raid. All of them were well-armored and one of them was hauling an imposing tower shield. They even had a rearguard, who'd occasionally pause to scan the surroundings. I thought I recognized her familiar braids: It was none other than Yumi.

She'd earned herself a cozy spot on the team of pros currently leading in the scoreboards. So, that must be Lance and his buddies. I think I even caught a glimpse of his white forelock in the crowd. They seemed to be at the top of the food chain at the moment.

Once the steps faded, we moved on. The idea of capturing the redoubt had seemed decent before, but now it felt like it was the only way we had to make it to the end of the quest timer and grind some XP in the process.

"They've dug in well," Simba observed.

Perhaps whoever designed this level had intended there to be an inn or a small market in the nearby houses. What else explained the two hefty peasant carts? The players had knocked them over, wheels inward, completely blocking the alley and forming a wall that was not too tall — about five feet — but certainly solid.

You'd have to climb over it with both hands and feet while a dozen people tried to stab you from the other side. If its defenders were armed with spears or bows, the barricade would have been basically invincible.

But with the primitive weapons of the given quest, a frontal attack could still succeed. I spotted only one long wooden pole among the defenders; the rest seemed to have swords, or perhaps nothing at all. It was a bit too tricky to judge their weaponry by some heads bobbing behind a wall of carts.

Nevertheless, as a defensive line, this one was effective enough. Evidence of this was the loot heaps at the foot of the barricade. At least a dozen of them, no fewer. Most of the defenders, however, were still at Level 1. I counted three Level 2s and one Level 3. Either they were the ones doing all the work while the rest were under their protection, or the defenders of the game's first fort were so organized they killed in turns, accumulating kills evenly.

The whole operation was led by the Level 3 — a guy with bright red hair and a matching beard, resembling a Viking. We could hear him barking orders and to the defenders who nodded respectfully. He was the one positioning lookouts by the barricade, and I watched as he directed some how to reinforce the wall with new boards, brought in by a special crew.

Another factor was that the alley they were defending was a dead end. After leaving Simba and

AngelCake on lookout, I circled the neighboring blocks and found no alternative routes. So the defenders weren't worried about their rear.

"Simba, how much Strength do you have?"

"Five. I've got 7 in Stamina."

I wondered what determined the ability to lift weights in this game: Strength or Stamina? Probably Stamina, as that's what usually does it in games. The "heaviest" player carries the heaviest armor. And Strength mainly affects damage output. That's the classic mechanic, at any rate.

"Squat down," I said, and Simba squatted. I climbed onto his shoulders, like we would do to joust or peek over people's heads back in childhood.

"Are you trying to scare them into fleeing?" AngelCake joked.

"Stand up," I told Simba, ignoring her teasing. "Can you do it?"

Simba, grunting like a heavyweight athlete, straightened up. It worked!

"Get off Andrew! I can't hold you long!" he panicked. "My Stamina is draining!"

My experiment was a success, but I hadn't reckoned that this maneuver would drain Simba's Stamina so quickly. And I didn't want to wait for it to regenerate.

"Go over to the wall, Simba! To the building!"

"Which one?"

I quickly scanned our surroundings... "That one on the right!"

Simba took a few steps, and I pressed my hands against the wall feeling the rough plaster for a grip. I shuffled on Simba's shoulders. One foot... the other... it was just a short reach to the window... I stretched out my hand...

"Andrew! You batty bastard! Get off my head!"

Stacy was laughing, watching us, her bad mood behind her now. I was trying to step up on top of Simba's head, but kept slipping off. A circus act in the works...

"Stand still! Don't you want to be a tank?"

We bickered, mostly in jest, blowing off the adrenaline that had built up.

The house I was trying to get into consisted of two stories and an attic. No doors were visible from the street. Its ordinary entryway was probably through some locked gates around the corner, which led into its courtyard and from there the neighboring buildings.

Even the first floor windows were high. Standing on the ground, you couldn't reach the window sill. The level designers had made it clear that players weren't welcome in there. But I saw no reason not to try anyway.

Reaching out, I used the hilt of my sword to break the window. Simba tucked in his head, fearing the shards might fall on him, and indeed I suffered a minor cut. I began to lose HP, but it was a slow bleeding and nothing to worry about just yet.

At last I grabbed onto the window frame, swung my other arm inside, and gradually hoisted myself into the room. The inside was pure smoke and mirrors. The house's rooms were entirely empty. It felt like when you step backstage during a play and discover that all the scenery — the grass, the houses, and trees on stage — are actually cardboard silhouettes propped up by sticks.

At least there were walls, that was something. Maybe in the future, during the next rounds of the beta, there would be furniture, chandeliers, wallpapers, or even inhabitants here. This was good enough for now though.

I ran up the stairs to the second floor and from there to the attic. There was a tiny, half-round window with a barred frame there. I struck it hard with my elbow, but it held. I backed up and kicked... again... and again... The window shattered. I was hoping Simba would distract our enemies in the meantime.

"Hey, y'all there in the fort!" Right on cue I heard Simba yell. "I wanna join up! Lemme in!"

"Who needs you? What're you good for?" a shrill, female voice yelled back. Had I mistaken the true leader? Or was there no set hierarchy at all over there? If so, they were in worse shape than I thought.

"I'm a good singer! And I know many jokes. I know y'all are bored in there!" bellowed Simba. "My friend Stacy here, can do a killer belly dance. Show 'em, Stace!"

A pang of jealousy stung me as I wondered whether Stacy really could do a belly dance. I'd never thought of her as my girlfriend, but now I was jealous that she might flirt with someone else. How odd. Maybe I was possessive after all...

Breaking the window, I slithered out onto the roof. Thankfully, Simba kept up his yelling, giving me a sense of direction. My high Dexterity allowed me to run across the rooftops, leaping from house to house. Although I almost slipped on my first jump, the subsequent ones went better. By my estimates, I should have circled behind the barricade. I inched closer and peeked out cautiously.

Our enemies were right below me. They were laughing and pointing at Simba, and there were more of them than I'd initially counted. Thirteen in total, including the leader. I wished I had brought Stacy's slingshot. I could have taken them all out from up here. But hindsight is 20/20.

Simba catches my eye, and I give him the signal. He immediately bolts towards the overturned carts.

"Where are you going, moron?!" someone yells. "You'd better stay away. We won't let you in!"

There's chaos at the barricade. Several armed figures approach the barrier, brandishing their swords menacingly. It's clear they'll skewer him the moment he tries to climb over. Stacy is closing in, but no one is paying her any attention.

I crawl up to the edge, ready to leap. This time, I know what I want: We're taking these guys down.

I gather myself and shoot down like a missile,

making no noise as I land. They only notice me when it's too late.

I land on a girl standing near the edge, right by the house. She's the one with a long wooden pole, likely meant to push away intruders.

We both hit the ground, but I get up faster. It's only in old kids' movies that no one hits anyone while they're down. I land two strikes to her chest. The system doesn't care about anatomy and awards critical hits for accurate blows. The girl yelps and vanishes, dropping a small heap of loot.

That's when the others notice me and charge. Two try to corner me against a wall. They move apart, trying to pincer me. One is a middle-aged man who keeps reaching for his nose, reflexively adjusting glasses he no longer has in VR land. Clearly a newbie.

The second is clad in quilted armor and holds his sword confidently. He might even be a seasoned gamer. Not every pro in here is top-tier. He presses forward, his strikes so powerful that even simply blocking drains my Stamina. A basic tactic: spam attacks until I'm exhausted then finish me off.

The first guy lunges with his sword as soon as he decides I'm distracted, aiming for a weak spot. He probably believes he's helping the second guy. A naive notion.

I raise my right arm purposefully too high during my swing. He sees that I have opened up and, putting his whole body into the blow, tries to impale me in the armpit on my unprotected side.

The only problem is that I'm ready for this and slide over, using his own body as cover from his partner's onslaught. Then, with one long, smooth motion I slit open his throat.

He wheezes and gushes blood. A terrible sight, especially for those who are not used to carnage in VR — those who are still fooled into thinking this is real.

I finish him off with a quick blow to the stomach, and immediately fall to my knees... My whole body is shaking... Crap! I've just gained a new Level! What a time for it!

On the other side of the carts, Simba roars and goes on the offensive. His main objective is not to get himself into trouble, and distract as much as he can. As for me, this might be it...

My opponent lowers his sword. I see the blade approach my neck in slow motion. This is not just a blow, it's an execution. I want to turn away, but my body refuses to obey me. It's wracked by the buzz of the game's main stimulant: a new level.

I take the hit! I don't really understand what's going on. The blade passes a millimeter from my throat, grazes my shoulder, immediately removing half of my miserable health bar. I see something bounce along the cobblestones... A smooth round stone. AngelCake has walked right up to the barricade and is shooting her slingshot pointblank, while Simba swats off anyone trying to make a sortie.

Having come to my senses, I simply roll away, somersault over my shoulder, making distance.

Here's five more unallocated stat points. Better look out now, ya bitches! I dump all of it into Dexterity as quickly as I can so as not to second-guess myself later.

A few points to Constitution won't help here. What'll it give me? The ability to take one or two hits without damage? That's just accident insurance. And I have enough Strength as is. High Dexterity, however, gives me the chance to be real OP for a bit — at least so long as there aren't any tanks or dps around.

My body is as light as a feather in the wind. My blades become extensions of my hands. My feet never seem to touch the ground.

The Level 2 who almost killed me continues his attack. He assumed that I was running away, that I was afraid. Funny. But his sword moves slowly, as if the air has become thick and viscous. His thrust peters out in midair. I just step back, letting it pass, and then hit him with an overhand left.

Inertia carries him forward. He falls through and opens up to me completely. Neck... side... shoulder blade... so many sweet possibilities... It's impossible to cut the neck with one blow. A bad target. Too slow. I correct myself and finish with several stabs to his stomach, my sword working like a sewing machine needle... two... three... four... there's a frag!

I move back to the barricade. There are more than a dozen defenders, but they are backing away in fear. Redbeard tries to restore order. He sends a couple more Level 2s against me, his shock reserve. Simba tries to climb the barricade. He is offended that we are getting the frags. He is the only one of us still at Level 2.

I don't care to fight on the Viking's terms. I slip past the Level 2s and start a bloodbath. The Level 1s scatter screaming. I don't know what gender they are or whether they are old or young. I slay three in mere seconds. The defense collapses, Simba clambers over the wall swearing. No one has any time for him anymore.

Redbeard the Viking turns, his face flushed with anger.

"Scum!" he sputters. "The hell did you come here for? This is my barricade! My fort! My redoubt! Die, you pigfucker!"

Redbeard rushes at me and I find myself facing three swords at once. I hold them off for a while but it's not going in my favor. I still have no Stamina after all.

Dropping to a knee, I switch to ground fighting and sweep the leg of one of the Level 2s. As he falls, I strike him directly in his groin. I'm not a sadist. It's just the closest soft spot. He doesn't just scream: He shrieks in horror. It must be difficult to comprehend that this isn't your real body.

I have no trouble with that however. I've killed and died many millions of times in cyberspace, practically non-stop since childhood. I don't envy an utter newb though.

Stacy finishes off the other guy. Her slingshot

has turned out to be a deadly weapon, especially up close. My opponent gets too caught up in the fencing and forgets about our dps.

Thunk! A smooth stone hits him in the back of his head. I kick his sword away and keep him down. *Thunk!* A second stone, the size of an egg, blows his brains out.

Redbeard clenches his teeth and launches one last desperate attack. He ignores one blow from me, then another... It's as if he doesn't notice them. He swings his sword wildly. One such hit would do me in, but I sidestep and slash his wrist in reply... the weapon drops from his hand, blood streaming from his fingers.

But he's still alive, still standing. He charges at me, knocking me down, strangling me. Both my blades are buried in his stomach... I'm soaked in his blood. Has he pumped all his stat points into Stamina? The damn coward, how much life does he have? My HP is draining away... Damn it! I only needed a little more... there's the red haze now... I overplayed my hand...

Thwack!... Thwack!... I hear heavy, meaty blows, like a butcher slicing meat at a market. I feel the grip on my neck loosen. The Viking pulls away from me, silently slumping to the ground and turning into a loot drop.

"Phew, that was intense!" said Simba coming out of his leveling high. "Better than coke I'd say."

"Coke as in cocaine? What are you talking about?" I said, half-laughing, half-wheezing, like an action hero who'd just saved the world. "You've never tried coke in your life."

"Let me roleplay in peace," Simba retorted serenely. "And anyway... I doubt any drug beats leveling up in this game."

He rounded up the remaining newbies. They didn't resist. To them, we were maniacs, killers, butchers. They just waited quietly for the nightmare to end. We lined them up and finished them off. We give no quarter in this war.

Our loot was four quilted armors, two pairs of boots, and eighteen swords. The barricade's defenders were no fluffy bunnies. You didn't amass this kind of gear by being helpful to random passersby who happen to wander into your alley.

We drew lots for the boots, and Stacy ended up barefoot. She sulked until we promised to buy her stylish shoes at the shop. Now we had the means. And everyone got a piece of the quilted armor. Simba and I looked like monks or bandits in it. The armor hung loosely on us, but clung to AngelCake's curves, so I tried not to look at her ass too much.

I was pretty sure there wouldn't be a repeat of yesterday's "random encounter" in my changing room. In my mind, Marina had completely eclipsed the much plainer Stacy. Marina was like a distant dream and I still couldn't fathom why she was getting so close to me lately. Either I was playing the role she wanted me to play very well or I had genuinely intrigued her.

It was clear I had caught Stacy's eye, but after our argument earlier today, she'd be cold for at least a day or two. Wistfully, I recalled Stacy's firm ass and how skillfully she had moved it, and sighed...

We piled the unwanted loot — the trousers and shirts — into one giant mound. Curiously, despite its owners' bloody ends, the loot always dropped fresh and clean. So I lay down on this mound of clothes to rest. I watched my HP regenerate, gazed at the clouds, and let my mind wander. Truth be told, I relaxed a little too much and almost dozed off.

"Hey... You on the wall!" I heard a girl's trembling voice through my half-slumber. "Your name's Simon, right? I remember you!"

"My name is Simba," Simon replied somewhat sternly for some reason, "and I don't remember you at all!"

"Scram, tramp, before we teach you a lesson!" AngelCake chimed in.

"Simba, is TargetAi here? Didn't they bring him back after the first round?" The strange girl sounded on the verge of tears. "Could you get him, please?"

Can't I get a moment's peace? Shaking my head to dispel my drowsiness, I got up and plodded wearily over to the barricade.

CHAPTER 19

ALL HER LIFE, Zoia Menshova considered herself special. In kindergarten, while other girls played with dolls or teddy bears, Zoia fell in love with Batman. From the boys, she stole an action figure of the mysterious masked man, who had either horns or ears on his head. At first she tried to introduce him to her other dolls — to her skinny Barbies, big-headed Bratz or curvy Winx fairies — but then she realized that none of them were worthy companions for him. So she kept Batman for herself alone. Every morning she'd go outside to the sandbox to see if he slept well. She cooked him dinners in plastic saucepans, took strolls with him, and eventually even grew so bold as to secretly sneak him into her bedroom and place him on her pillow before bed.

In Zoia's dreams, the tall, bombastic, caped crusader would take her by her hand and lead her into his world, which was full of secrets and adventures and so utterly different from the quiet little world that Zoia lived in.

Zoia's parents had worked in the same factory for 30 years — her father as a foreman and her mother in the accounting department. They would buy crystal during the holidays and go stay at their summer cottage on weekends. They never quarreled and they adored their only daughter. Yet they didn't understand her at all either.

At the age of eight, she painted all the walls in her room with water colors: green blots, yellow circles, red lines... She wasn't even punished. They just had room repainted. Light beige replaced the former gray so that the girl's eyes wouldn't get tired. A relative of the family, hearing of what had happened, remarked that their daughter had a creative streak, so Zoia was sent to music school where she studied the accordion.

In the sixth grade, her parents realized that they couldn't cope and gave up on Zoia. She was outgoing and smart, but her teachers at school only saw black nails and green hair.

And a year later, Zoia... Well, what kind of a name is Zoia anyway? Zoia passed away and Yumi took her place.

At first it was actually spelled "Yummy" because she liked the word, but then, when everything Japanese became fashionable, Yummy became Yumi and even made up a Japanese grandmother who had named her to the chagrin of her square, Russian parents. Since *yumi* means bow in Japanese, Yumi began to sometimes draw fake arrow tattoos on herself as a way to bolster her backstory.

She was a fan of all things Goth and K-pop, anime and Marvel, vampires and cyberpunk. She fell in love with Johnny Depp and then with BTS, all seven of them one by one...

And then esports blew up, and with it players like T-Rex and Xavier. In no time at all, Yumi's whole room was covered in their posters. And of course, the coolest, most awesome and legendary of all pros was Lance: as cool as a Viking, as handsome as a manga hero, as silver-haired as the Witcher. When he signed his name on her belly, Yumi forswore showers for next week or two.

But then everything worked out even better than she dared imagine. Later that day, Lance recognized her in the hallway after the beta test, decided that he liked her and wanted to have her right then and there. She gave herself up with delight, ready to fulfill his every whim, just to be the best girl Lance could have.

In Yumi's head, pink unicorns were already waltzing around their wedding cake. The first time she got into the backseat of Lance's new Tesla, wedged between Xavier and T-Rex, she knew for sure that she was in heaven.

Ten minutes later though her fantasy world began to crack. That was precisely when Xavier's hand reached under her skirt and began stroking her panties. Yumi blushed and straightened her skirt. Most of all, she was afraid that Lance would notice something and, god forbid, assume that she's a whore.

But Lance chatted calmly, discussing the beta with everyone except, of course, Yumi. The pros were deciding what they would post on their channels, whether it was worth posting screenshots on IG and whether all four of them should appear on the evening podcast, or only T-Rex, who had recently become the "face" of a new line of gadgets.

By the time they got to Lance's house, Xavier had practically fucked Yumi with his fingers, pushing her panties aside.

Lance's apartment was a large two-level loft with a full bar and even a small dance floor on the first floor. Lance put booze on the bar counter: whiskey, rum, tequila and a couple more bottles that Yumi didn't recognize, one bright blue and the other acid green. Then he muttered "have fun" and left the house, slamming the front door behind him.

Shugga, the silent guy with neon blue hair who'd sat in the front seat on the ride over, immediately turned his attention to the PlayStation.

"Do you want a drink?" asked Xavier.

Yumi shook her head.

"Too bad," T-Rex laughed. "You could use it."

He poured something clear into two glasses. Xavier and he drank in one gulp and slammed their glasses loudly on the bar counter.

"According to Lance," said Xavier, "you're a

hell of a lay. We're gonna have to verify that."

Amid the background noise of K-pop and console gunfire, they laid Yumi out on the sofa next to the dance floor. She found out that she got "a C for sucking," but that her ass was "as tight as a virgin's." They took turns fucking her, then double-teamed her, and then took turns again. At first she felt ashamed, then she felt good, and in the end she was simply extremely tired.

"Pour me a shot of what you're drinking," she said after it was over, approaching the bar counter.

She was still in her panties because Xavier forbade her to put anything else on, so that she would "please his eye."

"This is tequila," T-Rex explained, "you need to put a pinch of salt on your hand. You drink it, lick the salt and suck on a lime. It's good shit."

"Yeah, it's good all right," Xavier agreed. "Come on, bitch, cheer up! I already want seconds." And he gave Yumi a stiff slap on the ass.

"Welcome to the team," T-Rex tapped his glass against hers and winked.

Over the next two days, Lance never touched her again, although he let her join their team, spoke to her politely and sympathetically, and helped her complete the quests. Xavier, however, turned out to be a real terror of a fuckboy. It felt like she was his living sex doll and he couldn't get enough. Xavier could fuck Yumi day and night, in the car or in public, alone or together with T-Rex. In the second round of the beta, once the devs activated the mature content modules, he began fucking Yumi in-game too.

Now twirling a heavy dagger, the kind used for piercing heavy armor and critting tanks, Xavier approached his next victim, saying, "Well, well, let's see now..."

Yumi and he wore matching armor — cool-looking, tight-fitting, leather armor. "Black as night," he called it. Xavier didn't skimp on equipment. But he did tend to steal any frag he could. He'd say, "You get the next one," but then he'd take the kill anyway. His bloodlust meant he was always thirsty.

"Since you're the one fucking her, you can be the one to level her too," Lance had said earlier today. Xavier agreed. T-Rex whinnied and said he'd help — in both senses. Shugga, as usual, remained silent.

"Come on... Nooow..." Grabbing a kneeling player by the hair, Xavier pulled his head back andslit his throat, holding on until his victim bled out. "Come on... No...! FUCK NO! It's not enough... Again not enough!"

"So take the next one. Come on. Stop wasting time." Lance hurried him on.

They called other players "meatsticks" and they had worked out a system: They would drive a crowd of Level 1s, Level 2s and even Level 3s into a dead end and make a spectacle of killing one or two of them with especial cruelty, ripping open their bellies or quartering them. The guys had a good imagination for that kind of thing. Then they would promise a quick death to the rest, if they behaved in turn. At the moment, the remaining "meatsticks" were kneeling nearby, quietly awaiting their fate.

A short-haired brunette was up next. She shut her eyes, her thin lips trembling. Xavier stood behind her, bent down and slipped his hand under her T-shirt. He squeezed her nipple and when she twitched, he stabbed her in the neck with his dagger.

"Yesss... Ooh... Oooh.... Yasss..." As soon as "the meat" turned into a loot bundle, Xavier was overwhelmed with ecstasy.

He fell to his knees, savoring his orgasm. His eyes rolled back and his body shook like he was having a seizure. The five over his head changed to a six.

Yumi watched the others level up. She was already at Level 3 herself. Yesterday she had leveled up on spiders and noobs. At first, the new level had rolled over her like an orgasm — bright, juicy, unclouded. By her second and third levels, these sensations were not so acute and she could even suppress them if she wanted to. This wasn't the place to relax in.

In fact, Lance, the highest-level player on the team at Level 7, took the new levels quite stoically. He prided himself on his self-control. Xavier, however, savored each millisecond of VR ecstasy like some drug addict — and it seemed that his buzz only intensified.

"Can I get the next one?" Yumi jumped out in

front of Lance and folded her arms over her chest pleadingly. "At least one so that I can finish the quest?"

"First the fighters, then the comfort women," said Lance, and the others neighed obsequiously.

Yumi didn't know what a comfort women was, but she understood that she was being insulted. "*I'll have to google it later*," she thought.

"Your turn, Shugga," their party leader ordered.

Shugga flicked his blue bangs and stepped forward. Wasting no time, he began driving his sword into the base of his victims' skulls like an automaton. Hit, frag. Hit, frag.

"We're a bit short," he reckoned once "the meat" was gone. "I'll get my Level 6 with the next batch."

"Okay," Lance nodded. "Let's get a move on. The sun is still high."

"Go on without us," Xavier wheezed. "Yumi and I will catch up with you."

He was still staggering, his eyes unfocused.

"Okay, all right, hope you feel better," Lance grinned, looking not at him, but at Yumi.

The squad had not yet managed to disappear around the corner when Xavier ordered, "Let's do it doggy style."

Yumi looked around for a suitable spot. She walked up to one of the houses and pulled down her trousers and underwear to the floor, leaving her leather cuirass on just in case. She leaned against the wall, arching her back and sticking out her ass. Ready.

Xavier came up behind her and entered so abruptly that she yelped, and began pounding her without any further foreplay. Pain was barely perceptible in VR, yet pleasure was as vivid as ever. As a result, Yumi liked having sex with Xavier in-game much more. She began to moan and push back, arching harder.

"Undress completely," Xavier ordered. "I feel like I'm fucking a centurion."

Yumi removed her armor to her inventory. The humiliation and shame of the realization that she could be seen now by admins or technicians turned her on more and more...

"Bitch... That's it, take it like that, bitch..." Xavier wheezed.

"Ohhh... Yes... I'm your bitch... Your whore..." she began to echo back at him, knowing that it would turn Xavier on.

"Like this!" Suddenly she felt something around her throat.

A rope! Xavier had indeed picked up a rope somewhere today. Either it had dropped as loot or he had bought it in a store. He twirled it in his fingers constantly. A tight noose coiled around her neck. It was growing tighter and tighter...

DEBUFF RECEIVED (ASPHYXIATION): 1–5 DMG/s.

Her HP began to stream away in the log, still slowly, a trickle, but going faster and faster.

-1... -3... -5... -2...

"Xavier!" Yumi wheezed, "I've got a debuff!

You're gonna kill me!"

"Shut up, bitch! SHUT UP!" Xavier growled, "You belong to me! You'll die if I damn well please!"

Yumi began to struggle, trying to escape, but this provoked Xavier even more. Whereas in meatspace he was simply stronger, here in-game, he was several times stronger. A Level 3 against a Level 6 was no match: She was like a mouse in the paws of a depraved cat.

Back in meatspace, Xavier had already tried to choke her once. He said that choking a girl made her pussy shrink in fear, making it feel extra good. When he did do it, Yumi hadn't been particularly frightened. She even liked it.

Her life bar had already passed the halfway mark and turned yellow, the damage values growing larger. She suddenly realized that just a little more and she would DIE FOR GOOD — she herself would become a frag!

And that would be that. She would be eliminated from the beta and kicked off the team — a toy that'd seen better days.

"Baby! Baby — please!"

"Die you bitch!"

Yumi grabbed a heavy dagger from her inventory. She struck blindly, by feel, stabbing under the edge of his armor.

"Aah! You cunt! I'll kill you!" screamed Xavier. "I'll find you and I'll kill you!"

He should have grabbed his own dagger and finished off the rebellious girl. But instead, he began to fuck her harder and tighten the noose tighter and tighter, hoping that he would beat her to the punch.

Too late, however. Yumi's life bar was flashing red when she suddenly realized that she was poking at nothing. Without even getting dressed, she turned around and saw a bundle of loot — not the typical dirty white, but black: "Black as night."

Yumi got dressed, gathered what was left of Xavier, equipped a dagger in each hand and ran.

She ran, realizing that she had nowhere to hide. If they find her in the game, they would spend a long time killing her in the most terrible way. Lance would never allow anyone to just wipe out one of his buddies. She didn't even want to imagine what would happen to her back in real life.

She weaved through the alleys, choosing the ones they had already cleared. Time passed slowly, like the last day of school before vacation. There was half an hour left. She could hide in some hole, keep still, wait out the next 30 minutes. And then... then life would go on.

Suddenly, she saw something in her path. A barricade blocked her way — a heap of junk, overturned carts, but a robust and substantial barrier. Yumi approached to get a better look at the barricade. She wasn't afraid of any defenders; for anyone to attack her, they'd first have to climb over the wall, and her level and equipment made her a formidable opponent for everyone except maybe Lance.

Behind the wall, she saw a familiar face. It

was Simon — the one who had started the fight in the cafeteria. On the one hand, this was bad because he probably still held a grudge. On the other hand, at least she wouldn't have to spend much time explaining who she was.

"He also has a friend named Andrew," Yumi recalled. Lance had called him Ratmir, but when Yumi didn't see that name anywhere, he explained that Andrew was playing under a smurf called TargetAi. She thought Andrew seemed to like her; he might be the one to talk to. Plus, he seemed to be more level-headed.

"Hey... You on the wall!" Yumi yelled. "Your name's Simon, right? I remember you!"

"My name is Simba," Simon replied gruffly. "And I don't remember you at all!"

Just as she thought, he was still upset.

"Scram, tramp, before we teach you a lesson!" A nasty voice chimed in.

Who's this bitch?

"Simba, is TargetAi here? Didn't they bring him back after the first round?" Yumi knew that this wasn't the time to get upset and softened her voice. "Could you get him, please?"

At last Andrew's head popped up out from behind the wall. His hair was tousled, and his face looked somehow drowsy. Had he been sleeping? Amid this chaos? Some nerve. The girl's sensitive heart raced. Lance had talked so much about him — he wouldn't have done so for just anyone.

"Andrew!" Yumi stepped closer, addressing him directly. "Let me join your team. I'm Level 3, I have good gear, and I know how to fight. I won't be a burden."

"Why should we let you?" Andrew shrugged. "Weren't you hanging out with Lance? Go join his team."

"I can't," Yumi panicked. TargetAi also didn't want to help her, even though she had done nothing wrong to him! "I can't go to Lance. I killed his friend, Xavier... He'll just obliterate me now!"

"What's it to me?" If Andrew was surprised, he didn't show it. "That's your problem."

"Please TargetAi!" Yumi broke down in tears, this time for real. "You're not like them... they're animals... sadists... They'll flay me alive or impale me! I'll give you all of the equipment I have, all my gear, EVERYTHING you like — only help me please!"

Chapter 20

"I'M AGAINST IT," Simba dug in. "We know we can't trust her. She's deceived us once before blatantly. You think anything has really changed since then?"

"She's clearly bad news," Stacy sneered, glancing towards Yumi, "All she knows is how to lie. She's probably up to something."

"And what do you think she's up to?" I asked.

"She'll gain our trust now," Simba ventured, "and when Lance shows up, she'll stab us in the back."

"Why would he even need to resort to that? Look at her, she's already a Level 4. Lance must be at least Level 5 or 6 by now, if not higher. Why resort to Sun Tzu when smooshing us like flies is faster?" I pondered aloud. "Not to mention that there's five of them against us three, and they're all stronger than we are. This barricade certainly wouldn't stop them."

I wanted to add that Lance wasn't a strategist. He considered intricate plots to be beneath him. This whole situation didn't resemble his MO whatsoever.

"Why did you say she's a Level 4?" Simba asked abruptly. "She says she's a Level 3."

"Look at the handle over her head!"

"All the more suspicious!" AngelCake cut in.

"On the contrary," I disagreed, "It fits her story. She took out that Xavier guy and was so shaken up that she didn't realize she leveled up."

"Hey..." Simba suddenly shouted, "Why did you take out Xavier?!"

"Because he's a jerk," Yumi scowled, offering no further explanation.

"So, does this look like a setup?" I asked. "If they were sending her to us, they would've come up with a more complex story. And they certainly wouldn't have left her with that leather armor. Why give us expensive gear we don't have? They would've sent her in newbie rags."

"It doesn't matter!" Simba slammed his fist into his palm. "One minute they're her knights in shining armor — and the next they're jerks. When the going got tough, she ran to us, but tomorrow, they'll be wonderful again and she'll run right back."

"Exactly," Stacy agreed. "This is her problem. Why should it concern us?"

I understood that Simba couldn't forgive Yumi for the fight in the cafeteria, or rather, what had transpired before it. He was a proud guy and couldn't stand being made to look like a fool. Not that my friend held grudges. He just preferred to treat everyone based on their merits. And in his eyes, Yumi had already squandered her trust.

In Stacy's case, it was all even simpler. She didn't want a new girl on the team, especially one as attractive as Yumi was. And in her current chic leather armor, which was tight in all the right places, Yumi did make a hell of an impression. The armor did not look like the skintight biker suit Anna had worn the first day. It was composed of dense layers of leather scales, perhaps riveted with metal. It was completely black, but it was not glossy, but rather matte, absorbing the light.

Of course what armor looked like didn't really matter. It could be a full plate bra or fur panties for a barbarian; as long as it provided the necessary armor and stat bonuses, then it did its job.

Yet even from afar, Yumi's armor looked solid, reliable and expensive. Which, from my point of view, immediately and significantly increased her value to our team. And if she has another set in her inventory, well then that's just a gift. At the same time, the armor did not restrict movement. At least it was nice to look at Yumi in it. And her dimpled cheeks, coquettishly upturned nose and large, slightly slanted eyes perfectly explained AngelCake's irrational hatred of her.

"Simba, look at her armor," I said, "If your quilted armor gives you +5 to Armor and +10 against Projectiles, can you imagine the specs on the leather armor? And she's got two sets."

"Well, great," Simba adjusted his sword in his hand. "Let's go and take them for ourselves. We frag her and we get her armor."

"I call one of the cuirasses!" Stacy exclaimed. "I feel like I'm gonna suffocate in this blanket you've put me in."

It wasn't possible to overheat in the quilted armor that Stacy had equipped. It didn't feel heavy and certainly wasn't warm. But Yumi's armor looked far more sexy, making AngelCake even more pissy.

Yumi remained patiently waiting about thirty feet away from our redoubt. Her cautious glances already told me she wasn't lying. We needed to be cautious, but this didn't seem like a trap.

Taking her down right now and seizing her high-end gear was the easiest option. But not the most appealing one. Yumi actually had esports experience, making her a more valuable team member than, say, AngelCake or even Simba. She *had* already reached Level 4, so she was objectively better than any of us.

Moreover, and perhaps most importantly to me, Yumi had spent the past three days with Lance. Whatever had happened between them in meatspace didn't interest me at all, but I did want to know what she'd seen in game. Where they'd been, how they'd leveled up, distributed stats, and their long-term plans in general.

This wasn't just inside information; she was

the perfect defector. But she would only share voluntarily. Once she felt at home, she'd open up.

"We'll let her in," I declared.

"Andrew, no offense," Simba erupted, "But are you nuts? Why do you want to deal with her baggage? Do you fancy yourself a Robin Hood, standing up for the poor folk or something?"

AngelCake just shook her head in silence and pouted. I could've pulled rank and ended it there — and maybe that would've been the correct thing to do — but I wanted to persuade at least Simba.

"What does her baggage have to do with this?" I asked sternly.

"Because Lance will come looking for her and when he finds us, he'll kill us all!" Simba gestured emphatically.

"And if he merely sees us wearing his buddy's leather armor, he won't kill us? He'll let it slide? Water under the bridge?" I chuckled.

"Maybe he will, how do you know?" said Simba, out of arguments. "He'd have to prove it first!"

"Simba, he'll kill us anyway!" I said. "If he's looking for her, he'll scour every nook of this town. But if he finds us with her fighting on our side, our chances will be better than without her."

"Well you're the boss," Simba frowned. "I said my piece."

Stacy quietly distanced herself from us. It seemed I hadn't persuaded anyone. No matter. Time would tell who's right. No one judges a winner and the dead have no shame. We'd find out which group we belonged to in about thirty minutes.

"Hey, Yumi," I called out. "You can come in behind the barricade, but you have do as I say! No matter what I say!"

"Okay!" A smile of relief lit up the girl's face. "I swear to obey my liege in all his whims and wishes!"

Beside me, I could feel Stacy cringe from hearing this oath. If Yumi weren't a Level 4 with leather armor, I'd be worried about "friendly fire." A wayward stone could fly her way, followed by an "oops, my slingshot slipped" as an excuse.

As I helped Yumi climb over the wall, Simba and AngelCake turned away in protest, making their disapproval known to all.

"Okay, now, take the armor off," I said as soon as Yumi stood among us.

"Alright," said the girl flatly as the color drained from her face.

Lowering her eyes, she stashed the armor in her inventory, leaving herself completely naked.

"What the hell are you doing?" I was stunned. "Don't you have your noob linens? Put on your noob clothes. I'll give you quilted armor a bit later. It's worse than yours, but it's still armor."

Yumi hastily put on her starting skirt and top. She now seemed ashamed of what she had done and was actively avoiding eye contact.

"Okay, I get it," she tried to smile, but it didn't come out as nicely as the first time. "I'm sorry."

"Give the leather armors and weapons to me

and Simba," I continued. "Consider it payment for our protection. Maybe I'll give them back later, but you need to prove your worth."

Yumi nodded again and handed me the gear. Seeing the stat bonuses it gave me made me ecstatic: +10 to Armor, +15 against Projectiles, 20% Magic Absorption. Plus, a bonus +5 to Strength and +3 to Dexterity. I was effectively a level stronger in my new armor.

If I understand the game mechanics correctly, an attack from a Level 1 or 2 enemy wouldn't even scratch me. And in this unexpected way, I also discovered that there is magic in this world.

Simba was as happy as a kid, twirling a heavy dagger in his hands. In the inventory, it was simply called a "Good Average Dagger," although it looked more like a dirk — narrow and long but with a strong "reinforcing rib" that allowed it to pierce armor. It granted +8 to Damage and a further +5 against armored opponents.

It felt like we had entered a new Act of the game — one devoted to stats, gear, and leveling up. I was way more "lost" in these mechanics than in a fair duel. Translated into gaming genres, Gladiator Games was just a regular fighting game. Victory depended on a player's cunning and knowledge of weapons, not their stats.

Then again, whereas the difference here between Level 1 and Level 2 was huge — i.e. precisely double — the difference between Level 2 and Level 3 was only one and a half times. And these disparities grew smaller after that, so that the difference between Level 19 and Level 20 was barely noticeable.

"What level was Xavier?" I suddenly asked Yumi.

The most important thing now was to prepare for the upcoming battle. I had no doubt it would happen. This town was too small for our two parties to avoid each other. Meanwhile, we were eagerly unwrapping the gifts that our stroke of luck, Yumi, had brought us.

"Level 6," Yumi answered.

"And the others?"

"Lance is Level 7, T-Rex 6, Shugga is also 6. That's all."

Strange — I thought I saw more people on their team. Maybe I was mistaken, of course.

"Who's the one with the tower shield in your party?"

"*Their* party," Yumi corrected. "T-Rex. Lance is leveling him up as a tank. How did you know?"

"I know plenty," I said, feigning mystery.

I'd gotten good at bluffing and bullshitting lately, mostly thanks to Marina. As for Yumi, I'd rather she thought I knew more than I did. She might lie less as a result.

"So what's your class then?"

"Assassin," Yumi replied willingly. "I've got 13 Dexterity and 4 Strength."

"Nice," I nodded. "How did you manage to kill Xavier?"

"I got lucky," she frowned. "I think I got a crit at the right time. That was all."

Then we fell silent.

"Hey there, you lot behind the wall!" a brash voice called out suddenly. "What the hell are you up to? Come on out. We need to talk!"

"So talk!" I called back. "I can hear you just fine from here!"

"What's your problem!?" a voice exclaimed. "I'm about to wrap your guts around my sword and make kebobs!"

"Stacy, give that loudmouth something to chew on."

AngelCake took aim through a crack between the carts, drew back her sling and let fly. I heard the stone *thunk* dully against the leather armor. "-15 to Projectile Damage," I recalled, disheartened. If all their armor was like this, Stacy's slingshot would have little more than a psychological effect.

"Hey, what's your deal — jerk!" the voice squealed, confirming the hit.

I suppose if he wasn't a tank, even the attenuated damaged might sting. Healing took a long time here, after all.

"If you try to storm these stout walls, we'll take one or two of you down before you get to us," I said, finally peeking from behind the wall. "Who knows how it'll all play out after that. We have strength in numbers back here!"

"No need for heroics, Ratmir!" Lance stepped forward. "No matter how many, we'll tear through all of you like a flock of sheep!"

He hadn't changed a bit and neither had I. His forced bravado always made me wanna hurl.

"My name is TargetAi!" I retorted. "Get it right, you prim pretty-boy."

Yumi chuckled at this. It seemed any insult to Lance delighted her to know end. Considering what I'd witnessed in the bathroom, I wonder what he'd done to her.

"Fine, have it your way, TargetAi," Lance drawled lazily. "Now listen up, I've got a one-day special offer for you today: I'll spare your life if you help me. A girl of ours has run away. She's a rat and a traitor. She backstabbed one of us and ganked his gear. If you've got her, hand her over. I'll even let you keep the armor. I only want her. Give her up and we'll leave you alone."

Simba wiggled his eyebrows and gave me a thumbs up. AngelCake winked in agreement. Not a bad idea — hand over Yumi and part ways. All pros, no cons.

For her part, Yumi tensed up like a cornered animal. Even if she manages to fend us off, she'll have nowhere to run afterward. The quest timer had 20 minutes left on it. It was plenty of time to die. She had mentioned that Lance would deal with her gruesomely, and hearing Lance now, I believed her.

It sure wasn't pity that guided me then. After all, I'd slaughtered plenty defenseless players that day and had even killed prisoners without much hesitation. I clearly understood the difference between killing in VR and killing IRL, and yet I had no love for sadists. Most importantly, however, I didn't trust Lance one bit.

I was sure that if I sacrificed Yumi, we'd be next. Yet I had an ace up my sleeve and how it would play out, would determine everything.

"Yumi, no matter what happens, follow our lead, okay?" I instructed, waiting until she nodded in agreement.

I leaned in and whispered instructions to Stacy. She listened and smirked wickedly, clearly liking my plan.

"Hey, Lance!" I called out from behind the wall again. "Look here. Is this her?"

I gestured towards Stacy, who held Yumi out on display before her, a dagger to her throat.

"Were you planning to execute her or something?" I asked. "Well, you won't get her! Take two more steps our way, and AngelCake here will grant her a quick death. You won't get your sadistic thrill that way, Lance!"

I heard him growl in frustration. Lance loathed defiance.

"If you don't hand her over, I'll storm your garbage dump!" he screamed enraged. "I'll capture all of you alive, force-feed you your own testicles, then cut off your arms and legs. I'll watch you squirm like worms. We'll parade your girl with the slingshot right before your eyes! You'll suffer until the quest's last second and every minute will feel like an eternity!"

"He's lost it," Simba shook his head. "Total nutjob. Hopeless case."

"Do you want us, or your traitor?" I wondered aloud. "We're at an impasse. But if you really want her, I'll... sell her to you! A thousand coins!"

"Andrew!" Yumi twitched in AngelCake's grip. "You promised!"

"A thousand? That's how poor you are?" Lance laughed. "Fine, a thousand it is. Shugga will run to the store and convert it."

"I'll wait!" I shouted, taking cover.

Yumi sobbed.

"He's just stalling, you dummy," Simba consoled her. "While they run to the store and sell all their ill-gotten loot... We'll win five, maybe ten minutes."

"It won't save us though," AngelCake muttered.

She clearly didn't want to be paraded around. If it were up to her, Yumi would've been skinned by now.

"Notice how quickly he agreed?" I asked Simba.

"Uh-huh," he nodded. "Like he won't miss the money. He's planning to take it off of us anyway. You were right."

Simba knew business.

A skinny blue-haired player from Lance's party dashed off, leaving Lance and T-Rex.

My instinct told me that we should strike now. It was 4 vs. 2. They may have an advantage in levels, but Yumi managed to take one down after all! And yet no matter how I played out this scenario in my mind, it always turned out the same way: We would lose. Lance was a formidable fighter even when evenly-matched.

He didn't just have four levels on us, he was a seasoned veteran, a master of combat esports. I wouldn't be surprised if he purposely sent his man away to provoke us into attacking. So we simply cannot. Our only advantage lies in our hostage — and yet, the closer we get to the end of the quest, the less valuable she becomes.

We have 10 minutes tops. After that, they'll forsake all truces and storm in. And what then? Do we commit harakiri? It would be a fitting conclusion.

"WHERE'S MY ARMOR?"

At first, I thought I'd lost it. Large glowing letters appeared in all-caps over the gray stone wall, the overturned cart, and Simba's gloomy face. It was like augmented reality, like seeing a 3D movie.

Then it clicked. There's a chat feature in this game! You can communicate from afar, connect with anyone, without having to interact face-to-face.

Had I known this, choosing a rendezvous spot, hurrying to meet up with my team, and fearing for their fate would've looked completely differently.

"YOU PROMISED TO HAND OVER THE CARAPACE! WHERE IS IT? I'M WAITING!"

I mentally accessed the chat interface. All I had to do was focus on the chat function and think deliberately about wanting to use it.

"Are you Anna?" I asked.

"ARE YOU STUPID?" the chat responded.

Chapter 21

"Anna, I'm surrounded. I can't get to you."

"WUSS!"

I can't believe my eyes. Is this supposed to be sarcasm? In the next instant a simple idea forms in my mind. Sure, it's predictable, but you'd have to be an idiot not to take advantage of an opportunity like this.

"Maybe I am, but if they kill me, you won't get that armor."

She hesitates, probably weighing whether to waste time on me or indulge in some delightful slaughter elsewhere.

"WHERE ARE YOU?"

Bingo!

I quickly explain our location. Given how fast she is, she'll be here soon. We just need to buy some time.

"Listen Lance," I yell, "what did she do to you

anyway?"

"The witch fragged and robbed my friend!" replied Lance, fuming with righteous anger.

Well, there's no evidence that she did kill him. I've yet to encounter any friend lists, groups, or "living" counters in this game, so we could just as easily argue that Xavier found a new love and galloped away into the sunset. As the saying goes, "No body, no crime."

However, the robbery is evident. Xavier's stylish leather cuirass is now on me, while Simba flaunts another one just like it. Yumi cautiously peeks from behind the barricade. The evidence is clear.

"And how did she frag him?" I feign ignorance. "I mean, she's a Level 3 and he was a Level 6!"

"She seduced him!" Lance rambles. "She told Xavier that she loved him, then killed him for his top-tier gear."

Lance took my bait to talk man to man. He could've finished us off by now, but he felt the need to justify his righteousness. A clear case of Lawful Evil this one.

Shugga returned, and the chitchat ceased. The trio whispered among each other until Lance stepped forward again.

"I'll give you 350 coins for the bitch!" he declared. "Take it. It's better than nothing."

I squinted past him, delighted to know that my reply wouldn't matter anymore. A svelte figure was approaching us from the other side of the street.

Anna looked both magnificent and at the same time completely incredible in this gray medieval street. She was wearing dazzling white lace panties and a white corset that covered her waist, lifting her breasts and barely covering her nipples. Garter stockings and short white high-heeled boots completed the picture.

"Holy moly," groaned T-Rex.

Shugga's jaw just dropped mutely and only Lance, sensing something was off, drew his weapon.

"Guys, get ready, this is…"

But they ignored him.

"Are you here to see us, sweetheart?" asked T-Rex, who was the more talkative of their gang.

"You and only you," Anna smiled, thrusting her sword under his chin.

Oh, right! She had a sword! Oddly no one had noticed this earlier. Actually, she had two swords: a long katana and a short wakizashi. Defying all anatomical logic, the latter's blade emerged from the back of T-Rex's head. By his expression, he lived long enough to experience surprise. INSTAKILL!

It was my first time seeing a Level 6 get one-shotted. Then again, for a Level 17, it was a piece of cake. Anna didn't need to pull out the blade; her opponent vanished, leaving a gray loot heap on the ground.

Fluidly, she transitioned into a defensive stance. Lance and Shugga lunged at her from both sides, steel clashing. Shugga wielded a long sword, while Lance used twin daggers like Yumi.

Wouldn't the difference in levels let her to finish them both instantly? I soon realized Anna was merely toying with them. Dodging their thrusts and slashes, she was dancing to a rhythm I could discern: jagged, escalating.

Anna let them take the lead, studying their moves. I watched too, taking note for later.

Lance was skilled. Powerful, sharp, having honed his raw talents over years of VR dueling. A flawless defense paired with explosive attacks. Yet each strike missed; Anna was never there. She moved as if she were boneless, his blades grazing past her exposed body by mere millimeters.

Shugga's movements were more predictable. Eventually Anna grew bored and countered, sweeping his leg, and as he stumbled, slashing his throat with her katana.

"What the hell do you want here?!" Lance growled.

Anna didn't respond, she just smiled back. Her smile revealed fangs, as if she was ready to sink them into a victim. Maybe I'm twisted, but in that moment, I was completely captivated by her.

It's hard to imagine how, but Lance went faster. In a desperate attack, pushing his limits, he tried to strike Anna and...

Smack! With a stylish sweep, Anna knocked him off his feet, and Lance crashed hard to the ground. With one foot, she kicked the dagger out of his hand, with the other she stepped on his wrist and brought the edge of her katana to his throat.

"Not bad," Anna remarked, "I enjoyed that. Can't wait till the next time I get to kill you again."

A light figure in newbie clothes darted between us. Yumi wriggled free from Stacy and charged at Lance.

"He's mine!" she shrieked. "Let me kill this bastard!"

Smack! Anna barely moved, but her heel found its mark on Yumi's chest, sending her flying to the ground.

"Why should he be yours?" Anna looked at Yumi with curiosity, as if she was an insect that had suddenly begun to speak.

"This asshole looked the other way while his friends raped me," Yumi cried. "I endured all of it for... for him! Fearing he'd think less of me! And then what?!"

I saw Lance' eyes widen. What, he didn't know? Seriously?!

"Oh, what drama!" Anna feigned wiping a tear. "Sorry, girly. XP is XP. Sometimes it's painful, sometimes... it's Yumi."

She pressed slightly on the katana, Lance emitted a faint gurgling sound and turned to loot. Anna froze... squinted, her nostrils flared wide, and the number above her head turned to 18.

Anna stood motionless, if only for a brief moment, savoring the new level she had attained. Then she stretched like a cat, opened her eyes, and fixed her gaze on Yumi.

The latter instantly lost any desire to cry or

protest. Scrambling her ass on the pavement, she began to shuffle away towards the wall.

"I'll save you," Anna smirked, "from your suffering."

I had heard that a wakizashi could be thrown, but this was the first time I had seen it in action. The short blade struck Yumi in the chest. She coughed, choked on blood, and disappeared.

Good thing I took all the armor from her, was my initial thought.

"I see two more over there," Anna advanced, swinging her hips as if on a catwalk.

My gaze involuntarily dropped to her chest, then lower... A deadly trap for any guy. There are fewer female fighters after all, right?

"Hey, wait!" I stepped forward. "This is between you and me."

"So?" Anna genuinely didn't get it. "My deal was only with you."

Simba and AngelCake had already climbed over the barricade to join the conversation. They were shocked when the approaching monster actually stopped to talk to us, rather than causing mayhem like last time.

"Come on, don't be greedy," I exclaimed. "I could have just sold this thing at the store and ignored our deal. But I want to give it back to you, if anything to see gratitude in those pretty eyes of yours."

Anna snorted, unimpressed by my compliment about her eyes. She's an odd girl. Atypical. If anything, in the sense that others would be too shy to wear an outfit like that. But for her, results are all that mattered. Get distracted by her lace-covered curves for even a second, and it's game over.

To become both bait and hunter is a masterstroke. As for the rest, I'm sure her corset is as protective as my armor. "It's all just an illusion, Neo." It takes longer than three days to adjust yourself to virtual reality. I don't know how long it takes, but three days isn't enough.

"Why shouldn't I kill you right now?" she asked. "Or your friends?"

"Pride won't let you," I shrugged. "It wouldn't be fair for one and it wouldn't be interesting either. If you kill my friends now, I won't give you anything willingly. Either wipe us all out or none at all."

"You're a dumbass," Anna scoffed. "You believe in playing by the rules. She also always plays by the rules," she looked around mysteriously, "But she sets the rules herself. That's why she never loses."

"So, do we have a deal?" I asked, ignoring her rambling.

Anna pondered for a few seconds.

"Fine, I won't harm the three of you. But we're not even. Next time, I'll get a taste of you." She grinned, baring her teeth.

I wanted to make a flirty comeback but realized it might not be the best time. She might forget our agreement, and I'd be left picking up my guts from the pavement. Instead, I nodded, pulled out the odd item from my inventory, and handed it to Anna.

"Take it."

Simba's curiosity overcame his survival instinct. He had been eavesdropping on our conversation and, realizing that it was no longer dangerous, now came up to us. Anna was trying to store the loot from Lance's team into her inventory, but it kept falling out.

"Reached you limit?" Simba sympathized. "Want to make a run to the store? We'll watch it for you."

Anna looked at him, astonished, tried to pick up the loot a few more times, and grumbled, "No time. The quest will end soon."

Indeed, the timer was counting down the final minutes. There was still time to reach the merchant, but returning seemed unlikely.

"How about we carry it for you?" Simba went on in a friendly tone. "Or we can simply take it and pay you back later! Market value in cash! You'll save time and make money!"

"If you're lying, you're dead meat!" Anna twirled a katana under Simba's nose.

"I wouldn't dream of it," Simba replied, flashing his most sincere smile.

It was the same expression he'd use when peddling cheap airpods from Temu to girls in his class, claiming they were "better than the original."

Anna shot each of us a withering look, then turned and walked off into the sunset without even saying goodbye. Well, it's not like I planned to have kids with her or anything...

"What was that act of unprompted generosity all about?" I asked Simba. "What's your angle?"

"She told you straight up, dummy," Simba shook his head. "Didn't you see the prices the store offered? It's buy at one price, sell for half. So, what do we owe her? Right, the selling price... So basically, we got this here gear at half price and on credit. She'll still have to find us if she wants to get paid!"

"You should be our business manager, Simba," I exclaimed, impressed. "Let's gather our loot."

And so it was in perfect calm that we spent the remaining few minutes of the day's quest: picking up weapons, trying on gear, and figuring out how much money we owed to our sultry creditor.

Since Simba was our tank, he got first dibs on the loot and chose Shugga's gear: A sturdy round shield, a Carolingian longsword, and even a lightweight steel chainmail. I kept Xavier's armor, while AngelCake donned the leather armor that T-Rex had dropped.

In the midst of this, Simba remarked that AngelCake looked just as good in black leather as Anna did, but all three of us knew he was just blowing smoke.

3... 2... 1...

I came out of the game calmly enough, but pure chaos awaited me in the real world. As soon as the pod's lid slid open, I found four pairs of eyes staring at me: two security guards armed with tasers, Sergio the technician armed with a roll of gauze and a frightened nurse armed with a syringe.

"Hey, what's this now?" I blurted out.

What if the gig was up, the fat lady had sung, and the staff had been ordered to terminate all the beta testers to keep the cat in the bag?

"You looking for a fight?" Sergio squinted at me suspiciously.

"No, not at all." I shook my head for emphasis. "What's going on out here?"

I made sure not to make any sudden movements.

"It's utter bedlam," Sergio declared.

The others nodded in agreement, as a neighboring pod began to hiss open. Everyone rushed towards it, leaving me under the watchful eye of the nurse.

She brandished her syringe menacingly in my face, while rattling off the events of the past hour-and-a-half. No sooner had the round begun — and with it the massacre in the town square — than the VR pods began opening and fragged beta testers began to climb out of them. The first ones were calm enough — a few wept, others tried to hide their tears — but the next wave was much more aggressive. They attacked each other, got into fistfights, choked each other and bit each other... At that point security and medical staff were called into the VR halls.

By the time the slow-witted engineers reported what the day's quest objectives were to management, pandemonium reigned everywhere. Victims searched for their killers to vent their fear and frustration at being eliminated. There wasn't enough security, so they started locking down the pods. The testers inside the locked pods began panicking and breaking out from inside. By the time more security arrived, several pods had been smashed to bits.

No one required urgent medical care, although for some reason one of the male testers made his way into the women's VR hall and was rewarded with a hefty beating for his efforts.

As for me, I calmly climb out of my pod and throw on my robe beneath the nurse's watchful gaze. I've definitely become far less shy over the last few days.

Trouble is waiting for me right outside the VR hall.

Woosh! Lance's fist glides past my hair, as I barely duck in time... Immediately, without hesitating or coming back up, I punch him in the stomach quick and hard...

Womp! Lance bends over, gasping for air. Out here in meatspace, he and I have the same stats, yet I've seen many more fights than this pampered brat.

Next, I duck a haymaker from Shugga and then...

"Raaaah!" Simba comes up from behind like a linebacker and tackles Shugga to the ground.

The impact is painful to hear.

I'm left one on one with T-Rex. Under his pink bangs his eyes are filled with fear. It's clear he's never been belted in the face before and the mere fear of it has taken the fight out of him.

Security rushes over… they pull us apart…

"I'll find you, bastard!" Lance growls. "You'll die again and again at my hands!"

"Oh come off it. Your entire pro team got ganked by a couple girls," I laugh in response. "You're not ready for a real man!"

I'm not as cheerful inside, however. I've gained as many problems as triumphs today.

Security escorts me to my locker room under close guard. The two guards are polite but they don't allow me to wander off or talk to anyone.

I don't particularly mind. Fatigue hits me hard again, and I just want to shower, eat, and sleep for a couple of hours. And then think… think… think… While I was doing my best to survive in there, others were leveling up. A miracle saved me this time, but I can't always count on that.

The shower washed over me like rain after a long drought. I stood there, soaking, sighing, and just enjoying the water's warmth and repose.

At that moment, there was a hard knock on the door. It wasn't a gentle or polite knocking, but forceful, verging on pounding. Thankfully, whoever it was didn't barge in. I noticed once again that there was no bolt on the door.

This was peculiar. Random people couldn't be

wandering the halls at the moment. So, I wasn't worried about Lance and his crew. At the same time, I doubt security would let AngelCake come see me with her pastries. Only one possibility remained and I guessed it on the nose.

"The fuck did you stand up for that slut for?!" Marina stormed in raging.

I'd never seen her this furious. Even when Simba and AngelCake had spoiled her plans, Marina just pursed her lips and narrowed her eyes. Now, she was spitting fire.

"What?" I asked, taken aback.

"What do you need with her dead weight?" Marina went on. "You've surrounded yourself with nothing but floozies! One of them has tits big enough to smother you and whenever the other one opens her mouth, you can see the back of her head. Are you planning to start a brothel in there or what? Eek!"

The "eek" came out when she realized that I was naked. Completely and entirely naked. That's what a changing room is for — getting dressed and undressed and dressed again. So I had emerged from my shower without taking any precautions. Not to mention, that the last three days had given me a good deal of boldness.

She looked so good in that instant — all flushed, her hair undone, her chest heaving from the emotions that had overcome her, her little mouth a little open, ready to accuse me of some further infidelity.

Seeking to stop this torrent of loud and

senseless words, I pressed her to the wall with my body and stilled her lips with mine.

"Ooof..." Marina exhaled after a long and substantial kiss. "Let me go... You're getting me all wet..."

"Will you run if I do?"

"I was just gonna lock the door."

So there is a way to lock it?!

CHAPTER 22

I HAVE NEVER HAD SEX in the shower before. To be honest, it looks different in the movies. More romantic, perhaps. In real life the shower stall is quite slippery, very cramped, and the running water is more annoying than soothing, constantly getting into your mouth, nose and eyes. I might not have even enjoyed it at all if it weren't for Marina.

Marina's body was flawless. I have only seen such girls in glossy magazines or very expensive porn films. Her skin was completely covered with an even golden tan. Where other girls would have traces of their bras or panties, here everything was perfect.

I couldn't stop thinking about where she managed to sunbathe completely naked in winter, and how much I'd love to see her do it.

Marina was indeed more experienced than

me, but any insecurities I had about that vanished as soon as she knelt in front of me in the cramped shower stall and looked up at me as if she had dreamed of me all her life and wanted me with every inch of her body.

This one look of hers sent me into a frenzy. The blood drained from my head downwards, immobilizing me entirely, while my dick almost groaned from the tension.

Seeing my reaction, Marina flicked her deft pink tongue and began to tease me with it, looking up flirtatiously. Damn, she wanted to drive me into some state of madness and she had achieved her goal.

I tried to pull her towards me, but she didn't let me and went on rubbing her lips, cheeks, and nose against my throbbing cock. I bent my head back to distract myself at least a little to keep from coming right then and there.

Then she began to kiss her way up my stomach and chest, and I felt her stiff, erect nipples rasping against my skin. Her skin smelled of flowers and spices and this aroma only grew stronger as she rose to eye level.

She stood before me in the cramped shower stall, under the streams of water, pressing her whole body against mine, looking into my eyes, and the desire to possess this teasing bitch zapped me like an electric current.

To fuck her... to possess her... to subjugate her... to bridle her like a disobedient mare. I deftly grabbed her under her hips and lifted her against the wall, sitting her down on my cock.

She yelped... again and again, until I pressed my mouth against her mouth to silence her. In turn she kissed me madly, sucking and biting my lip until I tasted blood. It was as if wherever our bodies touched, we had merged into one...

Marina locked her legs behind my back. I pressed her back against the wall and lifted her over and over again, pile driving her ever further onto my cock.

"That's it, bitch... Take it, bitch... Do you like it, bitch?" I repeated like crazy.

The streams of water lashing my back distracted me enough to keep me from coming, yet kept me on the very edge. Suddenly Marina began to thrash in my arms, lowing loudly... I almost started to worry until I realized that she was orgasming violently.

"Oh my..." she said, sliding off and getting to her legs shakily. She turned to me, exposing her neat round ass, and began to slowly sway her hips, slightly rising on her toes, first with one leg, then with the other. I grabbed her by the waist, pulling her towards me and entering, this time from behind.

"Mmmmm... Yes!" Marina moaned. "Fuckin' amazing..."

She pressed her palms against the wall, bending over so that my dick felt cramped and hot inside of her. I thrust, feeling the head rubbing inside, butting up against something.

"Yessss..." I couldn't take it anymore. The

tension was growing. A tickling ascended from my groin up my spine and exploded in my brain...

"No need to treat me with kids gloves... I'm not made of glass you know... Pull my hair... Do whatever you like..."

I felt like a student, but I studied diligently and willingly. I ran my fingers through Marina's hair, clenched and pulled her towards me. I saw her crazed eyes, her lips half open in a moan...

"Aaaaaaah..." she moaned deeply and protractedly as I came inside of her and she clenched my cock as if milking me to the last drop.

I couldn't resist and forgot to pull out. I guess my fear was written all over my face.

"Don't worry, you won't be a dad..." Marina grinned, and it didn't sound evil, but on the contrary, somehow caring. "I'm on the pill."

Jealousy instantly adulterated my relief. Since Marina takes birth control, it means I'm not the only one. And why did I even assume that there would be more to this than just this?

Dull, senseless jealousy for a girl I didn't even consider mine. Even AngelCake seemed dearer to me somehow. And yet, I didn't want to let this ice cold blonde, who was clearly out of my league, go.

But the PR girl was in no hurry to leave, or even get dressed. We relaxed, lying on the couch. Marina somehow settled so deftly and comfortably on my chest that we were not at all cramped. I fingered her hair, and she drew patterns on my chest with a sharp nail. It seems that for some time I even fell asleep.

I'm back in the gladiator arena. Like a ghost I watch myself plunge my broken katana straight into Lance's throat. Crit! Again and again... Crit! Crit! I stab like a madman, pressing down on my victim until I'm the only one left, standing alone in the arena's sand. Lance's been eliminated. I am victorious.

As soon as I step out of my VR pod, Lance barges into the locker room. He's skinny and ungainly and extremely pale. Large ginger freckles spot his shoulders.

"Freak!" he screams at me. "That was so unfair, freak!!! That win was mine!!! That was my trophy!!!"

"Get the fuck away from me!" I shove him. "You died, so you lost!"

Lance shoves me, almost knocking me down. I catch my balance and jab him in the nose. It's not a strong jab, but it's precise. Lance's patrician nose crumples. Blood splatters on the floor and on my robe. People rush into the locker room, coaches and other players. They grab me, holding me even though I'm not resisting. Lance is led away...

Suddenly, I snap back to reality. Marina purrs beside me.

"If I'd known that this is what you're like," she smiles, "I wouldn't have wasted three days and snagged you back in your bedroom."

"Oh? So what am I like?" I ask, curious.

"Promising," Marina laughs. "Let's just say VR gaming isn't your only talent."

She stretches playfully, caressing me with her

entire body, pressing closer to me.

It feels good — even if she's lying a hundred times over — even if she has ulterior, darker motives — it's nice to listen to her lying here beside her.

I admire her, run my fingertips over her tummy, thigh...

"How soft your skin is..." I say banally.

I want to tell her platitudes, sweet nothings, and hear the same in turn from her.

"It's all cash money, baby... Cash money. Youth... Beauty... Comfort... Tasty food... Girls like me," Marina snorts with a laugh. "This is the world cash money buys you. And you're right there on the doorstep. Don't fuck it up, don't slip, and you'll be set for life."

"Do you think I'm fucking it up?" I asked what was most on my mind.

"Mmm... That's a serious conversation. Let's not mix business and pleasure." Marina stood up abruptly, her titties swaying in front of my nose. "Let's get out of here. I'll take you out. You've been laboring so hard as of late, all you know is work, work, work..." She giggled again.

The crowded hallways had thinned out. I don't know how much time had passed. I'd completely lost track of it. Glancing at my phone, I saw that an hour had elapsed. I had two missed calls from Simba, both forty minutes ago. Probably waiting for me after the end of the round. I had five more missed calls from an unknown number. A hunch told me it was AngelCake. And two from my mom, who had also sent a text: *"I'm worried."* What a model son I am: I haven't been home in a day and I haven't even bothered to check in.

I immediately replied to her: *"I'm at the university. Everything's fine. I'll be home soon."* It was a lie, of course, but it would reassure her.

To welcome the first snow of the year, Marina wore a short mink coat with a fur hood and high boots. Emerging from her office, she took hold of my hand firmly.

"Aren't you cold in that jacket?" she asked. "It's not the season for it. And it looks a bit tacky." She wrinkled her nose in distaste.

To keep from freezing, I had layered my autumn leather jacket over a thick sweater. I could hardly bend my elbows and I walked around like a hockey player or a knight in armor. Oddly, however, Marina's taunts no longer irked me, bouncing off like dull arrows.

I recalled what the Master had said at our first meeting. I had acquired Marina as a badge of honor to my status and was now enjoying the perks.

"The cold doesn't bother me."

This time around, I was handed the cash envelope posthaste. No one even ask for my last name. All I had to do was sign. The girl from yesterday was gone and the others were eyeing Marina warily.

Marina's boots slipped desperately on the stairs and she grabbed hold of me again. Or maybe this was just a sly ruse to remind me of her presence. The guards watched us pass and it seemed to me that they knew that I wasn't merely walking with this girl. No, no — I FUCKED HER! AND I WILL FUCK AGAIN AND AGAIN! SHE'S NOT GOING ANYWHERE!

I thought she would take me home, but we went to a café instead. Or maybe it was a restaurant, I'm not sure. A modest sign that read *Vinum et Pasta* hung above an inconspicuous entrance. I wouldn't have entered such a place myself, and I was amazed to find a luxurious dining hall inside, well-trained waiters, and the intoxicating aroma of fried meat, garlic, oregano, and something incredibly delicious.

"Do you even know how to cook?" I asked Marina.

"Why should I?" The girl skillfully twisted spaghetti onto her fork, spinning it against a spoon.

She had ordered an enormous plate of seafood pasta and was now devouring it with gusto.

"What guy would marry you?" I shook my head.

"Pfff, who needs any of youse guys anyways?" Marina rolled her eyes, still chewing. "I'm happy the way I am."

At first, I thought the PR girl had just decided to expunge the debt that the Master had saddled her with. Yet her enchantment hadn't ended there. Marina still acted as if I were the most interesting man on Earth, or at least in the city.

It was like "mind control spells" from fantasy books. I may not have known the reason for it, but I sure was enjoying the results, especially in this new form, where I could tease her to my heart's content.

"You'll die an old spinster surrounded by cats."

"Pfff... With cash money in the bank though. Or I'll marry a hot gymnast at fifty."

"At fifty, they won't even look at you!"

"I'll look better at fifty than your busty milkmaid does now!" Marina declared.

"Mine? Mine? Who said that?" I distanced myself from AngelCake.

"You think I don't know you're screwing her?" Marina laughed. "Remember, sweetie, women see through that shit straight away."

"Jealous much, m'crone?"

"Pfff... That's hardly someone to be jealous of," the blonde stuck up her nose. "What's your affliction anyway? Spermtoxicosis? You've got to get your spunk out by any means? That's treatable with regular procedures you know." She licked her lips demonstratively. "It's like you found the winning lottery ticket and are now blowing your millions before you claimed them."

They had just brought me a huge schnitzel, covering the whole plate with a pile of vegetables in a spicy creamy sauce and tiny fried round potatoes. I eagerly stuffed my mouth, taking advantage of the opportunity not to respond. Marina was in a talkative mood.

"Girls like her are always... The best word that comes to mind is 'troubled.' They're troubled. Some trouble is always happening to them: their phone breaks, they lose their purse, their moms get sick, they have nowhere to spend the night... They are very appealing to boys of a certain age. It's very convenient to save them, to protect them, to be a hero." Marina narrowed her eyes and flourished her fork. "But their troubles never end. They only multiply, until you're no longer thinking about your own goals and only thinking about how to get them out of the next mess they've created for you."

"Is Stacy like that?" I asked in surprise. "She brought me some pastries, by the way. Homemade ones, unlike the ones you got me."

"Uh-huh. She made you pastries after she killed you in-game." Marina snorted. "And then you have to save her from the rapists... She found herself a simp, so she whipped up a picnic and then used that as a way to get with you."

"What do you get from all of this anyway, Marina?" I asked directly. "You'll never convince me that you're doing all this out of the goodness of your heart."

"You're wrong," Marina pouted. "I like you. Especially after today..." She gazed at me seductively, like a cat.

"Marina..."

"Oh, come on!" She playfully puckered her lips and immediately became serious. "Did you check your envelope?"

"Where is it?" I didn't immediately grasp what she was talking about and started patting my pockets.

I found the envelope in my jeans, folded in half and crumpled. I took it out, opened it, and laid out ten bills of five hundred euros each. That was my mom's yearly salary. Or was it more?!

"The stakes are getting higher, Andryusha." Marina even stood up a little, leaning towards me across the table, and making me gulp as I stared right at her breasts framed in her blouse's neckline.

"And you don't even know what the prize money will be for the final round," Marina continued. "And I don't know either," she admitted easily. "But it will be fucking amazing. And if you think you're the only favorite, you're mistaken. There's Lance and there's your new girlfriend's fucktoy, Xavier. There's just 12 players left now. A dozen. You used to be at the top but you're almost at the bottom now."

"Why?!" I was shocked.

I thought I had done pretty well in the last round of the beta. I had kept my party alive and I got the equipment I wanted.

"You were saved by a miracle!" Marina started freaking out again. "You almost didn't get the level you needed! The top player in your party earned all her XP by sitting on dicks. What the hell did you take that floozy on for? And don't bullshit me about the benefits. You should have fragged her and been done with it Did you feel sorry for her?

Are you going to save her from herself? Make a decent woman out of her?"

Caught up in her emotions, the PR girl dropped her fork and dove under the table to retrieve it, giving me a chance to speak.

"Marina, who the hell do you think you are? The fuck would I report to you for?"

I don't like it when people shout at me.

"Think of it like I've made a bet on you," Marina replied, albeit more softly. "Ever since I first brought you to the Master, I realized that you didn't get this far by chance. The Master doesn't make mistakes about people. He saw something in you. And that's as good as insider information. Invest a buck today, get a million back next week."

Now this is a Marina I can believe. Cunning, cynical, and no less beautiful for it. It was odd but until that day, I had thought of her just another attractive girl; now, however, a single look from her made me swoon like strong booze.

"I propose an alliance," Marina said. "A business partnership. You once said we're in the same boat, and now I'm saying the same thing."

At the same time, I felt something touch me down below the table. Her quick little foot slid along my thigh, reached my groin, and started rubbing my fly.

A partnership?! Well what do I have to lose anyway? All I can do is gain by it. My partner would have access to the highest offices; she would be an advisor who understood the laws of these byzantine corporate jungles; a confidant behind the scenes of this experiment; and, of course, the amazing sex, let's not forget the amazing sex. It's hard to think about anything else when her foot is having its way with my crotch.

"Partners?" I extended my trembling hand to her.

The PR girl smiled and deftly withdrew her foot, jumped up from the table, took me by the hand, and led me into the back of the restaurant. A passage behind the curtain led to two doors with human-shaped signs. Even the bathrooms in this place were fancier than in most apartments: dark marble floors and walls, a golden faucet on the sink, a shiny black toilet.

Marina lowered the lid and sat on top of it, unzipping my fly, she began to furiously jerk my penis with her palm, swallowing it deeply from time to time.

"Partners," she said, smacking her lips. "You're the champ, you're the GOAT, you're the Alpha and you will be number one."

"Yaaah... Fuckin' Aaay!" My brain exploded from her fingers and her mouth and her words.

"Those other phony hating bitches can get fucked!"

"They can get fucked!" I agreed.

"And that dipshit along with them," Marina went on. "That mooch of yours, Simon... He's holding you back... There's only one champ!"

CHAPTER 23

"THERE'S ONLY ONE champ!"

These words pushed me over the edge. Marina noticed, wrapped her lips around my cock, and I nutted in her mouth.

"Aaah…" I wheezed. "Goddamn…"

Marina smiled slyly, smacked her lips, deftly returned everything to its place and zipped up my fly. She stood up casually and walked over to the washbasin. The water began to gurgle.

I stood there feeling happy, but also somehow empty. It's as if I just signed a deal with the devil. And he signed with his own dick, uh-huh. But why am I worried? Who actually got screwed here anyway?! I walked up to Marina, who was leaning slightly over the sink and diligently washing her sleek hands, looked over her reflection in the mirror and tightly smacked her ass with my hand.

Smack!

"Eek! What the...?!" Marina started in surprise.

"Let's go finish our food, pardner," I said without removing my hand. "It'll get cold. Obviously you already got your dessert... But I want some ice cream."

"You jerk!" The PR maven turned around and indignantly punched me in the shoulder with her little fist. "You're full of yourself! An impudent jerk!"

That's the feeling! Now I feel good!

Dessert was already on the table when we returned: some fruit concoction for her, and apple pie a la mode for me. The restaurant was empty; it was too late for lunch and too early for dinner, so all the waitstaff's attention was focused on us. Undivided attention. A couple in aprons — a guy and a girl — stood by the counter, eyeing us. Maybe it was a sign of their dedication or maybe they'd noticed the euros in my hand and were now showing off for tips.

I wondered who they've taken me for? A sugar daddy, maybe? Or perhaps a mercenary or a secret agent? A beautiful companion... An envelope of cash money... I leaned back and smiled. The waiters smiled back. They definitely wanted a tip.

"Marina, you said you didn't understand online games," I reminded her.

"I really don't," Marina agreed easily.

"So, how can you advise me on anything?"

"But I do understand team building, benchmarking, self-realization, and many other scary words," said Marina, picking pieces of fruit from the syrup and skillfully depositing them into her mouth. "All those dreadful corporate voodoos tell me that you're messing up big time. Look at Lance. His whole team's focused on efficiency. The other leaders are all solos. You're falling behind them in levels. Soon, you'll reach the point of no return and fall behind permanently. It's not me saying this, it's the analysts. I have access to the right offices and reports. If you don't get rid of the dead weight, you'll..."

"Who is Anna?" I interrupted her.

Marina understood me correctly. She didn't argue or insist on finishing her pompous speech. Instead, she carefully wiped her fingertips with a napkin, pulled a tablet out of her capacious bag, and squinted into it.

"Anna Falk, born in Switzerland, parents unknown. Age: 20. Citizenship: Germany. Entered the VR Gladiator Games at the age of 12. At sixteen, she made the EU's Top 10 Gladiators list," Marina raised her eyes. "You know, she's the only VIP who asked to join the beta. I had to cajole all the others for over a month. They all have training, tournaments, interviews," she frowned. "Of course, I accepted her offer immediately. Her name's well known. My only concern was that she didn't speak Russian. But it seems she can do that too."

"She knows Russian at least as well as I do," I remarked. "And did you know what your 'German citizen' calls our Master?"

"What?" asked Marina, startled.

"Uncle Eli."

"Seriously?!" Marina's eyes widened like saucers.

"Oh yeah," I nodded. "Saw it myself."

How about that, pardner? Which one of us has been hanging out in the executive offices more?

"You should find out more about the relationship between them," I said. "You understand the world of big money much better than I do." And to myself, I added, *"Earn your place, pardner. Put some work in before you spout off advice."*

However, Marina's tirade did make me think. Until now, I had been drifting along, like none of this was actually happening to me — like it was all an amusing dumbshow. Money... restaurants... corporations... fights... girls. It was as if I had been plucked from one life and thrust into another. It was high time I learned to swim in here, lest I end up drowning.

Marina poked around on her tablet for a bit, then set it aside and pulled out her smartphone.

"Yes darling, I saw your photos... Is that the Maldives?... Oh, Seychelles... Fabulous!... Tell me, are you still in the same place as in the pictures?... Yes, I want to steal you for coffee and pastries... and ask about the diving... Yes, yes, I'm planning to... Mmm... The main thing is to choose an instructor?... Ahahaha..." Marina rolled her eyes. "Well, you'll tell me, and I'll come by and pick you up! Ciao!"

She hung up with a look of disgust.

"I can't stand her. Do you see what I'm willing to do for you?"

"Not for me, but for our partnership," I corrected. "And one more thing, do you think they sell cakes here?"

"If they don't, I'll have them bake one specially for us," Marina declared and snapped her fingers, signaling the waiter.

* * *

"Mrs. Severyanova, I brought you a cake with my apologies!" Marina entered my apartment with a radiant smile and handed the cake to my astonished mother. "Please forgive me for keeping your Andrew away all day. Here he is now. I'm returning him safe and sound."

"Come in, come in... I'll put the kettle on now... Oh, how unexpected..." My mother grew flustered and rushed to the kitchen.

I took Marina's coat, hung it in the closet, and even found slippers for the PR girl. I can be quite considerate when I want to be.

"Hi, Mom!" I called out into the empty hallway, but it seemed like she'd forgotten all about me, occupied with her dazzling guest.

By the time I washed my hands, an idyllic scene had unfurled itself in our kitchen. My mother was setting the "guest" porcelain tea set on the table, while Marina was cutting an angel cake and plating the slices.

"I came here for a reason, Mrs. Severyanova," Marina began when the hustle and bustle subsided and everyone finally settled at the table.

"What reason is that Marinochka?" my mother asked anxiously.

"Our company wants to recruit your son," the PR maven said enthusiastically. "We really need someone like him, a sociologist with knowledge of computer games. He'll be working right in my department."

"We haven't agreed on anything yet..." I said.

"Andrew, hush!" my mother interrupted me. "You go on, Marinochka. Don't mind my stubborn son. He's very talented, but he's also principled."

"You can see for yourself!" Marina exclaimed, throwing up her hands. "He won't agree no matter what. He says, 'I have university, I won't have time.' And yet hands on experience is what counts in this job. Plus, he can start in a learning role for now... We'll help him. There's so much work ahead. And then he can transfer to distance learning in his university — what difference does all that make when he already has a career?"

"Here's your tea, Marinochka, it's steeped," my mother poured tea into the porcelain teacups, listening intently.

She was already imagining my brilliant career alongside this wonderful girl. She didn't ask about what position they were offering me, the salary, or what I would be doing... I guess this is how snakeoil salesmen and other conmen swindle their victims — over chitchat, tea and smiles.

"Mom, you said yourself I need to finish my studies," I interjected again.

"Well, you can see for yourself, the company will take care of everything, help with everything..." My mother was so decisively on the side of the PR maven that all further discussion seemed futile. "Just keep an eye on my Andryusha here. He's so direct that he could make a mess of things without meaning to."

"Don't worry, Mrs. Severyanova, he will be working directly under my supervision," Marina declared triumphantly, looking at me.

"And one more thing... They already gave me my sign-on bonus." I handed my mother the envelope. "It's like a welcome gift."

My mother opened the envelope and froze. She probably hadn't seen this much cash in her entire life. We had stopped at a currency exchange and converted the euros into good old fashioned rubles. I could have had them transferred directly to a card, but the effect would certainly not have been the same.

My mother counted the five-thousand-ruble bills, lost count, and started again. Even I was taken aback by the realization that I could earn enough for a used car in just one-and-a-half hours. Until now, I had seen the money as just numbers with zeros — colorful bills with stars and squares.

My mother didn't look up, even when Marina said goodbye to her and slipped away from the table — under the guise of having work to do. She just nodded in response and continued arranging the bills in stacks. Rent... loans... food... something else. She seemed to be suffering from slight shock. I'm afraid if I had brought this money myself and laid it out in front of her, she would have called the police out of fear that I had stolen it.

In the hallway, Marina patted me on my crotch and I gave her a light tap on the rear. That was the extent of our tender farewell. Leaving my mother to finish her cake and contemplate her new financial situation, I went to the stairwell, climbed the rickety stairs and found myself on my old weather-beaten rooftop.

Simba answered on the first ring, as if he had been holding the phone in his hand.

"Where are you?" My buddy asked as directly as always.

That's the very first question you should ask someone who's gone off the grid. If everything's fine, there will be time to talk about it later. If things are bad, there's no reason to delve into the hows or whys.

"The usual spot. Come on by."

While I waited, I untangled the knots in my cord and plugged in my earphones. Should I buy an iPhone now? I'm rich. As long as it wasn't from Simba! I know much too well where he gets his gadgets. Or should I hit up a fancy store, where rich kids buy all their stuff to fit in with the other rich kids?

"We can discuss tactics when we're all together. Otherwise, why repeat ourselves?" Simba suggested. "The girls decided to throw a housewarming party and we're invited. The four of us can talk there."

"Wow, uh, they're roommates?" I said surprised. "I thought they hated each other..."

In the game, when they first met, AngelCake was staring at Yumi like she was the enemy of the people. Given the chance, I was sure she'd have taken her out without a second thought.

"Well, that Xavier creep broke into the women's VR hall and started pestering Yumi," Simba chuckled. "So, Stacy beat his ass until security eventually pulled her off of him. She won't let Yumi out of her sight now. And with today's cash, they decided to rent a place together and already found one. It's not hard when you have the loot."

"*So they pay the others less than me,*" I thought to myself. Marina had told the truth then. The company brass were placing their bets on me, feeding me money, and steering me in the right direction. And yet they'd judge me based on my results and those were dismal at the moment.

"Simba, do we really know them well enough to let them in on our plans?" I asked. "We've known AngelCake like three days, and Yumi not much longer if you count by the clock, and even less in practice. Are you sure we can trust them?"

"How could we not?" Simon said with surprise. "We're a team."

How can I make it clear to him? "*So long, Simba, I'm going solo*" or "*There can only be one champion, you know...*" He's an entrepreneur by nature, cunning and shrewd, but he's also as naive as a toddler in matters like these. I don't want to part ways with Simba in the game. Logic tells me that the best way to move forward is solo, but my intuition screams the opposite. He's the only person in the game I can trust. That's worth something. But when it comes to the girls, we need to set some tough conditions: Either they have to earn their spot on the team, or out they go.

Dirty thoughts about how they would "earn their spot" immediately began popping into my mind. Well, one was definitely on board, and I think the other wouldn't mind either, but I needed something else from them. I have someone to have sex with now. Although... AngelCake's titties briefly eclipsed my other thoughts. Marina is beautiful, of course... but the way that Stacy moans and smacks her lips... Damn! Let's get back to the strategy.

"Simba, how do you think Anna reached such high levels?" I changed the subject.

I love doing this, throwing a topic at someone and listening to their thoughts from the side. Usually, everything they say turns out to be complete crap, but my brain gets fresh energy and finds a solution. Simba was perfect for this, he could discuss any topic at length and with gusto.

"She leveled up on players," Simon answered immediately. "You saw it yourself, she leveled up in front of us."

"Only after she fragged two Level 7s," I countered. "How many Level 7s do you think are at all in the game?"

"Fuck if I know," Simba shrugged. "Maybe not Level 7s, but something smaller? She went on a rampage. Did you see how she swung those blades?"

"She was Level 15 during the last round, remember?" I said.

"Nope, I barely saw her that time." Simba finally calmed down and sat beside me. "There was a flash and then a YOU HAVE DIED message."

"There weren't any high-level players at all back then," I mused aloud. "Everyone was farming spiders. Even she was taking down Level 2 or Level 3 elites… It still doesn't make sense.

I recalled the house we had cleared of spiders. The second floor was full of cocoons. Dozens, maybe hundreds of tiny spiderlings, each bringing experience points. And there was that strange room doused in spider blood.

"There was a boss in that house," I continued. "A real raid boss. I don't know what level it was, but it was seriously powerful. Like a queen bee or an ant colony queen, but for spiders. The house was recently infested. The new brood had just moved in."

"How would Anna know this though?" Simba asked.

He seemed persuaded right away, and I found myself increasingly fond of my idea. Everything fit:

the girl's insanely high level, the mysterious carapace — everything we'd seen in that house.

"Maybe she got lucky, or maybe she knew what to look for. She seems to know way too much about this game in general."

"How do you even know her?" Simba asked. "You guys didn't just meet in the game."

"We've crossed paths at tournaments before," I lied for some reason.

Otherwise, I would have to tell him the whole story of my acquaintance with the Master, my interaction with Marina... I trusted Simon, of course, but once two people know something, there's a good chance the pig knows it too.

Simba realized that I was holding something back, but he didn't press further. Instead, he suggested, "So then let's put together a raid and take down the boss. Are you going to the girls' place? They invited us at six. We could discuss everything there."

"Let's go," I agreed, promising myself that I wouldn't drink too much and that I would go home early. "But let me stop by my place first. I need to change."

"Okay, then call me when you're ready."

At home, I changed one pair of jeans for another and swapped my turtleneck for a dark gray shirt. I put on the same jacket, making a promise to myself for the umpteenth time to organize my wardrobe. I have the money, so why wait any longer? I need to buy pants and a warm jacket. Maybe I should ask Marina where I could buy some decent clothes?

I tucked ten thousand rubles for "small expenses" into my pocket. The two reddish bills warmed my heart better than any sweater. I won't freeze on my way from my apartment building to the taxi anyway. I downloaded the app, which I had no use for before, and called a cab. They promised to send a car in two minutes. I told my mom I was going out for business and that I'd be back soon and headed downstairs.

It was even colder outside. The snow was ankle-deep, and slush had accumulated on the street corners. It was already dark and large white flakes of snow slowly twirled in the light of the streetlamps like goose down falling from a torn pillow. I stopped, taking a deep breath, savoring the invigorating early winter frost.

Right now, I cleared my mind of all thoughts of future battles, tactics, and plans... I was heading to a party with two beautiful girls, I had money, the taxi was about to arrive, and my life was starting to come together. Soon enough everything would be awesome.

The snow behind me crunched and I heard footsteps approaching. *That'll be Simba, I guess,* I thought, turning around, and at that moment, a flash of pain exploded in the back of my head.

Whack! Darkness.

CHAPTER 24

WARNING:

Any description of medical drugs, diagnoses, symptoms, and side effects in this chapter is fictional. Any resemblance to actual medical conditions or practices is purely coincidental! The author DOES NOT ENDORSE the use of stimulant drugs without the appropriate medical advice.

MY CONSCIOUSNESS RETURNS in fits and starts. Here I am, lying in a car. "Watch out! You're gonna stain my seats!" the driver yells. Every word of his pings off my skull like the tolling of a bell. Simba stuffs something under my head. I think it's his scarf, but it hurts to think.

Then I'm being carried. I don't see by whom or where to. I only hear the snow crunching underfoot, and then a door slams, and footsteps echo loudly, as if in a vast and empty space. Bright lights, their glow visible even through my shut eyelids.

"Head trauma? Put him here, the on-call doctor will come soon..."

They lower me heavily, like a sack. I don't remember the doctor's arrival.

It's cold. I'm fucking freezing. The cold causes me to come to my senses once again. I'm lying next to a window, which has a plastic frame inserted into it, and yet Arctic level cold is blowing in from under its windowsill. I'm naked, stripped down to my underwear. I lie covered with a single sheet. A thin, ratty blanket hangs on the back of the bed. It's so far away, it could as well be in the Southern Hemisphere.

My body is sluggish, uncooperative. I try to get up and nausea overwhelms me, everything swimming in my head. The pillow is hard, as if carved from stone. Beneath the sheet, there's a piece of plastic, thoughtfully provided. If I were to accidentally piss myself, I'd be floating in my own urine, but at least I wouldn't have to do the laundry.

I turn my head slightly to confirm that my premonitions weren't wrong. I'm in a hospital. Not in some private, upscale clinic, but in the ordinary public one — of the "survival of the fittest" variety.

There are two more empty cots beside me. The wall, painted white with streaks of dripping paint, bears an electronic clock with bright green digits and a calendar from two years ago. That's the extent of the interior design. There's a square ceiling light with daylight bulbs. One of the bulbs flickers periodically and hums annoyingly.

I hear voices beyond the door. Both female. One is confident, loud, and shrill; the other's no less assured or forceful and somehow familiar to me.

The door is old, wooden, painted white, and peeling in places. It doesn't close tightly, either it's warped or it was hung crookedly to begin with. That's why I can hear their entire conversation as if it were taking place right by my bedside.

"When the doctor sees him, he'll tell you," the first voice insists. "I'm not obligated to tell you anything without the doctor, young lady."

"When will the doctor see him then?" the second voice asks irritably.

I recognize Marina's voice. But why is she here? It's no wonder she's irritated. Being called "young lady" would drive anyone to madness.

"When he makes his rounds on Monday." The first voice seems bemused at such a silly question. "On weekends, we only have the duty resident, but he can't make decisions like that."

"What the fuck?! It's only Friday evening right now!" Marina exclaims in frustration.

"Watch your language, young lady!" The shrillness reaches such a peak that it rattles the back of my skull again. "Would you look at her here in her fur coat giving orders! I'll be happy to call the police right now!"

"Why is he lying here if you're not going to treat him?" Marina retorts.

The full horror of my situation finally dawns on me. There's another round of the beta tomorrow morning. Anyone who doesn't show up is automatically eliminated. This isn't just a caprice of MosTech: The beta requires us to complete quests and keep leveling up. Who knows what else the Neural Network will throw at us? Missing out once means having to catch up forever. And here I am, unable to so much as lift my head and possibly trapped in this hellhole for the next three days.

I peer out of the window with longing. I see bars on the other side. It's clear that this isn't a prison; the bars were put here to keep people from climbing in from the outside, not the other way around. Nevertheless, my idea of escaping through the window is quickly extinguished.

Besides, I'm no Houdini. I try to prop myself up on my elbow and feel pain in my arm. Looking down, I discover an IV needle and a tube connected to a drip. Something is flowing into me from a large dark bottle. This realization causes a whirlwind of worries, and I fall back on my pillow, once again tuning into the conversation.

I'm rooting for Marina as hard as I can, but it seems like she's losing ground one argument at a time.

"He doesn't need anything right now." The nurse flatly rejects Marina's latest point. "All he needs is complete rest at the moment. He'll rest until Monday, and then the doctor will decide."

"Can I at least see him?" Marina tries one

more time.

"And who are you to him?" the nurse inquires. "A relative?"

"I'm his fiancée!" Marina declares.

This statement makes me sit up on the bed, despite my sorry condition. What a thing to say! Only later do I realize that Marina was only saying it for the nurse's benefit, not for her own... But it's still something to digest.

"In that case, you don't have a marriage certificate, so you're not a relative," the shrill nurse declares spitefully. "Your amorous desires are none of our concern. The patient needs rest!"

She barks the last part loudly enough to wake the whole ward. In this place, rest is the last thing I could dream of.

Rustling, the clattering of heels, huffing and puffing sound from the other side of the door. It seems Marina has attempted a desperate breakthrough.

"Where are you going, young lady? What do you think you're doing?! I'll call the orderlies! Tony! Tony!! Get this madwoman out of here! And lock the door. Visiting hours are over!"

A couple of minutes later, the door creaks open. Without understanding why, I pretend to be asleep, watching from beneath my eyelids. A woman enters the room, most likely the same nurse. The voice I heard matches her appearance completely. She could be anywhere between twenty-five and forty, with a square figure and determination on her face. She's not a woman, she's a battleship.

I lose sight of her for a moment, but when she comes back into my field of vision, she's holding a primed syringe in her hands. She bends down and inserts the needle into the IV port.

"Rest up now," she says with an unexpected amount of care in her voice. "You don't need any bimbos right now. You probably ended up here because of her in the first place, you poor thing you. I've dealt with young ladies like her before, they only cause trouble. You just sleep and recover…"

She takes a blanket, covers me, tucking it in from all sides. I slip away into a deep slumber before she can even leave the room.

* * *

I awake to further voices in the corridor. This time there are more of them, and they're shriller. They pierce my brain, dispelling the remnants of my medicated sleep. My head hurts even more, the spot where I was struck throbs, and waves of pain radiate to my temples and down to my throat, triggering waves of nausea.

I've no doubts about who clobbered me. It was Sullen all right. This has his handiwork written all over it. He's been blathering about brass knuckles since he bought some six months ago, and they've already found two guys with fractured skulls and stripped down to their underwear around the neighborhood. During the warmer weather, they'd be there in the bushes until some passerby saw them and called an ambulance. They filed police reports, but no witnesses or evidence ever turned up. In my case, however, I could have frozen to death. I don't know if he was lying in wait for me on purpose or just stumbled upon a convenient opportunity to settle scores, but it didn't change anything. I would deal with Sullen as soon as I could, but I'd have to get out of this solitary cell first.

"I'm telling you, we have the transfer paperwork right here!" I heard a girlish voice chattering confidently. "All the stamps and seals are in place, see?! He's being urgently transferred to the regional trauma center for surgery!"

"But how can that be?" someone objected. "We haven't even examined him yet. Why would anyone suddenly decide he needs surgery?"

"Maybe that's precisely why they made the decision — because you haven't even examined him yet," the first voice retorted and then switching to a loud whisper, added: "Maybe he's someone's son or grandson and his daddy made a call and the wheels started turning. Saturday or not, just get him ready for surgery and an examination."

The door to the room swung open, and the people having the conversation stepped inside. The night nurse had been replaced by a middle-aged woman with an unremarkable, elongated sheepish face and watery gray hair.

She was being crowded from both sides by

two very young nurses, their faces concealed by disposable sanitary masks. I noticed a tattoo of a colorful snake on one of their ankles, just below the edge of her uniform, while the other nurse's uniform was barely holding itself together, threatening to split at the seam due to her ample bosom.

"I need to clarify with the attending physician... I can't do this without authorization... It's not our standard procedure..." the gray-haired nurse protested.

"We don't have time," the tattooed girl argued. "Did you see the signature on the transfer papers? They've already prepped the OR and everything!"

The owner of the magnificent breasts leaned over me.

"Can you walk?" AngelCake whispered.

To be honest I had no idea, but I replied, "I can."

"Lean on me," Stacy said, placing her hand on my neck and helping me get up.

Helicopters were spinning in my head. They were doing maneuvers, their blades flashing, and then they nosedived, making my stomach churn. I managed to prop myself up, dropped my legs to the floor, and stood up with their support.

"What are you doing?" the nurse exclaimed, coming to her senses. "He can't walk! Let's get him to the attending physician, get a wheelchair..."

"There's no time!" Yumi interrupted. "Have your boss call our boss. Right now, we don't have time, there's a wait for the OR as it is and we're already running late!"

I listened to this nonsense and wondered if it had any basis in reality. Whose signatures were on the paper? Where had the transfer documents come from?

Yumi lifted me under my other arm, and the two of them, stumbling, dragged me towards the exit. The gray-haired nurse ran alongside.

"What about the discharge papers?" she lamented. "What about the discharge papers?"

"They'll send them to you by mail," Yumi brushed her off.

"But I need them from you!"

"Then we'll send them!"

We tumbled out the front door. A beat-up, snot green van stood waiting at the hospital stairs. It looked like it had been pulled from a junkyard or a collection of automotive relics. Someone had slapped red cross stickers so sloppily onto its doors that the duty nurse refused to believe the ruse any further. I guess she figured that a regional hospital's ambulance would look more presentable.

"That's it! Stop right there! Stop, I say!" she yelled. "I forbid it."

The girls swung open the rear doors, practically tossed me inside and hopped in themselves. The van roared to life, jolted and took off.

I stretched out on the floor, relishing my immobility. The pain in my head now felt like molten lead sloshing around inside my skull, threatening to spill out at any moment. I didn't get a chance to relish this sensation for very long because, just as I was starting to appreciate it, the van hit a bump and I slammed my head on its bare metal floor!

"Damn it! Could you be more careful?!"

"Hold on, Andryusha!" Simba, who was behind the wheel, replied. "If it hurts, it means you're alive!"

"Where did you find this wreck?!"

"You think it's easy to find something decent overnight? Marina found it among MosTech property. It was listed in their janitorial motor pool."

"Andryusha, be quiet and conserve your strength!" AngelCake interrupted. Then she turned to Yumi and began to order her around: "What are you waiting for? Cover him with something. We don't want him to catch a cold along the way, do we?"

Yumi snapped out of inspecting my underwear or whatever else it was she was staring at down there, grabbed her jacket and Stacy's jacket from the seat, and began to cover me from above.

I emerged from the hospital empty-handed and practically naked.

In the meantime, AngelCake kindly cradled my head, obscuring my view with her chest.

"No one thought of bringing me some clothes?" I asked.

"Well, things got a bit hectic..." Stacy

stammered. "It never occurred to us."

"We didn't want to bother your mom," Simba added.

The van we ended up with was not only ancient but also stripped down to its bones. The cabin was separated from the cargo area by a solid partition, and there were no seats to be found anywhere. They placed me directly on the floor, which had been covered with a beach towel. Stacy sat on a fold-down wooden bench fixed to the van's wall, while Yumi had to make do with a wheel well.

"Lift me up, please," I requested. "I can feel every bump in the road in my head."

Stacy slid down to the floor so that I could rest my head on her lap. Yumi, not wanting to be left out, also pressed against me, apparently intending to keep me warm with her hot body. It's like I'm in heaven, surrounded by angels who're also valkyries and harpies all at once. Only the pain in the back of my head reassured me that I was still very much alive.

The van roared and revved, maneuvered somewhere, and came to a stop. The driver's door slammed shut. I knew I was about to have to walk again, just as I was getting comfortable... Please, either leave me here or put me out of my misery.

The rear doors swung open, and the scent of snow and cold rushed in from outside. It was already dawn. The girls helped me get up and out, where Simba hoisted me onto his powerful shoulders, narrating the story of my rescue along the way.

"It was Sullen all right! I'd recognize that sour mug of his any time of night! The rat was riffling through your pockets when I got there!"

I was incredibly lucky. Simba had come out of our apartment building shortly after the attack. I don't know what was going through Sullen's head, but I wouldn't be surprised if he had decided to settle the score quietly. However, his greed got the better of him, and then Simba scared him away.

My buddy didn't wait for an ambulance. He loaded me into the taxi I called and rushed me to the nearest hospital. The taxi driver complained about the change in destination, but a couple of bills quickly changed his mind.

Another handful of bills ensured that I was assigned to a private room in the hospital, and a tip at the nurse's station got me some initial attention. But after that, Simon's generosity backfired. When Marina rushed into the emergency room, the last thing the nurses wanted was to give up such a profitable patient. "*A cash cow like this had better stay under our care,*" they figured.

As I listened to Simba, I tried to get a look around to see where we were. It seemed we had reached the MosTech office tower, but from the backstreets. AngelCake rushed ahead to open a steel door painted gray, and then the three of them dragged me up some stairs that were either a fire escape or for maintenance personnel.

"How did you get me out?"

"That was Yumi's idea," Stacy babbled. "She's in med school. She interned at the public hospital and saw how patients are transferred for surgery. Marina came up with the paperwork. With all the equipment and design professionals they have in this place, they can whip up any document you like in a half hour."

Yumi remained modestly silent, batting her eyelashes coquettishly.

Behind another door, we found a familiar office corridor. A few more steps, and I found myself back in the medical examination room.

"Here, here... Bring him in... Lay him down gently... Be careful with his head..." Two nurses bustled around us.

To my delight, they were the same ones who had examined me on the first day. Simba laid me down on the couch and slipped out into the corridor to act as lookout. I found myself alone, surrounded by four pretty girls in sexy medical robes.

"What a good set up for a porno," I ventured. "Don't you think?"

Fucking was actually the last thing I felt like at the moment. The thought of moving made me sick, but a leader must lead by example.

"You just worry about getting to the beta on time," Stacy replied decisively. "If you do, we'll all take turns blowing you."

"I didn't sign up for that!" one of the nurses piped up.

Amusingly, the other one made no objection.

The door swung open and Marina burst into the room. She was in a state of extreme agitation.

"What the hell are you doing?!" she set upon me for some reason.

"Leave him alone!" AngelCake shielded me with her chest. "He can't get upset right now!"

"Damn! Am I the only one who has to worry about everyone?!" Marina covered her face with her hands for a moment. Her shoulders shook as if she was about to burst into tears but then taking a deep breath, she went on calmly: "What can we do to get him on his feet? All we need is like three hours. After that he can rest as long as he likes."

"Theoretically..." said one of the nurses and all ten eyes converged on her. "Theoretically... nothing."

I was afraid Marina would kill her. The PR maven's stress level was so high that she could beat a man to death with a tea bag.

"We need to raise his adrenaline level," Yumi's voice cut through.

"How?" Marina jumped up to her. "Is that even possible?!"

"Tendrozipine should do it," Yumi said a bit uncertainly. "Do you have tendrozipine?"

"We should," answered the nurse. "We have a full set of pharmaceuticals. We keep them on hand just in case. And we almost never use any of them, because all we do is measure temperatures and blood pressure and sometimes prescribe aspirin. The only issue is that we have to document whatever we use."

"Oh we'll document it," Marina said decisively and somehow even aggressively. "This is war. Documents aren't an obstacle."

"Oh wow, you've got Sirestal too!" Yumi rummaged through the cabinet like a child in a Christmas stocking, selecting the tastiest candies. "That will stimulate his nervous system and give him a burst of energy. You need a prescription for it... but it looks like you guys just have it... Wow, you even have this one too!? This is technically designed for horses, though, so I don't think it's a good idea to..."

"Is this what they teach you in med school?" I said in disbelief.

"Nope," Yumi shook her head. "I saw that on an episode of *House.*"

"Well, I suppose as long as it wasn't an episode of *Breaking Bad...*"

Yumi giggled, turned to me and stuck out her tongue. Just the tip. I immediately recalled the first day of the beta — how her tummy with Lance's autograph and heart trembled under my hand...

"You lot want to kill him, right?" AngelCake jumped up. "You didn't finish the job yesterday, so today is your day, huh?"

"Are there other options?!" Marina stepped up to her. "Do you think you will last longer than five minutes if Andrew isn't in the game with you? All he does is save your cellulite ass!"

"Speak for yourself, you skinny bitch!"

"Hey!" I tried to shout over both of them. It

turned out to be harder than I thought in my condition, yet after some further effort, they quieted down. "Ladies! Isn't this my choice to make?"

"Depends. What do you choose?" Marina narrowed her eyes.

"Andrew!" Stacy folded her hands in supplication on her chest.

As for Yumi, I don't think she gave two shits. She just couldn't wait to try her pharmaceutical experiments on me. When else would she get the chance to play Dr. House?

"All right, hit me with your stimpack," I gave up.

There really were no other options.

CHAPTER 25

YUMI BROUGHT FOUR SYRINGES over to the couch: two large ones, one smaller one and one very small one. I've hated needles since childhood, since elementary school. "Come on, Andryusha... You're a big boy now..." I'd rather tear my finger to the bone than feel this thin metal spike enter my body.

I closed my eyes and turned away. Let her do what she wants, as long as I don't have to see it.

"What are you, a toddler?" Yumi lived up to my worst expectations.

She tied a tourniquet around my arm and began her experiments. The one good thing was that she had a light touch. The teachers at med school aren't bad and I guess she got a lot of practice. I didn't even notice the first or third injections. The second one left my hand very numb, however, and the fourth one suddenly sent a torrent of heat coursing up my vein, making the back of my head tingle as if I had just swallowed a spoonful of wasabi. I twitched, breathed through my nose, and then the pain went away, as if someone had suddenly flipped a switch. Just like that — completely gone. The back of my head stopped whining, the helicopters stopped spinning their rotors and settled at the edge of the runway. And beyond that edge, the grass was green, so green... and the daisies were swaying, so swaying...

I opened my eyes and jumped to my feet.

"What time is it now? Are we late?"

"It's 9:42," Marina glanced at her Apple Watch. "We'll still make it if we hurry. Can you walk on your own? Eek!"

I looked down at my hand and found that it had attached itself to Marina's ass, fingers tightly clenched. My other hand was on AngelCake's ass cheek, who had stayed quiet about this detail.

"Mmm... Marina..." I said pensively. "We'll go in a second, but before that, you're not dressed right." This detail seemed extremely important to me at the moment. "If you were to put on the same uniform as the others... Then there would be FIVE sexy nurses here at once!"

"Are you high?" Marina looked at me incredulously. "Hey, Zoia, what did you inject him with?"

"Girls, do you have another uniform?" I continued. "For her?"

"You're the one who told me to get him back on his feet, Ms. Marina," snapped Yumi, who seemed to hate her real name. "And so here he is — on his feet like you asked. I suggest you put on the uniform. There is no use arguing with him now, you'll just be wasting your time."

Marina ground her teeth loud enough for everyone to hear. I looked at her with a cheerful grin and nodded.

"The universe must be in harmony!"

A nurse's uniform was soon found and it was even appropriately sized, though a little tight in the chest. Wearing black lingerie with white tops isn't recommended. It wouldn't be visible normally, yet if you stood in front of a window, it could look... intriguing.

"Are you satisfied now? Can we go?" Marina addressed me in a tone reserved for the injured or the insane.

Probably both applied to me to some extent.

"I was waiting for you!" I jumped up from the couch, pulling AngelCake along with me and replacing my other hand on its rightful place on Marina's ass.

The three of us tumbled out of the nurses' office, waffling at the narrow doorway and having to turn sideways to fit through the door without breaking up our trio.

"How ya feelin' Andrew? Did you get some meds? Where are you taking him?" Simba ran alongside, bombarding us with questions.

I no longer had to be carried. In fact, I was the one dragging the two chicks after me. They were simply too slow on their beautiful legs. The hallway lights winked at me, showing me the way like a runway. The lights seemed like arrows to me directing me onward!

"Go, go, go! Rush the bombsite!" I yelled, reliving my CS days.

The security guard on the second floor did not recognize Marina, forcing her to shove her badge in his face enraged. For my part, I saluted him, while feeling around the back of my head with my hand. "An empty head needs no treatment," my father used to tell me. However, I could feel a clump of bandages, plasters and gauze back there.

What I really wanted to do was flick the security guard's nose like the Master had the first day. I never got my chance though because AngelCake pulled me away, despite my protests. I managed to snatch his glasses off, however. I needed them more. Everything around me was too bright: too bright, too loud and too fucking slow!

The security guard just stood there, blinking dumbly.

"Have him jump on one leg, Marina!"

But the girls preferred to drag me onward. "*Well, to hell with him then,*" I decided, immediately forgetting all about him. There were other guards stationed along the hallway and I started flashing them peace signs and flicking them birds, depending on my kaleidoscopic mood.

"I'll stay with him!" Marina declared at the door of my changing room.

"Oh yeah baby!" I pulled her to me and burst out laughing.

"I'm staying too!" AngelCake intervened.

"Are you nuts?" Marina bore down on AngelCake. "Go change. I'm just going to make sure he gets to the pod."

"Don't fight on my account, ladies!" I struck a foppish pose, leaning against the door.

Stacy shot us an incredulous look, turned around and walked down the corridor.

In the locker room, I pounced on Marina, pressed her against the wall, and began to paw her body under her thin uniform.

"Not now," she whispered to me. "After the beta... Anything after the beta... Whatever you want... Do you want me to wear a uniform like this? And stockings? Do you like a girl in stockings? Only after the beta... OH CUT THE CRAP ALREADY! WE'RE GOING TO BE LATE!"

In my bathrobe, slippers and glasses, I looked like el Duderino. But what mattered was that I felt good about myself. When all this is over, I should take a vacation. Go to the Maldives. Or the Seychelles... Where is it that the fucking rich go these days? I should ask Marina. And I could take her with me. And AngelCake... And Yumi as my personal pharmacist... And Anna... Wait, why would I take Anna? Oh that's right, to make her jealous!

"Is he, uh, good to go with that thing on his head?" mumbled Sergio the technician staring at the floor. It seemed like raising an objection to someone as high up as Marina was the most daring thing he'd ever done.

"I will assume responsibility!" Marina snapped.

Sergio nodded without looking up and opened the lid of the VR pod.

"To infinity and beyond!" I quipped cheerfully at Marina, climbing inside.

By the look of apprehension on her face, you could think that she really was sending me off into space. It was silly of her, however, because I felt GREAT!

DEEP IMMERSION SESSION INITIALIZED.

Hypnotoad fixed me with his eye.

HAVE A NICE GAME, TargetAi!

But suddenly the spiral stopped! It froze in place, becoming an ordinary striped circle, divided into segments. And then system text started scrolling in front of me:

DEEP IMMERSION SUSPENDED!

PLAYER CONDITION UNSTABLE!

CRANIAL-BRAIN TRAUMA DETECTED!

HIGH BLOOD PRESSURE DETECTED!

HIGH HEART RATE DETECTED!

UNKNOWN MEDICATIONS DETECTED IN PLAYER'S BLOODSTREAM!

Through the VR pod's sealed lid I could hear Marina's muffled screams:

"Launch it, I said! I'll fire everyone to hell! I will assume responsibility! I'll have you cleaning toilets until you retire!"

ERROR OVERRIDE: FORCE DEEP IMMERSION!

CONDUCTING PHYSIOLOGICAL ANALYSIS...

ADJUSTING IN-GAME PARAMETERS TO MATCH PLAYER CONDITION…

DEXTERITY: +100%.

STAMINA: -50%.

INTELLIGENCE: -50%.

APPLYING PERMANENT STATUS EFFECT: "RUNNIN' ON FUMES" (CHANNEL HP INTO STAMINA AT -0.1 HP PER 1 SP).

If I understand these numbers correctly, I've become twice as fast. Not a bad boost. Though, the changes to my Stamina remain a bit unclear. Not only have they cut Stamina in half, but now it's also draining my life. I need to keep an eye on my stats lest I accidentally die during battle. As for the Intelligence debuff… I haven't found any use for that stat anyway.

I spawn in the familiar alley. I'm wearing leather armor and I have daggers in my hands. Excellent, I still have my gear then. There's the fence and the boulder… Something may have changed about them, but I'm not interested at the moment because there's a voice yelling so loud that it drowns out all other sounds.

"HEAR YE, HEAR YE! ATTEND NOW TO THIS ANNOUNCEMENT AND CLAIM NOT LATER THAT YE HEARD IT NOT!"

First thing I do is check the quest screen. It's empty! There are no objectives. Either yesterday's massacre quest is still open or… the Neural Net has evolved to assign quests in a different way.

The voice is shouting from the town square. Our party's rendezvous point is the merchant's store in the opposite direction. At the moment though, the announcement seems more important. I locate the chat interface and as soon as I concentrate on it, an exhaustive list of every player currently online appears before me. Fortunately, all I need to do is think of the players I need to select their names.

"*Let's head to the town square,*" I write.

Simba: There's a chat feature?

AngelCake: omw

Yumi: Okee!

I dash out of the alley and reach the town square within a minute. There are quite a few beta testers already here — around 200 or so. The previous round seems to have thinned out our ranks quite a bit. The various parties stand around the plaza in islands. Everyone's mostly Level 2 or 3 and wearing quilted armor which gives them a motley, thuggish appearance. But there are also some in leather armor like the one I have and even a few who are sporting chain mail.

The players who are still solo, who managed to survive last round, huddle nervously at the edges of the square. They seem terrified of their own shadows. They stand there meekly, pretending to be innocent and peaceful, but I know the curse and mark of Cain must be on each of them. They've all become killers to be here. They'll stab their nearest neighbor in the back if they have to and do it without remorse.

There time for killing is past however. Those players who have tasted the blood of others for the first time — and the easy XP that came with it — are eager to resume the slaughter then and there, but the very first words that thunder across the square forbid them: Order has returned to the town.

"KILLING WITHIN TOWN LIMITS IS PROHIBITED!"

"KILLERS SHALL BE DECLARED OUTLAWS!"

Following the best traditions of medieval urban design, a platform of timber has been erected in the center of the town square. This is typically where they'd put a scaffold or a gallows, but there are no such devices here for now. Instead, the mayor paces back and forth on the platform.

He looks stern and officious. In his hands, he holds a long scroll rolled up into a tube. He stops and begins reading it loud, his proclamation filling the entire square.

"WE HEREBY COMMEND THE BRAVE WARRIORS WHO ARE HELPING US CLEANSE OUR TOWN OF THE REVOLTING MONSTERS THAT..."

Guards armed with pikes surround the platform. NPCs! They wear steel breastplates and helmets. They glare around themselves sternly, showing that there's real force behind the mayor's words. Here they are — to serve and protect! Their level labels shine above their heads: Level 2s and Level 3s. Their levels may be relatively low, but they must have leveled up somehow.

We, the players, outnumber them tenfold. We could overpower them if we wanted to. And I don't know why I keep thinking about it, but I want to crush this display of authority at its core. Burn, shatter, and kill the lot of them. Somehow, today's order seems scarier than yesterday's chaos.

The guards have similar faces, with thin mustaches and pointy beards. They all look like brothers. Or clones. The mayor puffs up his cheeks seriously. His face doesn't seem very comical anymore. It won't be so easy to get a quest from him — he might even call in the pikes if you don't address him correctly.

Two black specks, Simba and AngelCake weave my way among the crowd. Their armor is jet black like mine. Yesterday, I thought it was sheer coincidence, but now I realize that Lance deliberately had this gear customized. I wonder how much extra he spent? Thanks anyway, Lance. There's a sucker born every minute.

An empty space quickly forms around our all-black party. No one wants to get close, except...

"Are you going to return my gear to me?" Yumi murmurs.

I hadn't noticed her among the crowd. For some reason, every sound she makes reminds me of a cat. Barefoot and in her starting gear, she looks like a shy cutie, and when she notices me looking her over, she folds her arms and bites her lip... Damn it...

At the same instant something dull slams into my head. At first, I think someone's attacked me and drawing my daggers, I spin around, casting about for my assailant...

"What's wrong, Andryusha?!" Simba asks tensely.

DEBUFF RECEIVED (SEXUAL AROUSAL): -20% to ALL STATS.

"Uh... I think I'm okay," I reply. "I mean, everything's fine."

I can't really tell him that I have an excruciating BONER — one so tight that it feels like all the blood has rushed from one head to the other.

"So, what about my gear?" Yumi insists. "Meow, meow?"

Damn it!

"Give her the armor, Simba!"

I oblige her request, seemingly showing her how much I trust her, but in reality I only do it so that she covers her boobs. Then, to distract myself, I scan the crowd. I never thought that so many girls would survive last round. Turned out that plenty of them were bloodthirsty enough to make the cut. I see fat butt cheeks peeking out from under short skirts and cute little butt cracks in leather shorts...

"We need to buy stones for my slingshot, TargetAi. We're running out."

I turn to look at AngelCake. I watch how the globes of her cleavage heave above her armor... up... down... with every breath... how she puckers her lips, saying TargetAi... how her pink tongue flickers... Motherfucker!

DEBUFF RECEIVED (SEXUAL AROUSAL): -40% to ALL STATS.

What cursed concoction did Yumi inject me with anyway?! Most worryingly I don't know how to remove this debuff... Or, well, I know one way, but I can't really try that here in the town square!

"WE HEREBY GRANT YE BRAVE WARRIORS WHO HAVE TRIUMPHED IN PAST BATTLES PERMISSION TO STUDY COMBAT SKILLS IN OUR TRAINING CAMP!"

Hearing the mayor's words, I immediately open the map. There it is! Right beyond that dead end where our barricade had been... The dead end is gone and the alley leads onward to the Training Camp. Meanwhile, an envelope appears in my quest log. I'll read it on the way...

"Follow me!" I take off.

The Training Camp is on the other side of the square, but we'll get there faster if we take the surrounding streets. Plus I've already memorized the way. And yet as quickly as I went, I still made sure to get a good look at the crowd on our way out of the square. I didn't see Anna or Lance in the crowd. Of course I might not recognize Lance or his crew in the newbie rags they must be wearing after getting fragged, yet I doubt I'd miss their foppish hairstyles.

By the time I reached the first corner, however, I was forced to slow down because my Stamina had dropped into the red and was now consuming my HP. I'll have to allocate a point or two to Stamina at my next level, but for now...

For now, I feel terrible. My lack of Stamina wasn't just consuming HP. It felt as if I had just finished running cross-country and was ready to heave my lungs and stomach out onto the cobblestones.

I am forced to crouch down and lean against the fence, waiting for the others.

"What's wrong with you?" Yumi asks. "You look so pale."

Being Level 4, she's the first to catch up to me. The others are coming up behind her. Yumi presses her palm to my forehead, checking for a temperature. I doubt it'll work in the game, but old habits die hard.

DEBUFF RECEIVED (SEXUAL AROUSAL): -60% to ALL STATS.

"Yumi, what kind of concoction did you inject me with?!"

"What do you mean 'concoction?'" Yumi pouts, offended. "What's your problem? I didn't hear you complaining when your head stopped hurting."

"What's my problem? I'll tell you…"

I tell them about the debuff. Simba neighs like a parade horse. AngelCake blushes unexpectedly and very attractively. Yumi flashes her eyes at me, either guiltily or flirtatiously.

"Well this isn't a normal situation. Side effects are possible," she says. "I did warn you."

"Why don't you just jerk off?" Simba suggests.

"Are you fucking serious?!" I explode, irate.

"Yumi started it," says Stacy, "so she should

help you dispel your debuff."

"How?!"

"Why anyway she can! Isn't she a... medical pro-fessional?" AngelCake almost chokes getting the last word out. "Let her treat your 'side effects.' I'll look away and wait."

Stacy pointedly turns her back to me. Yumi giggles into her fist and then licks her lips. The sheer sight of it overwhelms me.

DEBUFF RECEIVED (SEXUAL AROUSAL): -80% to ALL STATS.

"Simba! You turn away too, this ain't going into your spankbank!"

"Sure, sure, I understand... The priestess will now bless you. What a party we have, what a priestess! Just don't take too long you two! We need to be grinding here." Simba turns away, facing the same way as Stacy, "Listen there, Stacy, do you know how to cook borscht?" he says casually, striking up a conversation.

I'm struggling to stay on my feet at this point. I have to lean against the wall because I've got less Strength than a Level 0. Every movement causes me to shed HP. My dick, however, stands as stiffly as a battering ram on a war galley. Wasting no time, Yumi deftly kneels before me.

I fiddle with my belt clumsily, unable to figure out how to undo it... How *do* I get these damn game trousers off?

"Just unequip them into your inventory," Yumi tells me, reaching for my crotch.

Chapter 26

AT THE SAME TIME, three floors overhead in meatspace, Doc had convened a meeting in the boardroom. Then again, it would be a stretch to call what was happening a meeting. The people in the boardroom were simply yelling at each other — so loudly that even the heavy oak doors couldn't dampen their louder and more colorful expressions.

Dr. Kotov's secretary, a young, curly-haired brunette named Julia, had twice endeavored to deliver a tray of coffee into the boardroom but had been frightened away by the screams coming from within. You could easily find yourself looking for a new job if you got caught in an executive crossfire like that... Like that blonde from PR who had just entered the boardroom as if she were heading to her execution.

"What do you think you're doing, you idiot!"

Doc was yelling, pounding his fist on the table. "You sent a drugged up player into deep immersion! You impersonated a medical professional! You overstepped your authority and forced him through security despite all medical advice and threw him to the mercy of the Neural Network? Do you know how badly you've exceeded your authority?!"

"*So the nurses didn't snitch,*" Marina thought. She had already shed her tears while sitting in the waiting room, unashamed to cry in front of the curly-haired secretary. Marina had cried not out of sorrow, but out of anger. Everything had been going so well! She had sprung Andrew from the hospital, seen to his miraculous recovery and gotten him into the game in time. Who had betrayed her?!

Two security guards had come for her. They escorted her upstairs as if she were under arrest. Various worst-case scenarios swirled in her mind... the loss of her bonus... a stern write-up... a demotion...

"She threatened to fire the technicians," Benjamin helpfully poured fuel on the fire . "I have the report on my desk. 'I'll fire everyone to hell,' she told them."

"Oh, I see," Doc said slowly, almost syllable by syllable. "She said, 'I'll fire everyone to hell,' eh? In that case, your punishment is that you're fired! Gather your belongings and make yourself scarce!"

Marina clenched her fists until her fingers

went white. How could this happen? She had just been following orders and she had followed them well. She had put her heart and soul into this job they'd assigned her.

"Andrew will come out fine," she said aloud, unexpectedly even to herself. "Please, wait until the end of the round. You will see that everything will be fine."

"What?!" Doc exclaimed, his eyes bulging, as if an insect had suddenly spoken to him. "You dare argue with me?! Have you seen his indicators? What if he has a breakdown in there, in the VR pod?"

"I believe in him," Marina said stubbornly. "He won't have a breakdown."

She didn't understand herself why she was so confident. From the very beginning, Marina couldn't figure out what the execs saw in this Andrew. He was just an average guy. She'd never give someone like him a second look. But he kept coming out unscathed, time after time, and she herself began to believe, not in his incredible luck, but in some special character trait that she couldn't identify on her own. Maybe that's what people meant when they spoke of men having a "backbone?" He just exuded confidence that, no matter what nonsense happened, everything would turn out fine in the end.

"I said get out of here!" Doc raised his voice again. "Or should I have you escorted out? I want you gone within the half hour! We'll see to your current assignments without your help... YOU

ARE DISMISSED!"

"I was just following your orders!" Marina burst out, her voice rising. "YOUR orders! You approved the ruse with the street fight. It was YOUR security service that was supposed to protect him, instead of spying on me. I was just following your orders: to get him into the game at ANY COST!"

Marina glanced around at the assembled group. Dr. Kotov sat there, clenching his fists in rage, his face turning red, a swollen artery pulsing in his neck. The Master puffed away, staring at the ceiling. Benjamin grinned mockingly and Dr. Skuratova doodled flowers in her notepad. Seeing their indifference, the PR maven burst into tears, covered her face with her hands, and stormed out of the office.

"Is it me or is she making more sense lately?" Doc asked in a completely different, utterly calm voice.

"Unlikely," the Master replied. "She's probably in love."

"Oh!" Dr. Skuratova perked up. "There's a condition called Florence Nightingale syndrome... when a caregiver falls in love with her patient."

"Isn't that something that afflicts nurses?" the Master wondered.

"Well didn't you notice how she was dressed?" Dr. Skuratova triumphantly raised her finger. "A clinical case."

"Will this TargetAi guy hold up?" Doc mused.

"I think he will," Benjamin Zvyagin shrugged

expressively, as if to say, *"If he doesn't, he's a weakling."*

"Can we see him for ourselves?" Doc persisted.

He couldn't stand letting things run their course, and if he showed interest in some issue, he made sure to delve into all its details.

"Of course." Benjamin began to clatter on his keyboard. "I'll have the stream sent to the screen right away."

He picked up the remote control and turned on the massive wall-mounted screen. The entire game town could be seen there from a bird's-eye view, although no one in the game had ever seen a single bird there.

At a keystroke, the image split into many smaller screens. Benjamin highlighted one of them and zoomed in.

"Oh, that's curious," Dr. Skuratova remarked.

The Master let out a loud snort to suppress his laughter, and asked, "Benny, are you intentionally choosing the juiciest angles?"

It was clear that TargetAi had no intention of kicking the bucket. To the contrary — with a most satisfied expression on his face, he stood, leaning against the fence, while an attractive girl knelt in front of him, eagerly performing oral sex on him.

"I think he *will* come out fine," Doc summed up.

He liked having the last word, even in a situation like this.

* * *

A torrent of sensations washed over me as Yumi's fingers wrapped around my e-cock. It was as if a tantric sex specialist was caressing my entire body with an intimate massage. Well, I've never seen a tantric sex specialist, but that's the only thing I can think of comparing it to. My arousal was off the charts and needed an outlet.

"Wow, is it always so huge?" Yumi asked, surprised.

I heard Stacy snort at this and noticed that she was trying to get in a quick peek to see if dimensions in meatspace matched dimensions in cyberspace. In fact, there's a good chance that Yumi had said this not to flatter me, but to stoke curiosity and friendly competition.

"I make sure to assign him stat points with every new level," I retorted, relishing the look of wonder on Yumi's face.

All this talk and foreplay was great for titillation and building self-esteem, but time was running out.

I seized the initiative by placing my hand on Yumi's head and pulling her towards me. She took the hint, willingly wrapped her plump lips around my penis and started to work on it.

"Arrrrrgh..." I gurgled from excitement.

There's no way I'm going to let this debuff get to 80% again... I could die from an orgasm right now!

"Don't get carried away back there," Stacy muttered loudly, "there's no time for romance."

This remark irritated me. We were already forced to do all of this in the field, improvising, and here she was distracting me further. Yumi just winked at me however, glancing up, and loudly smacking her lips.

"Chmuff... chmuff... chmuff..."

"Oh-oh-oh yeah!" I understood what she was trying to do and also turned up the heat.

Yumi grabbed my penis at the base with her fingers and caressed it in time with the movements of her mouth. Faster... faster... Her lips were tight... and wet... and hot...

"Fucking A..." I tensed with my whole body, e-nutting in her mouth.

Yumi licked her lips roundly like a cat, shot me a sly look and rose from her knees.

"We're ready!" she announced to the party.

I realized that I felt... GREAT! All I had to do was equip my pants on and I'd be ready for battle!

The map led us straight to our destination. There was no trace of the two carts which had served as our redoubt last round. Even the dead end was gone. The alley had been widened into a street that led straight on down to a set of tall and sturdy wooden gates that stood wide open, welcoming the approaching players.

Before entering the training camp, I made sure to get a good look around. Thick stone walls stretched to the right and left, a block in each direction. The training camp seemed vast and, judging by outward appearances, quite intriguing.

It appeared even larger from inside. To the right of the entrance was a massive courtyard where some guards, much like the ones I had seen in the square, were currently training. There were no fewer than fifty of them. To loud but incomprehensible commands, they practiced wielding short swords and massive rectangular shields, a bit like real life riot police.

Next to them, I noticed a few players diligently mimicking their movements. Were they also training or had they signed up for guard duty?

A little further away, there was a platform with life-sized dummies and training equipment for practicing strikes. Even farther, there was a shooting range and an obstacle course. All of this was surrounded by various buildings, perhaps barracks or utility structures — it was not immediately clear.

Directly across from the entrance, a handsome and businesslike NPC with a plushy mustache and a slicked-back hairdo sat at a desk. Surely, he was the local heartthrob, the fixation of all the local belles — none of whom I had encountered so far.

His appearance even suggested some familial resemblance to the mayor himself, but I attributed that to the stereotypical appearance of machine-generated characters. The guards, for now, all seemed the same to me too.

And, most unfortunately, there was a fairly long line of players already waiting at his desk —

no fewer than fifteen at a glance.

"I hate lines," grumbled AngelCake. "No matter where I go, there's always a line, even in here."

I didn't tarry for too long. Pushing aside the last person in line, I made my way through the waiting players with my party following behind, occupying the newly cleared space. I could even hear Yumi apologizing for the way I was acting.

Most of the players were Level 1 or 2, so I had enough strength to push them out of my way. They looked around in annoyance, but seeing our well-armored group, they kept quiet and lowered their gaze. Yesterday's events had made many reconsider their attitudes towards common human values in this place.

"Where are you going?! Are you crazy?" one of the players, a Level 3, protested.

I was so surprised that I didn't even respond, I just punched him in the stomach. He doubled over but quickly recovered, as this wasn't real life after all.

According to the genre's conventions, the surrounding guards should have been alerted and immediately moved in to eliminate the offender or at least demand that he sheath his weapon. Yet none of this happened. So, "killing" meant annihilation, not merely aggressive behavior. That was good.

I immediately drew my daggers, prompting my party members to draw theirs behind me. The overly impulsive objector seemed taken aback.

"You can't kill me," he declared.

"Who said anything about killing?" I replied. "We'll disarm you, and then we'll lop off your right arm... and your left leg... for symmetry. Then we'll see how well you can balance."

"You can cut off his ears," Yumi added helpfully, "and keep them for trophies."

Lance sure had left a mark on her... though right now, her bloodthirstiness was quite appropriate.

"Forget it." The player spat at our feet, sheathing his sword.

I turned back to the line and saw that the path was now clear. The others had decided not to get in our way and had made themselves scarce just in case.

"What's your profession?" the NPC asked me, dipping a goose quill into the inkwell.

"Sociologist," I blurted out.

"We don't have that," he said, casting me a bored look.

"How is that possible?"

"Scout... Sniper... Spellcaster..." he began to read from the S section in his list of classes. "There's no mention of Sociologist here."

"So, these are classes?" it finally dawned on me. "Can you list all of them?"

"There are 352," the NPC frowned. "I'd rather not."

"Do they each have unique skills?"

"No, of course not," he laughed. "Many have the same skills. It's just that each specialty has skills that complement each other. You wouldn't teach a Samurai how to use a shield or a Paladin how to shoot a bow, would you?"

"So there's a Samurai class too?" I exclaimed in amazement.

"Of course. It's quite popular."

I completely forgot that I was talking to an NPC. He answered my questions and gave advice, while displaying entirely human emotions. I kept bombarding him with questions for another five minutes and found out that "professions" were not rigid classes but more like builds. Once you reached Level 10, you could choose a skill from any specialty, so multi-classing was the way to go!

At that moment, however, I was faced with the difficult choice between being a Samurai or an Adventurer. Both classes had a dual-wielding skill, but I liked the one of the Samurai a bit better due to its name: Kendo... and *daishō* and sake with geishas under a sakura tree... Meanwhile the Adventurer class sounded vague and poorly defined, but I liked its description: "A street fighter willing to get an edge in battle at any cost." I'll be damned if that isn't me in meatspace!

But then I spied a skill that made me make up my mind on the spot, sacrificing my passion for no holds barred fighting.

"Samurai," I quickly declared, before I could change my mind.

"Go straight ahead and to the left," said the whiskered NPC with a nod, "to the field with the training dummies."

I didn't set off right away, however, since I wanted to see what the others would choose.

Predictably, Simba chose the Paladin class. He was practically drooling as he listened to the buffs and skills that it came with: "reduced pain threshold," "provoke," and even "divine invincibility." The Paladin sounded downright OP, but there was one catch.

"As holy warriors, Paladins must abide by a set of strictures," the NPC said with almost like a sinister grin. "Here's a reminder of what these are."

"What?!?" Simba bellowed like a wounded bear. "A daily ten-minute prayer I can endure... But A VOW OF CELIBACY?! Are you serious?"

"What's the big deal, Simon?" AngelCake hurried to console him. "A VR session doesn't last that long. Surely you can handle being celibate for a few hours. It's only in-game after all..."

"And IF IT ISN'T?!"

"And if it isn't, you'll have to deal with it anyway!" AngelCake insisted. "The party needs a tank!"

"Does this mean I'm not allowed to get married?" Simon asked hopefully.

"That's right," the NPC nodded sympathetically. "None of that kind of business whatsoever."

"In-game, you mean," Simon gave in. "Meatspace doesn't concern you lot!"

AngelCake tried to interrogate the debonair NPC about how magic worked in this game, but encountered cold incomprehension. It was the same story when it came to healing and support mechanics. I wouldn't be surprised if these skills would be introduced after Level 10, as abilities for multi-classing. There weren't any players in here who couldn't fight by now anyway.

Despairing, Stacy was going to be an Archer, but at my suggestion, she changed her choice to Scout. Our party could use someone who could set and disarm traps.

As for Yumi, she knew exactly what she wanted to be.

"Assassin," she said with her usual suggestive glance when her turn came.

"A sassy Ass-ass-n'!" Simba burst into uproarious laughter.

DEBUFF RECEIVED (SEXUAL AROUSAL): -20% to ALL STATS.

"Oh damn it... Simba, shut up!!!"

Yumi didn't bat an eye though, and I approved of her choice. Booby-traps and poisons... It was definitely her thing.

Then, to my dismay, our party was forced to split up. I had hoped to supervise the different builds in our party, but I was having difficulties focusing on that now. The cursed sexual arousal debuff had reared its horns again. Dispelling it there in the training camp would be difficult.

The training session was boring and formal. The taciturn instructor asked what skill I wanted to learn. Dual-wielding, of course! He silently handed me two wooden bokkens — a shorter one and a longer one. A katana and a wakizashi.

This guy preferred not to communicate verbally at all. He had a long wooden whistle hanging around his neck, and that's how he drew attention to himself and issued orders.

The art of fencing invented by the legendary Miyamoto Musashi had taught samurai to wield a katana with two hands. Later on, however, they reverted to wielding it with one... the lazybones!

The instructor showed me how to strike, and then walked away. For about ten minutes, I pounded the dummy until a message flashed in the interface:

DUAL-WIELDING (Passive Skill): Allows fighting with a weapon in each hand without penalties to Dexterity or Damage.

Skills were unlocked at each level, so I had two more to choose. I chose "PRECISE STRIKE" next — the ability to find vulnerable points in an opponent's armor. The skill had a 30-second cooldown and delivered a blow that ignored my opponent's armor.

Lastly, I unlocked my third skill — the one I had chosen the honorable path of Bushido for.

"LEADERSHIP," I said.

This skill allowed me to create a party and redistribute XP within it. It was available to Knights, Samurai and a few other classes.

I was curious about how the instructor would go about teaching me leadership skills, but he simply removed the whistle from around his neck and hung it around mine. That was it. A "party" section immediately lit up in my interface, though it remained empty. I thanked him with a slight bow as befits a newly-anointed aristocrat and hurried towards the exit.

There were rows of dummies to the right and an archery range with targets to the left. As I walked, I caught sight of a slender blonde drawing her longbow. The way her thin, green, archer's costume tightened over her muscles, she'd make a great elf... A finely sculpted figure, frozen in the instant before she releases her arrow... Every muscle taut... every tendon... even her... Oh damn it!

DEBUFF RECEIVED (SEXUAL AROUSAL): -40% to ALL STATS.

Familiar faces were waiting for me at the training camp gates.

"Well, well, Andrew, are you ready to become the next shogun?" Simba laughed. "What skills did you choose?"

"Not now," I interrupted. "That damn debuff has got me again."

Yumi chuckled and feigned modesty.

"Aren't you two taking it a bit far?" Stacy looked at us suspiciously.

"Would you like to take her place?" I suggested.

"No way!" AngelCake retorted.

DEBUFF RECEIVED (SEXUAL AROUSAL): -60% to ALL STATS.

We dash out of the training camp, run along the stone wall and take cover behind the corner of the first building. I instantly unequip my pants, while Yumi drops to her knees and gets to work.

It truly feels like a healing procedure the second time around, albeit no less enjoyable. An oral blessing, indeed. I should have asked if they had a class with such a skill. Yumi could use it.

We're almost done. Purring, Yumi licks my dick clean and I let out a satisfied sigh — when we realize that we have an audience.

"Look at that: This slut's already found herself a new fuckboy," I hear.

"Yeah, her mouth's custom-made for cock. She sucked us off for our loot, now she'll suck the rest off the beta testers for XP."

Lance's entire party is standing there watching, while Xavier and T-Rex practice their wits.

"Jealousy's no good, kids," I calmly equip my pants.

"As if there's anything to be jealous of!" Xavier explodes. "You better look out you don't catch anything from that slut. I'm warning you, she likes it rough!"

Yumi gets up. Her eyes are two narrow slits. Without saying anything, she turns to the scumbag and heads his way.

"Don't you dare, Yumi!" I yell. "Don't do it, he's provoking you! Calm down, they'll get what's coming to them! We'll get plenty of chances to tear these bastards apart!"

"Stop, you idiot!" Stacy calls out, moving to cut her off.

Yumi goes around her as if she's standing

still. Catching a Level 4 Assassin is not easy. I sprint after her. One more step, and I'll be able to grab her by the waist, and hold her back...

Pop! Yumi vanishes into thin air. Stealth!

"Run!" I scream at Xavier. "Get out of here!"

But he doesn't understand what's happening and just stands there grinning. Yumi appears behind him, soundlessly, like a shadow. By the time she's fully visible, her stiletto has already entered the base of Xavier's skull. Critical hit! A backstab from stealth with some additional skill heaping on further multipliers. The damage is monstrous. She's one-shotted him.

DONG!

A tolling reverberates through the streets. It presses against my eardrums and resonates inside my skull, breeding panic and alarm. It is a death knell.

"PLAYER YUMI HAS KILLED ANOTHER PLAYER! PLAYER YUMI HAS BEEN DECLARED AN OUTLAW!"

I see the first of the guards come rushing out of the training camp gates.

E N D   O F   B O O K   O N E

Want to be the first to know about our latest LitRPG, sci fi and fantasy titles from your favorite authors?

Subscribe to our **New Releases** newsletter:
http://eepurl.com/b7niIL

Dark Paladin
a LitRPG series by Vasily Mahanenko

Galactogon
a LitRPG series by Vasily Mahanenko

Invasion
a LitRPG series by Vasily Mahanenko

World of the Changed
a LitRPG series by Vasily Mahanenko

The Bear Clan
a LitRPG series by Vasily Mahanenko

Starting Point
a LitRPG series by Vasily Mahanenko

The Bard from Barliona
a LitRPG series
by Eugenia Dmitrieva and Vasily Mahanenko

Condemned
(Lord Valevsky: Last of The Line)
a Progression Fantasy series
by Vasily Mahanenko

Loner
a LitRPG series by Alex Kosh

A Buccaneer's Due
a LitRPG series by Igor Knox

A Student Wants to Live
a LitRPG series by Boris Romanovsky

The Goldenblood Heir
a LitRPG series by Boris Romanovsky

Level Up
a LitRPG series by Dan Sugralinov

Level Up: The Knockout
a LitRPG series by Dan Sugralinov and Max Lagno

Adam Online
a LitRPG Series by Max Lagno

World 99
a LitRPG series by Dan Sugralinov

Disgardium
a LitRPG series by Dan Sugralinov

Nullform
a RealRPG Series by Dem Mikhailov

Clan Dominance: The Sleepless Ones
a LitRPG series by Dem Mikhailov

Heroes of the Final Frontier
a LitRPG series by Dem Mikhailov

The Crow Cycle
a LitRPG series by Dem Mikhailov

Interworld Network
a LitRPG series by Dmitry Bilik

Rogue Merchant
a LitRPG series by Roman Prokofiev

Project Stellar
a LitRPG series by Roman Prokofiev

In the System
a LitRPG series by Petr Zhgulyov

The Crow Cycle
a LitRPG series by Dem Mikhailov

Unfrozen
a LitRPG series by Anton Tekshin

The Neuro
a LitRPG series by Andrei Livadny

Phantom Server
a LitRPG series by Andrei Livadny

Respawn Trials
a LitRPG series by Andrei Livadny

The Expansion (The History of the Galaxy)
a Space Exploration Saga by A. Livadny

The Range
a LitRPG series by Yuri Ulengov

Point Apocalypse
a near-future action thriller by Alex Bobl

Moskau
a dystopian thriller by G. Zotov

El Diablo
a supernatural thriller by G.Zotov

Mirror World
a LitRPG series by Alexey Osadchuk

Underdog
a LitRPG series by Alexey Osadchuk

Last Life
a Progression Fantasy series by Alexey Osadchuk

Alpha Rome
a LitRPG series by Ros Per

An NPC's Path
a LitRPG series by Pavel Kornev

Fantasia
a LitRPG series by Simon Vale

In order to have new books of the series translated faster, we need your help and support! Please consider leaving a review or spread the word by recommending *Kill or Die* to your friends and posting the link on social media. The more people buy the book, the sooner we'll be able to make new translations available.

Thank you!

Till next time!